the other shore

Also by John Fraser
and published by
AESOP Modern Fiction:

Animal Tales
The Answer
Behaving Well
Best Friends
Black Masks
Blue Light / Starting Over
The Case
Confessions
Down from the Stars
The Ends of the Earth
Enterprising Women
The Future's Coming Everywhere
Happy Always
Hard Places
An Illusion of Sun
The Magnificent Wurlitzer
Medusa
Military Roads
The Observatory
People You Will Never Meet
The Red Bird
The Red Tank
Runners
'S'
Short Lives
Sisters
Soft Landing
The Storm
Strangers and Refugees
Thinking Scientifically
Thirty Years
Three Beauties
Tomorrow the Victory
Wayfaring

the other shore

a script for four voices

john fraser

AESOP Modern
Oxford

AESOP Modern
An imprint of AESOP Publications
Martin Noble Editorial / AESOP
28a Abberbury Road, Oxford OX4 4ES, UK
www.aesopbooks.com

First edition published by AESOP Publications

A catalogue record of this book is
available from the British Library.

First edition 2010, revised 2014, 2020

ISBN: 978-0-9561409-7-5

main characters

Feodor – lives in an industrial city not far from Moscow; active in the Komsomol (Communist League of Youth); writer and journalist.

Leo – lives in Canada, is a Czech who lived in Moscow several years ago and who has worked in Canada as an industrial worker; writer and propagandist.

Aleya – agricultural economist; now lives on a *sovkhoz* in Central Asia

Aleya's diary – was written in Moscow some time before moving to Central Asia.

note

Felix Dzerzhinski (pseudonymously 'astronomer'), 1877–1926, was the historic head and founder of the GPU, the police arm of the Russian Revolution. In Moscow the square which bore his name is today renowned for its big toyshop, Children's World.

the other shore

'Valorous daring is sometimes better than wisdom. I very well know that it is not easy: it is no trifle to part with everything man is accustomed to from the cradle, with everything familiar from childhood. The people in question are ready for terrible sacrifices, but not for those which the new life requires of them. Are they ready to sacrifice modern civilization, their way of life, their religion and moral conventions? .... to prefer raw youth to polished senility, untilled soil and impenetrable forests to exhausted fields and cultivated parks? Are they ready to pull down their hereditary castle from sheer enjoyment of participating in the laying of the foundation of a new edifice which will doubtlessly be finished long after we are gone? Many would say that this is the question of a madman.'

Alexander Herzen, 'From the other shore',
April 1850, 'Voix du peuple', *Selected Philosophical Works*,
Foreign Languages Publishing House, Moscow, 1956, p. 380

feodor

Yuri and Ilich are playing volleyball behind the repair shed, and I can hear them shouting. They are playing for drinks, and when they are finished we will all go and get drunk. On the table before me there are two bowls – one with sweet cherries, one with sour. I have enjoyed the whole day – there is a smell of ozone and sweet heavy oil from the bus repair shop. This morning I had the memory of a taste – the taste of a Georgian wine I have not drunk for months. Sophie came back to town today.

'I cried when I saw the birch trees,' she said.

All day I have been sitting at the window, watching the traffic run by like water, thinking of the South and the sun. Thinking of writing a novel about the sun and the South to keep me warm. The ice is already pushing out shelves beyond the reeds to the boyars' island. All day the yard outside has been full of workers, and I must think of something to say about them.

I was thinking too about my America. They will be playing college football, and the police will be trying to stop them drinking in the stands. The militia will be trying to stop us drinking too, but I have no sympathy for the Americans.

Well, yes, I have. But our priorities are different. I want to get drunk as a Soviet citizen, to be punished – if they catch me – as a responsible Party member. Where is the America I know? They could kill me as I sit here at the window. They could kill Yuri and Ilich, they could kill Sophie and the wolf Sophie tells us she saw in the forest. But they will freeze their ignorance in the little snowpile of our remnants ... Could they understand these four things that I do – the work for the Komsomol, the thinking of the southland (the dog split open by a truck in Samarkand, sweet and stinking), my America, my life with the welders and the intensity of the slice of the vodka to my heart ...?

And my Sophie, who likes me to think because it makes me quiet. 'My girl, my girl, don't lie to me ...' If only she could ... Her new fur is honey and black, a wolfdog: and she is sweet as these cherries to my sour breath ... she is the blasting wind off the desert which sweetens those long pale grapes – what do they call them? Sophie believes that innocence drives out dialectics – but she believes this because she is not innocent. I say too, 'I submit to discipline because I agree I must submit to discipline' – and this annoys people. 'But you know I'm a good communist,' I say.

'Just be a communist.'

But I am a good communist.

*

There are days when the intensity of isolation nearly rattles the rivets out of my head. 'Transcending the necessity of necessity,' a friend of mine puts it ... Today there is the scent of snow and apricots on the wind – last night the militia shot a cougar in Great October park. I wrote a letter to Sophie: 'Can you reconcile your modes with mine? Do you think we can all hug together and stand close – there not being very many of us, and it needing all the heat and warm breath we can muster to keep out the frost and the cougars ...' But I did not send it.

This had been the longest week in my world. Sophie had gone to Yaroslavl'. Here I am with what I call my honesty. With my lecture for the Komsomol on intra-bloc relations. With that slow slow clock in my head, audibly counting off the minutes. I can survive the loss of Sophie, if it comes to that: I can survive a winter without honey and a soft warm song from the south. In the street two of the girl construction workers, come to tease us all the way from Georgia, are dancing. One of them likes me, and I like both of them.

I know the limits of necessity this week. This produces a certain austerity, and a certain arrogance. Sophie understands this, and is proud of me. But as I move from austerity to austerity, I think, 'Perhaps Sophie will not come back, despite being proud. Perhaps she has plans so big I just cannot show up on their scale. Perhaps the plan of her life has no category available for me. I can understand that.' But when I think this, the austerity shows through as bitterness, and I see myself for a fool.

And yet I will survive. As a communist, that is what I have been taught, that is what I can practise. If you survive as a stone, survive: as a talking stone. And in my case, survive with a vestigial nose turned to the stinking tripes of the shattered dog in Samarkand, survive with a bare crack of an eye to catch the thin wolves running flick-flick through the birch trees.

Always the sticky-sweetness of things past. Why do I think of the horsemen of Montenegro, riding into the sky, riding alongside the little Zastava, its engine boiling as it climbed the mountains? Of the girl – my girl – who cried when she came back from the south and saw her birch trees again, who showed me the ants which ran like water under the poplars?

So, I wait in my room, the sad piles of newspapers and periodicals building up like bones on a cave floor. Will Sophie take the time to explain why she is leaving me, as I speculate on my America – hockey players, cops, the sad tropics of the 'south of Louisiana' ... small towns linked by chains of motels, two strangers in every room sharing the bottle of rye in every suitcase ...

But I am in the Soviets, and the only life of any significance I have is my life in the Komsomol, not my life looking out of this window at the workers in the yard.

Yuri and Ilich are nearly finished: there are only three sweet cherries left in the bowl. Now I will go and drink.. But it is in the Komsomol that I must work. I remember the old man who told me, 'When your quest is for truth, you don't have to bustle about like everyone else.'

The voices of the Georgian girls are harsh and challenging. Perhaps they will come to drink with us.

I remember someone singing a song in French – 'I have never seen China – but I can imagine it ... in my street there lives a Chinese who carries his country inside himself ...' I would be like that.

So, is it true then, that honesty costs more than truth? What a mistake Sophie was (already I sense that the vodka will lift the images of Sophie off my memory like stamps soaked off an envelope) – to have mistaken spontaneity for sensibility – how pitiful! And yet again – all as meaningless as patterns of smoke. Regrets without an object are onanism, as old Marx said. How fortunate the stores here are never out of vodka.

Am I even so good a communist? If I were, why ask the question? Am I a moralist without a conscience – for whom both doubt and certainty are equally self-indulgent and paralysing? Do I have the courage to explore, and the courage to conceal my discoveries? Does that concealment really require judgement and courage – especially when self-doubt twists like old ivy round judicious loyalty – or judicious humbug and priggery ...

So my mind is a squirrel's cage. Sophie once had a squirrel and had it killed when she was tired of it. How many excuses I made for her when I loved her ... 'Why not set it back among the birch trees you like so much?' 'It was a black squirrel, honey: they get tame frightfully quickly. It would have missed me.'

What nonsense it has all been so far. Each of us must reject the old ways. And I shall do so tomorrow – or the day after, when my head is better.

The thaw is dead and buried in the summer heat we are now beginning to forget. The birches stood knock-kneed together like fawns' legs, a little yellow-green fuzz on the branches, so pale it looked disembodied. The ice unlocked the bodies of dogs and pigeons for their season of corruption – the morgue on clearance day. In those days I could go home and make love with Sophie, crouching and gnawing like a fox with its trophies of the forest. But all that is past.

leo

Leo started to awake from forty years of solitude. Outside, the spume from the boilers of lodging houses stood up straight in the silent frost, like the plumed lances of the Teutonic knights. Police cruisers crunched up a crust of yellowed snow as they patrolled past the loan companies and *caisses populaires*. In Lafontaine's Surplus stood a dummy dressed as an urban guerilla – Soviet-style helmet, set of duck and moose calls complete – '*tout pour la chasse*'. A sign flashed like a pulse 'Heart of the Northland'.

He dreamt a real-estate agent was giving him a tour of French literature, the authors transmogrified into drab half-timbered houses. Stendahl, who covered a whole district, had for-sale signs 'the will is reason'. Flaubert too extended for several blocks. The agent said seriously 'every-man makes a journey through Lukács' aesthetics to reach the other shore'. They passed streets of shuttered antique shops, and at last, where he had to catch the bus taking him to the next part of the dream, there was a silver-gilt statue of Queen Victoria, no more than four feet tall. The houses smelt of mutton and jam, and in some of the back rooms were men wearing caps and oversized moustaches, who looked like syndicalists.

In the desert his job was to milk the goats – but were the villagers really guerillas, or was he simply a goatherd? No one seemed interested in the problem. Descending the street of a town built like a ziggurat – a counter town spiralled upwards helically through the heat haze – he saw green, black, purple lumps of buildings like stage rocks. They were mostly jewellers' shops, selling uncut gems in the shape of clenched fists. The conceits twittered away into zigzaggurats, and he smiled and woke up.

A sad birthday, a sad forty years. He remembered the proverb of the four soldiers who could choose to spend the devil's riches either while they were young, or by the time they were forty. Not much hope of that chance now.

He remembered Moscow in the spring – the streets surging with the vast assembly of all the silent people in the world. Then, in the shade of a syringa, hearing Miaskovsky played as if all the bustling was to get to this universal conservatoire and discourse with profoundly serious intensity.

Leo had been explaining Baku to his wife: the dead rats, the sweet red wine, the little tugboats from the Caspian fleet spelling out NINEL, on the eightieth birthday. The open-air ballet with an instant of total menace when the khakhan's stage army went in unison hop-hop-hop like an eagle in a private game. And saying to his wife – 'Look at those children – we're living lives like hot wires laid across one another, who knows if the heat is sufficient to fuse them into a fretting...'

And his wife saw only a little boy, wearing next year's cap and boots, persuading his dog to carry home a report card with a '2'. By him, a girl skipped with the ferocity of a boxer. The little courtyards of central Moscow were gold with the soft light of weak naked bulbs. The capacity for maintaining impenetrable privacy had been established by the children, even though they were playing a shared game. Leo smiled at little Feodor and little Aleya, thinking of the two political lives he had already lived, and of the third he was contemplating. Or rather, of the two political lives he had not quite experienced, the lungs never properly inflated. Leaving Czechoslovakia in '47, and missing his revolution, translating in Moscow and seeing only a society silently bitter at its losses.

And his wife looked at him and wondered only if he would like her to have children – seeking to please him by self-effacement so complete, she had arrived at a terror that she bored him. But then, one was lucky to have a live husband ...

But not lucky, Leo thought, to have a husband who was so skilled a dialectician that staying comfortable in adversity and obscure in isolation had come to replace the stouter-hearted political virtues. And now, with his wife twenty years dead – dying of self-effacement, losing the moral fervour even for reproach, lying like a sick mole in the snow-light of their tiny room – he felt his moral impotence no longer subjective. It had become a kind of cosmic knowingness, the finger of one of the long-service administrative angels laid forever knowingly along a mountain ridge of nose:

'We get all sorts here, you know: I do my bit to bend the rules.' When God died, did they have to open up His gulags? What matter the re-instatement of eros, the rehabilitation of a part of the fallen host when Lucifer himself is still excoriated?

At his party the previous evening, Leo had proclaimed, 'The trouble with we rational, I might even say classical, Marxists, is that we know the aim is not to make mistakes. If the struggle does happen to nought avail – why struggle? That is, why hope, even if you do struggle, that it will bring any biological satisfaction? Of course, as old Herzen said, one must issue the call to work on the foundations of buildings – in an architectural style yet to be devised – to be completed long after our death. But one often wants to erect some of the thatched huts and paper temples that the peasants build, even to join in the jumping about during the tiger festivals, the fly-past of paper kites. To be a monumental mason is fine, the comparative study of architecture a noble calling – but in order to build foundations you need a rich patron, or a number of men with stronger backs than mine.'

'That doesn't sound like Marxism to me,' said Shirley. 'It's more like a perverse spinelessness. You're getting to be one of those foul old pundits who have lost all indignation to become merely querulous.'

'But I'm in exile. I'm exiled from my historical moment. My wife died in a Moscow winter, crying for ice-cream. "Just a little ice-cream," she kept saying. In memory of all the other ice-cream I'd not bothered to buy her. Sorry for the bathos.'

'Poor old bugger,' said Shirley. 'But you were very young then, weren't you? And a tricky kind of time and place to be married?'

'I think we felt we had to get close to someone. I was very proud of being an intellectual, and being able to make quixotic gestures without being charged for them. And she was very simple, very sweet. And you're quite right – it had nothing to do with politics. And my politics has nothing to do with politics.'

Leo used to say to his friends – who aspired to become a coterie – 'My children! when things are tough on the plain, starve in the hills as bandits,' but they did not catch, or ignored, the irony. At forty, he had turned iron-grey all through. There was a toughness and a wit – but more in the set of his nose and eyes than his remarks. Like the comedian who starts by telling jokes only on stage for the sake of economy of effort but ends by being unable to tell them anywhere else, Leo teetered near the same half-ridiculous professional over-refinement. His performance had become so polished that nothing could adhere to it – not even a snigger. His bookshelves were immaculate, his heterodoxy no deeper than the servant's nod and wink rooted in intimacy with the pious and dogmatic. Though his might now be a party of one, its discipline was mordant, its criticism paralysing, its purges surgical.

Leo accepted that the line between the ascetic and the obsessive was almost obliterated through being so often crossed. But he retained a genuineness – just as the toy soldiers on parade know how to make their entrails go splat on the battlefield.

He remembered the first play he had written for the guerilla theatre – *On the Side of the Angels* – a kind of inversion of Bulgakov's *Beg*. And Shirley's criticism – that the sardonic grin was more like the rictus of a death mask.

'But, my dear,' he had said, 'the whole point about a hall of mirrors is that the *one* mirror you look into gives the whole effect. You *look* into one, and you see the rest only *through* the one. Do you understand me?'

'But in guerilla theatre, only the actors have to be real – it doesn't matter about the writer.'

'You think you are the first people in history: in Europe, by the time I was six I knew that the cannons never really fire off-stage, and that when the trap in the stage opens, you keep on going down.'

And he thought too of the poignancy, of his life with the steelworkers – of the anxiety of his comrades to resettle him in a bourgeoisie to which he had not been born, and never belonged.

'No, Shirley,' he said, 'I don't understand these workers. They've no future and they don't care. If they reach the middle class, they'll do so as philistines. Who cares if there are a few more bourgeois? Not the existing bourgeois. In Chelyabinsk the men I worked with had a greater gentleness, a greater wistfulness. Here in Canada they despise me – I'm one of the old guard who's too stupid to learn the new ways. They've forgotten the days when they too in thin suits, with nothing but the clenched fist to protect them, marched behind the red flags against the uniforms and the batons. They've forgotten the days when a party, not necessarily ours, offered them a discipline, a loyalty to their potential which was stronger than any exploitation or betrayal by the leaders. They were a chain which had to be snapped link by link, and when the need came everyone, students, intellectuals, party bureaucrats, linked their arms in the chain.

'And whatever mistakes and betrayals and evasions we'd committed – every link had its own time of test. And now the chain seems broken. I remember before I left the Soviet Union – a drunk in the theatre was dragged out shouting – but he shouted 'comrades', and everyone listened, because without knowing him, whether he was French or Tatar, drunk or sober, he appealed to us as if we were devoted to him.'

'But you didn't help him – because the cops were comrades too?'

'That's as naive as my remarks were romantic.'

And Shirley thought how, after all, Leo's pain did spring from a genuine absence of wounds, the hurt and guilt in his eyes from an admission of crimes he had not committed – like the only survivor after a bomb-blast his wounds were borne by others. She looked at the kids on the floor – just kids, she thought. At least Leo travels clean, she thought, like an old soldier – even if he did miss all the battles.

And Leo thought of his dead wife, plump as a bird till she tried to gulp down his demands in a lump and they stuck in her throat. But I have experienced much, he said to himself. Remember the delegation to Denmark – was it there I saw the seals? A man and his dog like two thick brushstrokes watching us against the white wall of their croft, black basalt cliffs covered in sheep bones, a farmer liming the thin soil in sea-fret? Wasn't it there we saw the stone rings that had been houses – ruins rounded by habitation – in the sour green of the turf, where they cut the peat like potter's clay, and the sky rolled in all day like the sea – or like the magic red cloud in Suzdal which saved the nuns. Except that these people hadn't been saved – they'd been allowed to survive: among the cairns to the resistance – some land league or other. But they knew the Italian songs and the Soviet ones. And a poem about a wolf who hid a rabbit in his ear, which they said was Czech.

'"Paris with no mountains inspired me with a distaste so profound that it went almost as far as homesickness ..." – how much like my ambitions, to live in Paris – or Canada – and write comedies,' said Leo. 'And how much like "now I am witnessing something difficult" could my political epitaph be …'

*

The group wandered round Leo's apartment. Photographs of Leo in Georgia in a Hungarian student cap: engravings of Armenian rock churches (breaking away from the cool dark, you saw an eagle outside, a half-forgotten lizard in its beak – and beyond the stream, groups of collective farmers roasting sheep, dancing to clarinets which bubbled like birds. An unread book in Italian, *The Collective Intellectual.* A letter from on old friend, 'I do not like what you have written. You have gone a long, way down a perilous and dangerous pathway: I tremble for you.'

But out of cosmopolitanism, only anonymity seemed to be asserted. Leo had built what he called the 'something difficult' room. Based on his reconstruction of a battle some years after the revolution – out in the dunes beyond Bokhara – between pan-Turkic revolutionaries, and local basmachi, under licence to the Bolsheviks, the lines of cleavage were as pungent and stinging as the blasting sun which filled half the sky. Riding out on donkeys in their caftans for a day of sweat and slash.

'Drink,' said Leo, 'is always the wine of remembrance. I remember somewhere in the wet west a whole community getting drunk – the most drunk being held up by his friends, a huge curling circle of mutual aid, of slip and slurp, a long whirl of damaged gyroscopes, until the drink rubs away the distance between Danish and Russian ... And waking in a vomit of crustacea I'd not eaten, and wearing expensive fouled clothes not my own ... Still, every silver lining has its cloud.'

And dancing, twirling with the fat local girls until they became beautiful, wrist to wrist and leaning back to make the faster balance, galloping like little heavy horses over the broken glass and the sand that looked like the sand around Bokhara, mixed with shards and green glaze, cool blue glass ...

'You talk as if the singing and the fighting is all over,' said Shirley kindly, 'but you know we'd like to make you sing and fight again. You're not a victim of imperialism – only of nostalgia. You're so serious, sitting here like a fox counting the bones of its kills: be a bit naughty! Look around at us rutting and boozing – fiercer gnawing at weaker. Not so much of the love stuff now – more like compliance with one another's schemes. Are we living in the shadow of fascism (*aren't we all, always*, thought Leo) – and if we are there's no party, no Red Army coming in from the wings like the khakhan's to help us, you know. The only hope is to leave the steelworkers, leave this museum – come and take the guerilla theatre over Canada with us.

We value your intellect, and your sadness. You make us gentler, and sentimental, and this has its place on the stage...'

'But not in politics or aesthetics – and I feel we must distinguish the two, especially if we're tottering on the edge of the new world. A friend once said that "Islam is an area five or six times the size of the known world" – my own known world is several times the area of yours – no offence – and it takes me longer to move about in it.

'I've recently devised a new formalist theory – restoring it to populism where it belongs, basing all on the social rhythm of class argots. How can an idea like that fit guerilla theatre? Forty years of living in the margins of other people's maps – no preparation for being a grand old trouper on the retreat from Moscow: All I've learnt is that the late quartets prove that things are not what they sound like. I'd rather die in bed with my boots on than twice nightly in empty shopping plazas ...'

But Shirley was nice. And Edgar and Lorraine. All the names the English had long since stopped calling their children. And L, Leo, is for loyalty.

He stroked Shirley's dress, and she followed his caress nervously, as if a noncommittal tenderness was a new love-play to be learnt. 'Come on,' she said, 'that's easy enough. The hard thing is playing the end of the world to the burghers in their station wagons and plaid trilbies.'

Leo wondered how the colours of Shirley's hair managed to avoid a match with all those of her raw silk tunic – an impression of meticulous near-misses, carelessness raised to an obsession.

'OK', he said, 'I'll try anything three times. I'll stage the last continental farce of capitalism. At least leftism is an infantile disorder, not a senescent one. If we can't simply be unavailing, let's at least be decorative ...'

And now, the day after, Leo was one of the last desperate men in the land of the desperate.

aleya

It was a morning in one of the indeterminate seasons of Kazakhstan – perhaps the full blast of the heat was still lurking in the low rake of the mountains. Men on horses were riding out to ranch sheep maned like lions. The *sovkhoz* included an area of semi-steppe, and shepherds crossing a corner of it were raising dust which hung in the dry air like corn-dust over a threshing floor. Aleya looked at the photograph on her desk of herself and her father. She thought she had been five or six – the child's features seemed to have been conventionally blocked in on the negative by some assistant who knew how many parents had died, remembering their children's features only as a denser white in their bleached faces ... But this was after the war – and you could just see St Basil's rearing in the background like a parody of the largest cauliflower in the world.

Aleya awoke thinking proudly that she had slept well and not thought of the letter she must now write. Five years of life in Asia had hardened her discipline – she never let herself stray out of her sight. 'How I regret my dependability,' she thought. 'People mistake my control for austerity, they feel they can exploit what they see as my lack of passion ...' But Aleya needed politics as if it were alcohol – her intensity intimidated, and men felt her seriousness must hide an unconcern for the trivia of human relationships. Even her concession to bad taste, the beech-tinted lustre of her hair, seemed calculated, an almost patronising pronouncement of unnecessary compromise.

'Let me think of the most honest things to put in my letter: that "I have been devoted to the cause of our Party for as long as I can remember." Certainly to the extent that its errors and omissions can't be separated from my own – its face and my own have the same lines, and I desire to judge myself as the Party would judge me. That "life on the *sovkhoz* under the present director is intolerable" – well, certainly intolerable to me. But to the others – a little slackness, a little insanity, it's familiar enough. Irksome for the technical staff and the administration – but not intolerable.

'"I have on my own initiative decided to approach you directly, since my complaints and requests must also be taken as an expression of disquiet at the actions and lack of comradely self-discipline of our Party organisation here. All other ways of bringing matters to your attention seem likely to cause more damage and delay ..." After all, the question of correct procedure to start an investigation must come after the revelation of the problem ... True, the procedures were instituted to stop people like me taking up time – but this itself is a recognition that the duty to speak out is an urgent and demanding one ...'

She wrote and thought, following her phrases till they died on the page.

She felt dissatisfaction with herself, impatience with those who tolerated laziness, who were content to see the workers on the farm grow slow and docile like the sheep. She had a horror that the technicians who looked after the breeding would – by an orderly process of reconciling contradictions – blur the distinction between the animals and their handlers. She wrote, 'I am not a perfectionist, nor I think especially aggressive. But I cannot stand to see our resources wasted on projects for the administrators while some of us still work sixteen hours a day ... especially as this is done with the approval and encouragement of Party members. "Service before everything", as Tolstoy says – let our chairman remember this ...'

In the court three children were reciting the story of the four legends – of the good and evil birds, of the panther, of the tower of the five winds, and of the fourth legend. An old man with yellow eyes was trying to fit together the pieces of a bowl from Kashan – dark blue scimitar shapes – like birds or clouds or just denser patches of sky on the lighter, summer-night blue of the body of the bowl. He thought:

the bowl of my komuz
can play melodies today
– round as the sky or this bowl
my uncles brought: from Kashan ...

feodor

The first shots of vodka are disappointing, an old friend revisited who fails to burst through into intimacy – as Yuri says, he prefers food and drink to affairs of the stomach, but for my part I enjoy the dualism of drinking, the indulgence and the hurt.

'Here, Ilich,' says my Ilich to the waiter, rolling rouble pieces to him, 'champagne and some decent glasses.'

Outside it has turned thundery, clouds like pale yolks seem to be pressing round the restaurant. There is a firework display, and they are firing rockets to disappear into the clouds which shoot back lightning. When our gunners miss, we have the more beautiful shells, but their weapons are of heavier calibre.

Yuri says, 'Like Saigon,' but no one laughs. It is hot, and I remember a summer in Tbilisi, lying on a mattress in a blue balcony, overhanging a street where men and women in black clothes bent under the heat like crows. Smelling the cooking of the little dishes of mutton and apricot, the soft pink flowers scented at dusk like caves, the dark amber wine forever at my elbow – listening idly to the chatter of two sisters outside – 'old enough to be independent', 'drinks all day and then carouses'. To be able to take the bus to the mountains, the wind so powerful it was like an engine trying to launch me over the rocks and the brownstone churches – and strain to hear a shepherd talking, laughing, in his language I didn't understand. They would joke and describe their huge high sheep walks as I watched the broken scraps of their epos (all hooks and broken circles) whirled away – like the script on old maps to label and excite. And they would laugh at me as I gobbled down their bread and sheep cheese and bitter little cucumbers, nose pricked out into the wind like a young dog's.

But the vodka and the champagne are beginning to bite. I tell them – 'Remember what Blok said, "There are not only two conceptions, there are two realities; the people and the intelligentsia ..." – and among the intelligentsia "a hasty fermentation, an endless change of views, of state of mind and fighting banners" and we come forever to Kukilova. Or rather, the battle is over – except for this thunder.'

But why can't I remember what happened in the fighting? Am I part of a collective intellectual? I hardly think so. Nor did Sophie. 'Why don't you do something?' she'd ask. 'You'd probably be quite good at writing.'

'As good as who that you've read?'

'Oh, I don't know – I've not read very many people. You're not quick enough to be a sports writer – but you could interview people.'

'Do you think I could write about communism?'

'Well, of course, everyone does that, don't they – I mean something lighter.'

So I've never bothered.

My friends are dancing a ballet in a language I do not understand. I have appropriated myself to myself so finally that I can make no public statements, live out no public actions. That is our problem – whether the people give us privileges or whether we take them notwithstanding, the kind of professional returns expected are not forthcoming. Money to buy vodka may be an earned privilege – but drunken fantasies are inescapable consequences.

Travel doesn't bring us closer to the people – as my friend said when he came back from the St Petersburg they have in Canada – 'They might at least have called it Petrograd.'

We are like the rich Americans who come to Moscow demanding to be treated as the very rich – and then resent having to pay. Just to be wealthy is not enough – they must also be inappropriate. Do I want the truth, or just a variety of analyses? To keep silent when one is in error is the hardest thing – and for me to demand an analysis which does not change anything, and does not commit me to action is absurd. Perhaps I am not a good communist, but a quiet one.

I remember the autobiography of a Soviet Muslim officer who had studied under Ryazanov, and fought in the desert. He described an evening like we're having – a legless drunk crawling on his arms to the urinal and each time wetting himself because no-one would lift him up – the usual stuff. And a comrade told him – or spoofed him – about a dream of a return to a battlefield for treasure: the railway official and his retarded daughter, hovering over the dead railway lines like curses. And a military attack on them as they dug for a buried truck – or was it simply a mined truck? And how he himself had to do the same in real life two years later. Like an actor who learns a part in prose for the first time, and decides to improvise instead, because the language is so much more ordinary than verse – then discovers that his improvisation is word for word that of the written part ...

Yuri does not like my stories. A woman came up to us. She was drunk, and said, 'Would you like to see my daughter dance?' A man began to fight, but the manager sent a waiter over: 'Tell him he's to call and see his mother urgently ...' and the fight stopped. A girl at the next table told the man she was with, 'You don't have to change your opinions just because you disagree with me,' and Yuri said, 'Love at first offer.'

I am massively drunk. My head and legs have the gravity of the rarer metals. 'God makes lots of rocks and hides presents in some.'

Must have cherries: and the girls from Georgia are over there somewhere. And Ilich is saying, '... write our history then. Write the history of the repair shop, and discuss it with the Komsomol, our children.' And I can only see the pale acanthus holding up the ceiling – 'Yes, I'll practise my praxis. And how about Sophie?'

I think I am crying, but it does not matter. I try to remember the story of the four legends. Really, this is too much of a scene. There is a pale alcoholic looking at me through the mirror, blinking his red eyes like a ferret. Disgraceful – yet amusing, because he looks like I would if my suit were older and my hair longer, and his companions are taking him outside and how good the air feels out here. The orchestra is still playing, and the pavement is spotted with wet syringa blossoms.

And now it is morning, and I am still going to write the history of these workers.

*

When I went down to the repair sheds, they were burning the tarry logs of the flatbedded sledge which gives us rides in the snow, the little snow-tractor pouring fumes back on us – making the vodka taste resinated. In the distance I could pick out the source of other memories – of burning musky lime-trees, a few cows by the plank bridge, a watchman with his rifle walking slowly, whistling. In the yard only a few sparrows, dust. Yuri passes me, suddenly courteous, asking seriously of someone else what he should do with a generator. Does he even remember me now? His work absorbs him completely, and there is a symmetry and a modality about his life that I don't have. When I work I am involved twenty hours a day – but when there is nothing, there is only a limping speculation. Does Yuri resent my life, that it is so pre-mechanical, that I live the life to which these workers, I suppose, aspire – and yet draw so little comfort from it? One day soon I must ask.

I feel at times like this so much like someone in Blok. '"Not only is it true that no one can deny himself, it is also true that one can affirm his weakness to the point of self-destruction,"' I used to say to Sophie. 'Of course we live like drunks, and truly we don't look much like Soviet man, but inside (where it doesn't matter), we are filled with courage and resolve – we are communists and would fight alongside the best. Every imperialist must at some time perform acts of self-sacrifice and generosity...'

But how harsh my new life is. From the manager's office I can see the trees struggling with the first cold winds. Through the windows of the sheds you can see the glimmer of the welders' galaxies. Grigor, the manager, is only in his late thirties, but already his face looks like a potato left too long in the ground, all shoots and cavities. I remember when Sophie told me he had been her lover. I felt like a soldier who has just been blown up, inspecting himself for wounds, and finding no blood on the outside, but pain inside. 'It's my body, and I'll do what I like with it,' she said, swishing it like a tail. 'It's not a question of morality, it's a question of taste. Or pride.

Grigor has a picture above his head which he calls 'The Hidatsa and the eagle hunt' – they look like walking fringed sea-anemones, the eagles more like parrots. 'Grigor, could you let me use the records of the factory, interview some workers, especially the older ones? I thought I'd like to write an account: of the strengthening of socialism and of communist attitudes to work in the plant ...'

'It doesn't sound much of an idea to me. Who put you up to it?'

'Most of the work on this is either too empirical or totally unlikely. I want to write an essay in social perception, the flowering of personality, awareness – or not – call it what you like.'

'Look Feodor, you're just trying to tart up a shoddy and perfunctory idealism by making it an obscure – more complex if you feel hurt – idealism.'

'But even if that's true, Lenin says an intelligent idealist is closer to us than a stupid materialist ...'

'No one's very close to me today, and everyone I meet is stupid ... You want to take the time of the men and turn up all the old nonsense – and for what, self-indulgence? Frankly, anyone else could do the job well. And when I finished work here I could go home and check on the year they built the third shed, and what a fine fellow I am. But yours would be a mishmash of dialectics and objective contradictions – your theoretical apparatus would be so heavy and so burgeoning it would topple over and completely squash our poor little factory.'

Grigor looks so proud: as if he has managed to say, 'Well, Mr Herzen, I would say, yes, your trouble is you take yourself too seriously – why worry about other people? – you may be sure they don't worry about you…'

'And how is Sophie?' he asks. I ought to find the situation as they say 'richly comic'. In a moment he'll start discussing general moral questions ... How ridiculous – the discarded lover and the former lover – neither knowing for sure what Sophie has told either of them. To me the Sophie business still hurts as a rejection, but to Grigor it's just an episode; I'm no better a man than him – or alternatively Sophie enjoys the full rich life. After dark, anyway. It doesn't say much for either of us – but Grigor's delighted.

'Well, why not, Feodor,' he goes on. 'We've gone through a lot together. Sure, root about as much as you like.' A crow is riding the wind like a surfer, and topples clumsily into the yard below us. The hoardings from the Lenin centenary are coming adrift and blowing about the yard. I have a history to write, and no Sophie. It will be hard.

leo

'Do I really want to know these people?' thought Leo. 'Ah well, too late now.'

They used his home as a kind of summer yurt – not burdening him with friendship, and supposing a congruence of their lifestyles, a symmetry of obsessions, which was not really the case. Young workers, older students, girls coming around from the first bite at the cherry – all frolicked and bickered around Leo's intellectual hegemony, like the Young Hegelians round the feet of the master, or on the figure in the carpet. And Leo felt seven times as large as life – but still dead and speechless. So this was what being stood on one's head was like!

And he thought of a poem a friend wrote for him when he left Moscow, saying, 'Wherever you go, remember, you cannot afford a country …'

'Wrapped in granny's shawl for his last ride
the sick dog scented the syringa, quietly stirred his tail
and died, crossing the river into Moscow.'

And Leo longed for his dead and desolate friends, for Natasha who went to Riga and died of pleurisy, for Konstantin who was persecuted by his wife and became a mystic. I am alone and in exile, he thought, and Shirley is a soldier in a completely different battle. To me, everything private is subsumed in the one public act – for her, every lover is a campaign, every triangle a schism. I couldn't live that close to scrutiny – and she spends herself too freely. But then, I'm a chronic leaver-out myself ...

aleya's diary – five years ago

'No, no, no,' I shouted – it was in class, and I feel I pounded the desk with my fists. It so surprised us both that the teacher and I laughed. I said, 'All right, I agree that this Scott Fitzgerald is the last – the most perfect and the most complex – bourgeois novelist. So, what next? Why isn't the end of the novel like the end of philosophy? Suppose I write a diary – what can the praxis of the diary be? The diary records praxis ...'

And the teacher, pink and confused, said, 'It could well lead to a refinement of praxis.'

'I say, "Good! – we are now past perfection and can start to write about what matters. Unless Fitzgerald was really not interested in writing for the bourgeoisie but that his bourgeois should want to meet up with intelligent and intense people – not other bourgeois?

'"I think you'd like the 'end of the novel' to mean 'no more novels'. But it doesn't. You've been misled by your own enthusiasm. You see, Marxism is a language of survival. Occasionally it is able to come out of the cave and make unequivocal statements – but they have this tendency to be runic. Look at the Philosophical Notebooks, how speculative and compressed they are – you must not mistake a simple reading for what is needed, a naked reading."'

I understand that we were both talking about myself. I have this tendency to harshness. The other day I interrupted another lecturer – he used the analogy of an eagle, needing histomat and diamat like two wings to keep him aloft. And I said no, like two eyes to see in three dimensions, but just the one brain. He was angry and said, 'Why waste time on perfecting analogies when we are trying to understand something which has nothing to do with eagles, when the perfection of analogy leads only to people rooting the analogy in their minds?'

Now I have started this diary, I should be able to decide what is important to me. Am I becoming tough beyond my nature? I would not want sex to be a problem when I am working.

'Don't you feel any emotions?' asked one boy – I think it was his first time, and he was so proud of his athlete's body. I think he was frightened of me, and disappointed by my calmness.

'I feel emotions – but why should I feel them for you? You are a part of our cure for fear and illusion. You are strange to me, that's all. Everything I do I do seriously. I don't like to have to lie. I feel nothing for you, but I am not disappointed ...'

How I would have to be tough – but how easy it is to be isolated. And how easy when you are isolated to have 'the will to die', to move aggressively and violently against people who will need me, and be happy to use my services. There is something powerful and ruthless in so many of these students – as if strength comes from a refusal to suffer, and what suffering there is must come from small, private causes. They want to be fire-hardened without being charred … I am afraid of this hardness, because it is a carelessness about precision in human relations; it shows a lack of concern for oneself, the brutality of the bull who does not mind being trampled by the rest of the herd because he too is trampling them ...

But this evening, when I went to the concert in the great hall of the conservatoire, and saw these people sitting and working – the music was as quiet as power looms in a cotton mill, muffled by the concentration of the audience – I think we were happy to be all together, going further and further in silent intensity – so many voyages to the end of the mind ... And afterwards in the soft golden light, families clustered like moths round the night-scented flowers, youths playing with their samoyeds, the exasperated solemnity of radios where no one is listening – I felt all round me the solidity of us when we relax, when we can reflect …

But I have to be able to live without love, with only public satisfactions, without regrets, without compromise.

*

Later I had gone in to talk – 'in the English manner' – with a teacher about Hegel and Spirit. He thought me very young and innocent, and this was his bond with me – he is young too, and shy, and the excitement between us rested on what he believed to be his superior *savoir vivre*. I said, 'But do you really believe that all this can be materialised – all these categories made concrete? That we are just set down in a corner of Hegel's perfection and invited to explore the rest?'

'I think it is necessary we accept this, or something very like it – though I agree psychologically it may be unsatisfying to someone as vigorous as you,' he said.

'At least you don't think I'm unreflecting.'

We went on to argue about sacrifice and love – and he told me to read more Gogol – 'if that doesn't make you react against idealism, nothing will …'

And he said too, 'Don't shake yourself to pieces. No one has to "go to the people" any more, they're all round us. I mean, that we are the people. We've solved the old narodnik puzzle.'

I said, 'Perhaps we just solved it by waiting till it went away. A friend said to me yesterday, "Neither the Russian nor the Soviet intelligentsia solved a problem – it deals only with oppositions and conflicts which can't be reconciled. When it starts to reconcile these irreducible contradictions it has 'an attack of the vapours, it falls into a swound', it talks of the unity of minds, movements of vast and lowering forces."

'And this friend said, "Marxism was the worst thing to happen to the intelligentsia, just as communism was the only possibility for the Russian masses. It is a fatal and humiliating conjuncture ..."'

In fact, I have no such friend, and said this to show that I was not a fool, and not an idealist.

And the lecturer said, 'You worry me – you treat quite ordinary courses like guerrilla training. You're like a coyote suddenly put down in a picture gallery – eyes and nose going ten ways at once. You don't know whether to look at things or sniff them. You follow ideas as if they are scent trails, you're so intent on them you don't notice where you're going, or even that you've started to follow a quite different animal – and often one stronger than you are.'

'Yes, I realise I'm quite undisciplined. It's my worst fault.'

'You can give away too much in your desire to get close to people ...'

'I think you overestimate what I'm willing and able to give. I see my life as a solitary and often frightening adventure, with brief, rather harsh lyrical breaks – like bird calls in Mahler. One thinks, "What can that bird be doing so far from the shore, or so deep in the forest, or so high in these summer clouds?"'

'You like Mahler, then?'

I think in the end he was disappointed – I seemed to win my independence from him too violently, and I had his respect at the cost of his sympathy. I stood in the middle of the bridge looking up towards Red Square, later that day, and watched the soldiers with their girls – everyone was carrying flowers. Some soldiers in trucks went past, and they threw me a flower too.

What will my life in Asia be like? Dark green trees standing firm in the heat, gardeners turning the earth into chocolate paste around them – everywhere the clattering of *dutars* and *komuzes*, little boys carrying drums to music lessons. Buildings blue as the sea with here and there a yellow tiger's head in the tile, like the sun. And will all that be Spirit too? – or what we would be well-advised to think of as Spirit?

I went for an ice-cream – and that set everything right!

feodor

I am obsessed by the shape of the buildings, the fishy smells of the puddles which glisten in the yard. Not a history of welding shops, but a saga of fixation. The yard seems always full of serious people caught in the full flight of solemnity, bustling away to do nothing in particular. You can see two little churches over the roof of the largest building, the crosses on their domes twisted – it looks as if the wires meant to stay them are pulling them down. These green domes are a comfort during the snow, they are like a quintessence of crocus ... But I must stop dreaming, and open the first page of the living book down there.

But what do I expect to find? Quality forever turning into quantity? Unique and specific situations exemplifying something I can call socialist working relations? Is my purpose really serious? My need is to 'speak loud' as they say. But could what I find be spoken any other way – and with more effect? Questions, always questions, like smoke and steam rising from a pot into which the cook has forgotten to put the meat. Today I feel bad about Sophie – how one misses her enormous selfishness, that self-absorption so complete it infects everyone else. I remember her saying to an Italian, 'What, you don't speak Russian? Well, that's all right: it doesn't matter.'

I'll start with Benjamin: 'What changes do you find around here – say, from twenty years back?'

Benjamin is the clay from which the figures of the prehistory of all politics are made. He's so full of rugged wisdom and loyalty he has difficulty in stringing together three words. But he's amiable, he has no curiosity about my reasons for asking these questions.

'Well now: I remember there was never enough goose. I love a bit of goose – a little in the soup is excellent, and there's some that likes just the fat.'

'But apart from more goose, change has been minimal?'

'Ah well, things are better all round now, eh? Twenty years – well now – I'd a dog then, but it soon had the smell of death about it ...'

Well, perhaps Benjamin had the more acid wit. A book saying 'A man's mates are a man's mates', circling round like a Tatar dance-song – this would say as much as most books.

But Sophie wants 'to talk things over' – she'll enjoy it so deeply. Looking teasingly at me, like a big warm animal that one longs to spend the winter with, curled up in some burrowed-out bed – she studies me intently when I'm speaking, but I'm sure only to see if I brushed my teeth. I can imagine my rationalisation now – 'Some people are *quite objectively* victims of their partners' wit.'

There's nothing more ridiculous than being faithful to a woman who has gone off on her own.

'Well, Sophie. It's not often we can lunch to Shostakovich's "Leningrad". Makes one think of hope, force, don't you think? Well, you must – everyone does. And so do I.'

'You sound very odd, Feodor?'

'No, I was just listening.'

'I didn't want you to mope without me, you know. It was all a bit abrupt, so I thought I'd come back and do things more slowly and deliberately – give you time to adjust slowly.'

We played around with Sophie's self-indulgence for a while, and I felt better. Life with Sophie would be no better than life without – I was able to start fearing life in society before I'd stopped fearing the incursions of my neighbour.

Sophie said, 'I really think if we were not so secure – you call it the "kittens in the basket syndrome" – that I'd have stayed with you. But it is inertia that flings us apart. I'm the feather and you're the lump of lead falling in the vacuum ...'

'Whatever became of those, I wonder? Sophie, you're freeing me every minute. And I can't even thank you. As Mably said, "Lift from man the fear of tomorrow" – you've done that. The guard dogs are starting to bark. I'll confront life like a wolf from now on – a little timid and solitary, but snug and weatherproof.'

And I thought with sudden pleasure of looking through a haze of pungent mutton smoke in a tea house, teapots like glazed oranges glimpsed through the silver leaves, dust speckled with mica, and men in silver caftans ... and I am cured of Sophie. And now, I know what I must investigate and write.

leo

'It seems to me,' thought Leo, 'that reactionaries got so used to using the language of democracy and objectivity that we assumed they'd forgotten the language of barbarism. What our theatre must present is the picture of a world deep in the primal scene. For instance, the whole of capitalist society must be our stage, with immense tricks of scorn and perspective. Great plaster snails on suction pads swooshing down the sides of the Toronto-Dominion building – and ourselves wearing huge padded heads walking over freeway bridges – like Cossacks off to join the Red Army. It is a terrifying thing to imagine.

'How secure, somehow, when Engels talked of the Paris Commune as being a transitional form of the state – meaning transition to statelessness. And now it is hard to escape a Samson complex – when the whole thing comes crashing down, where can one be but out in the fields away from buildings, preferably with all one's friends and trinkets gathered round? We're not a guerilla group, but a survival group – our political message is fear and trembling.'

And Leo thought of how frightened his wife would be – how she'd loved the serious cheerfulness of the Soviet election campaigns; only she could mistake a heroic mode for a lyrical one. But that whole story was too complicated.

Even today an impostor in the management had been unmasked. The level of imposture had been so low, and gone on so long, it was below self-parody. It had been an imitation of the worst incompetence conceivable. He had been cut down in a story which began, 'Her and me was bunkies ...' and the notion of 'bunkies' haunted Leo all day.

As he looked down the streets he thought, This is a country where in winter they have to use dynamite to make a grave. And remember that little man who said, 'I've just had some shots in my knee', drinking in the tavern for an hour, then screaming up, slithering and fighting like a demented fish – waiters and chandeliers of beer going down like a pack of acrobats, till the chief barman pounded him with a tray.

'Lively little sod,' said the waiters. How different all this was from the workers he knew ... Here it was the intellectuals who talked of hope and the future while the workers grimly fought for air.

'I miss the kindness and the gentleness of the men I worked with in Europe,' he said half-aloud.

Even the little village clubs he'd seen in the Ukraine – a feeble red flag flying over mud and broken fencing, the village centre marked by the deepest puddle in the road – there was a sense of slow rhythm, and never anything like the despairing frustration and bitterness of these taverns. The men here had the look of animals given a few hours' reprieve from the slaughterhouse ...

How difficult too to talk of the things which concerned and moved him – in simple and honest terms. These people could not hear simplicity – even the countryside was just a place to hunt wolves in ... And Leo smiled at his self-pity and homesickness. After all, everyone realised how desperate things were – and that was why there was no time to make the finer perceptions. It was just subjectivism and fatalism that made him shrink from calling his friends '*les copains*', of admitting them to a more intense collective intimacy.

'We must see what can be done about that, then.'

Leo thought briefly of his wife crying for ice in winter, and his running savagely downstairs and making a kind of snowball for her, furious at the flabbiness and unreasonableness of her dying. But she'd died all the same.

aleya's diary

I heard Dimitri protesting as I came into the room – heard with pleasure, 'No, I'm sorry, I can't agree' – for he's the most vulnerable of my friends. He was discussing one of his compositions. How could he be so foolish? He insisted on a scherzo, and I said, 'How can you have a scherzo in the middle of a revolution?' And he replied that whether I called it 1905 or 1907 made no difference to him, or to the formality of the exercise.

'So I wrote a scherzo, very high and fast and almost inaudible, like the wings of birds above the clouds. I'd annoyed him too by saying that I enjoyed the minor works of Janáček so much that I didn't need any major works … I have this picture of working myself to exhaustion, my creative life a headlong race to recognition or insanity – flogging myself along like a tired old centaur galloping down into the abyss – and always a wife weeping in the kitchen. Do you see what I mean, Aleya?'

I said, 'I wonder if friendship is based on understanding or on agreement? And then I wonder about the working conditions of Musil, or of Canetti. This precise turbulence, the long billowing conversations in coffee houses unravelled at home like hundreds of yards of thin faded silk … our own lives seem certain to be full of concentration, activity, so full that when we reflect we merely find fault, and then shrink from intelligent criticism of one another. We end up without a culture – for our culture is too precise and technical, too measured, to nurture complex reactions to our friends. And we end up without friends. It scares me to think of a life in which friendship is slowly replaced by mortality. To see you and Alexei and Nina – all of you, smaller and smaller, stiller, monochrome ...

'Do you remember the big party at the Institute last year – the professors discoursing among the lupins, everyone self-consciously beautiful, constrained by the necessity of enjoyment and the importance of retaining the memory – the two quick thunderstorms, do you remember, swooping fiercely down on us like hawks. And how I found Alexei – you know how his hands shake on the nervous days – sitting under the big waxy flowers with fat red bees fumbling all over him, and crying with frustration. "Oh, Aleya! It's like fighting in my head. I can't stop the shaking, I can't enjoy the depth of things ... I want to bury myself in you like an axehead in a tree, the wood quite healed up around the metal, slowly rusting with sap ..."

'And I told him, "Yes, of course sleep with me. But I can't give you comfort, you need strength, not sleep." And he could only say, "Why do they press us so hard?" until I lost patience, and thought he looked foolish sitting there in his suit at my feet, as though I'd just knocked him down. You think I'm hard – but you remember there was a fiddler, from the southern Ukraine I think, making his violin purr and growl like a lynx.

'And suddenly someone beyond the flowers started discussing Dobrolyubov's "What is this Oblomovshchina" – where he talks of the word "forward", how long and wearily Russia had waited to hear it. And I thought of living on a farm, somewhere in the south, sheep yellow and black, perhaps with big leathery udders and fierce amber eyes, of proving that I could survive without all of you. And wondering why I am so concerned that my love for you all should not be dependency.'

Sergei had not spoken all this time. His mind is so secure it is constantly reaching its limits. Sergei once said to me, 'What I see I see so clearly – that your rushes, your impulsiveness, seem a waste of effort. I admire your "onwardness" – but you're like a wave looking for a rock to break on.'

He said now, 'Alexei feeds on sympathy as if it was nectar. Perhaps that's why the bees were all over him. He's a spoiled poet – his parents indulged him by letting him stay up and look at the moon. He should have been asleep with his teddy. But I thought we were talking about writing. And to me it's all formal exercise. I don't have this mystique about style and uniqueness. It doesn't matter that the mystique leads to subjectivism – and to *folie de grandeur* – it leads to frustration and distortion. It leads automatically to falsehood: this is a crime against literature before ever it becomes a breach of Soviet reality ...'

I was angry. 'Your reality is vulgar common-sense. You can't give complexity its due by cramming in every element of trivial normality. I say, "Long live Soviet travesty and distortion!" – we're intelligent enough to judge ourselves, our own weaknesses and errors. The reason drunks remember hangovers is because it hurts. We must remember what hurts in literature, not base everything on saying, in effect, "Milan was an alcoholic, but nonetheless was sober much of his life, especially when young. Although he took a knife to his wife once, most of the time he didn't hurt her, and in one of their many evenings of lovemaking started a child!" If you're so alarmed about aesthetic crimes, you should be a policeman and track down real criminals. You seem to be obsessed with the things that don't suit you – and instead of endless searching you want to create a quite spurious reality – which corresponds to nothing but your wishful thinking!'

Dimitri laughed – 'Aleya will only be happy when she's wearing a peasant smock and struggling to lift two sheaves – mice and all – onto the cart. But you know, mechanisation has set in.'

But I have a concern for Alexei. He is so tormented. He has written a novel which he won't show me. Tomorrow I'll try to get him to show me it. He said it is about a group of young musicians, all of whom for some reason decide to renounce music and take up other responsibilities. And they get no satisfaction from their new lives, but they continue because of the sense of enthusiasm and struggle, of continuing movement and forcing of their own natures and capacities – an epic of people who live their whole existence at the limit of their capabilities, and constantly fail. The dialogue has a kind of musical springiness and tenseness – a light voice floating *parlando* over a large orchestra playing in one of the flattest keys. Or so he told me, and I can always trust him.

aleya

How vicious these mornings are, thought Aleya. Wasn't it Serge who was exiled around here, describing the poverty only a generation ago, the plagues of flies, the children black with dirt? In face of these vast tilting plains, the sheep forever running about like little blobs of dusty quicksilver – to her the work of the shepherds was a huge, rather cruel, child's puzzle. Slotting these balls of bleat and instinct into pens – as if they were figures in an immense living ledger, with the steppe beyond, yellow, brown, white and rust, the inside of a flayed panther's pelt, with the odd tuft of hair poking through the holes and tears of the skin.

The slowness of life dismayed her – the director of her institute told her before she came – 'Anything you do – even managing to stay – will provide continuity. You are a woman of sophistication and not quite sufficient education or ambition to give you perspective. You have the capacity for encouraging and sustaining a great unhappiness, most probably about some unalterable condition. I know I'm sounding tedious and paternal – but you must realise that there are periods, long periods, of consolidation, and even of retreat. These are the times when only discipline and comradeship can encourage us to examine our mistakes, so that the next forward movement carries us further than we were before. You know this, but you must learn to accept this principle into your life.'

Perhaps isolation had coarsened her – certainly she felt unfitted for urban life. Her memories of Moscow were now those of anyone visiting briefly from the East – stores, the confluence of people from every one of the Soviet legions ... Her friends were forever caught in the excitement of leaving the city – they had become a throng of uniformly genial faces bidding farewell. And on the *sovkhoz* she had only come to accept a distance between her and her co-workers, one reached and measured by friendly consent, but which excluded understanding as it prohibited also hostility or dislike.

There was an elderly Russian woman who helped her in the educational work. She had interminable stories of being cheated by waiters on rounds of raki – her husband had for a time been a toothless waiter in a big Istanbul hotel, forever trotting for his two per cent. They lived under the walls – 'Ah, the walls of Byzance' – selling melons and stolen mosaics to tourists, their home a box of charred sacks and galvanised iron – 'So snug, just like two little kittens ...'

Her first husband had been a White refugee, lingering on proudly among the ambassadors and churchmen, generals and station masters until such time as he could find employment in petty crime. They had then been persecuted by Armenian neighbours, 'Until I took a shotgun and climbed a tree – so, like just a small bird, hop hop from branch to twig, and *blasted* at them' ... It was a life of such regular literary and social form that Aleya prized it not for its quality of suffering, but for its visual imagery – 'The sea, my dear friend, like catarrh in all its moods, the cemeteries where the dogs went to get their *bones*, my dear. The wrestlers *basting* themselves in corn oil like chickens ...'

So to Aleya, life had ceased to be one of action, and become one of adventure. The adventure of 'struggling against tribalism', of 'antagonistic contradictions in Moslem national movements and the creation of Soviet power ...' But over and against the feeling of struggle, of participation in changes of almost frightening audacity, there was too a sense of oppression by the enormity of the forces and resources involved. The physical adventure too required a reconciliation with the improbable that Aleya could not make. The trips by truck to the mountain streams, meadows covered with flowers like starfish on beds of spinach, to sing songs in difficult and archaic languages, and cook mutton pilaf – to watch the surreptitious wizards in the park, to all this she felt only a response through her eyes.

So her action, precise and passionate, against the director demanded a reassertion of the indignation she had learned in Moscow. In local terms, what had he done? Minor abuses of privilege, major distortions of priorities, a measure of intimidation through intrigue and refusal to communicate and discuss major policy decisions affecting the farm and experimental stations. If there was exploitation involved, it was only exploitation of good nature and apathy. But there was contempt for the feelings and intelligence, a squandering of human resources for symbolic and merely prestigious effect ... New buildings built and unused – some slight but sufficient deterioration in working conditions. Hard to distinguish between errors of judgement, megalomania, and obedience to inappropriate directions from higher bodies.

But she said to herself, 'If I'm wrong, I suffer either way. It is better to use just a little courage – irrespective of the consideration that one has the duty of doing so – since passive acceptance is not passive, nor acceptance. It's a withering away, an acceptance of incursion.'

'So you've sent a letter – at last,' said Yusan. 'Better than grim silence and contemplation. But they won't judge the whole policy. If they get rid of Milan, they'll blame all of us for not acting sooner. The motto seems to be, act instantly, or not at all. Mind you, I respect what you've done. But if you were a little less isolated, you'd realise that we all look foolish now.'

'There's worse than merely looking it,' said Aleya. 'If Milan goes, we'll have more power over ourselves. We're not objects of administration – if I'm wrong and unsuccessful, then we'll still all have learnt something.'

'But what if you're right and unsuccessful?'

'It seems to me you introduce these scruples at the wrong end. If they'd been in the mix from the beginning, no one would be objecting now. If you're saying that people accept a lax kind of despotism because they fear every alternative, then all I can say is yes, of course despotism causes fear! Of course the cure is the cure of something sick, the state of becoming cured is a transitional one, with relapses and weakness. Doesn't everyone in the Party know that? Aren't you saying that all diseases are worse than cures because one accustoms oneself to the luxuries and indulgencies which arise from being bedridden?'

'But don't you make the mistake of self-dramatisation and a kind of historical megalomania yourself? Translating modes of inertia into gigantic political strategies?

'You talk as if I expect gratitude – I don't expect transformations and apotheoses swinging down like bunches of grapes ...'

feodor

I think the question 'Why do I write what I write?' wholly inappropriate, at least for what I've written. Secure in my freedom from Sophie, pure potential once more, I was discussing the matter with one of the factory's research workers:

'Someone I once met from England told me a story about a policeman off-duty, too drunk to tell his comrades not to arrest him for drunkenness. Writing about people who know exactly how much you know about them is rather like that – you either know "the quality of their lives", or else from delicacy you have to preserve the knowledge – "They are good sorts", "They do their duty as it appears to them" and so forth. Honesty at these times could be a huge disincentive – to frankness and to further effort.'

He seemed surprised. 'I would prefer to talk of complexity – even as a prelude to further complexities – than everlastingly of integrity, responsibility and all that. There are some things I want to be left to judge for myself – for instance you making apologies, or letting me off with a warning about "certain immaturities and errors" before I've finished the last page.'

'But for complexity one must have patience,' I said, weakly.

'Well, then, perhaps for once you will be lucky in your subject and your readers ...'

I remembered then how keenly the 'idiocy of rural life' suits me – and the cretinism of rural pursuits. The sombre possessiveness of ants, the brooding senility of even the youngest toadstools, the wild cherries hidden in isolation like buried treasure. Playing this public role demands so much effort – and we are allowed service, 'service before everything', as such an honourable alternative to inventing the unknown ...

Sophie once said to me, 'You've no idea what being a communist and a man of action means. In fact, you seem to think these are contradictions. Lots of my friends are communists, and they're all more active than you, and they don't drink as much. You get away with it because no one can think of anything much for you to do. You seem to think a communist is someone who stands behind a pillar and conducts the heroism of the masses from inscrutable obscurity – and security.'

'Well, and what if you're right, Sophie?' I replied. 'Suppose I am this private and misguided person, what then?'

'You have many qualities,' she said. 'For instance, there is a kind of jaunty sadness, a desperate conviviality, an acceptance of crisis and seriousness about you – you're a doctor with a quick ear for an early symptom, but your fearfulness and optimism compel you to tell the patient to cheer up, and you never try to cure anyone.'

I felt Sophie had trespassed on our intimacy. Too much talk about one's qualities diminishes their suppleness.

We were at a meeting to discuss initiative and economy of effort. The manager, Grigor, would, I'd been told, circle around the general deficiencies of the place – like a vulture over a field of rabbits. Sometimes he would toss down some of his own shortcomings, but there were never many, since he had a keener eye for shortcomings than most. On good days everyone left relieved that they now knew what to avoid – but on bad days they left with the certainty of their inadequacy and a nostalgia for a future they were unable to embrace.

Grigor spoke, and I resented the silence he commanded – if he could enjoy Sophie, then he was enjoying this pedagogy for sure. There was a frightening docility beneath the gentleness and attention of the veterans, the old Party workers. Having seen so many comrades die, we survivors seemed merely wary and alert. Members of the strongest army in the history of the world – but with too many sentries. A big round laugh floated through the window like a bubble of helium as one of the process workers celebrated his immunity from the tiny punishments we were to have. I thought of my America – men and youths on the street corners watching the police drive past, drunks in doorways forever fumbling with the latch, 'gotta hustle down some of this booze', and all day on television Hollywood riding in its funeral procession, millions of feet long – a nation goaded into self-immolation by contract.

'Feodor, perhaps you'll tell us the terms of your research project. It will save us time, and allow you to have our full encouragement if you'll just tell us what you intend by your history – of us, as I see it.'

So, the squirrel has to stop its pedalling and run through its act on the biggest stage in the world. Sophie is in the audience. She looks amused, as she should. Grigor can make everyone in the room his accomplice. We can all share the joke. Except me.

'We hear a lot about socialist working relations, and in the transitional period we are in, we should understand the process of development ...'

Someone asks, 'But surely this has been done exhaustively? Surely this kind of work forms the basis for our whole policy here? You won't just discover a history – you'll find you're living in it!'

It's quite true, and that is why the task was really so undemanding. An attempt to devise an aesthetic, that's all.

'I shall, of course, use quantitative techniques in my research.'

'To establish qualitative changes? But either it's been done, or it's banal, or it's impossible – depending on your patience and skill! Look, I'm not concerned so much about your qualifications or your ideas. Or your procedures, which as Grigor told us were, shall we say, informal. I'm just struck by the difference between your grandiose schemes – and the small scale on which you propose to test them out. Also, I'm wondering why you describe your aims so generally – and in such ordinary terms – if you think you have something new to discover. Are you being quite straightforward with us, comrade – as we wish to be with you?'

I have lived my life for this moment of honesty. Perhaps our reasons for our solemnity are a kind of collective bad conscience, relieved by suffering and effort— a kind of institutionalised torment. And yet, to think this lets me escape. That is the purpose of the thought. My doubts and exhaustion – what my Americans would call my dissidence – is simply a lack of courage. That is why I want to write the history. To get courage, to rid myself of this nineteenth-century nonsense. To be able to speak loud, At whatever cost? No, because to estimate the cost requires also courage. All I have to do, then, is to admit my lack of courage, my failure to proclaim my honesty. This is a silly dilemma, but a real one. I don't think it's the last resort 'either ... or' of a vulgar dialectician.It is an invitation to complexity – but I can't break it out of my head. Don't they have this problem – won't they have this problem in America too? True, it is above all my problem – but I'm supposed to know better. Why don't I then?

'I accept the comrade's strictures, and also the friendly terms in which they were put. I have no wish to take up time or ask for support from whimsy. May I start work, and submit a chapter to the suitable authority? I ask no help beyond mere tolerance ... It is true that not every example in our history forms a chapter. But where the examples are collective, the acquisition of self-consciousness as a key to self–leadership is important.' But why could I not embarrass everyone by talking of courage – which after all I don't really need.

Everyone accepts my nonsense indulgently enough. Who knows, I may find something of interest.

leo

There was another large party to send off Leo and his group. He remembered a party in farewell in Moscow – he and his wife leaving for a few months for the south, she to wander through the fields of raspberry bushes ('One red berry for every one of us that was massacred'), he to sit in libraries in turbulent ecstasies of boredom. Little Feodor and little Aleya coming up for a few solemn sips of leave-taking from the apartments below.

His wife whispered, 'Will our children be as grave as that?'

Leo, irritated, said, 'We can't expect to be parents of every mode and mood ...' because he did not really want our children. It was too hard to pick them up and run. And he thought of the potential for activity of all those little Feodors and Aleyas – requested to give whatever effort they had, whatever mode of action they preferred, and sombrely making their choices.

Modality – that was the notion. And what fractured modes in his own life – like the time after his wife's death. An English girl, sitting as they do, not a ripple on that great reservoir of passion. Intricate voids, keyholes only to be entered by some curly and unique key fancied up by some locksmith, dead long and faraway.

She smiled at Leo in some pub and said, 'I'm really rather wild!'

'You don't look it,' Leo said,

'You won't need to take my word for it,' she replied sharply.

How easy that infidelity, how simple it seemed, and it was this which gave it its rank as infidelity. How odd, he thought, because I don't believe in regrets or immortality, or self-indulgence. But perhaps I live as though I do.

The girl had said, 'Human relations are made not by the normal and healthy – when they meet they just touch together, there's no friction, and no lingering. They're made by the incongruous and the exaggerated.'

'And that's what makes them so hard!'

And all this conversation which lasted two days, framed in the sickly memory of English summer afternoons, the air so heavy and fragrant it was like living in a jar of pot pourri. Leo found summer in the English countryside ridiculous, grotesque. He was exhausted by the lush abandon of the people, too, their fantasy, their love of jokes, their noisy and undiscriminating enjoyment.

'Look at Leo,' said Shirley. 'Throw a party for him, and he only thinks of all other parties.'

'You need cheering up,' Peggy said, 'you look as if you've come to the end of something. In fact, something like dirt pie, and can't quite crunch up all the grit. You look like you're dying, for Christ's sake.'

I suppose, thought Leo, that if that can conceivably be said kindly, she said it kindly.

Leo asked Peggy, 'What makes these people so constrained? They drink together like it was taking communion ... only the Finns seem to start naturally from such restraint, and can end by becoming fairly cheerful. It can't be class which cuts everyone up like this – all the women over there, electricians here, realtors somewhere else ... It can't be money they're after, because theirs is all the same ... they're not exchanging technical knowledge because they all do the same job in the same way. How can we bring a theatre to these people? You can't turn your back on half the people on a stage, and you can't sit back and say, "It takes all sorts to make a world ..." These people don't seem to want to interact: coexist, yes, profess mutual admiration and respect – but reveal nothing, admit to nothing. Don't admit there's poverty, because quite inadvertently that might mean blaming someone – political crimes are all crimes of omissions, neglect, ignorance. When Canada's Old Bolsheviks confess they'll say, "I'm sorry, I didn't know," "I'm afraid I didn't know I could make the choice ..."'

Peggy was hurt: why did people go into politics if they didn't want to help people, and the country they lived in? Alternatively, if you decided there was nothing to be done about some structure or other, like the professor said, you must force people to be free. Guerilla theatre was the perfect political vehicle: either people responded freely and openly, or you had to be shocked and alarmed into free and open response.

'Peggy,' said Leo, 'you are a very nice, a very honest girl. I would not like you to think, though, that your honesty is proof against error, your own even more than other people's. The question of improvisation, of participation, is basic to our political work. If we are a guerilla theatre – you understand this is my position – then we train other guerillas, we do not "put on a show". We also have a battle plan – though our weapons and objectives must be symbolic – which is not drawn up on the spur of the moment. We may live communally – up to a point – because it is expedient and efficient. But we are not demonstrating to ourselves that it is possible to live in a commune. That is not at all our purpose.'

Shirley said, 'But Leo, you have to take us as you find us—'

'On the contrary, Shirley, one must never take anyone as you find them,' said Leo angrily.

'Well, I don't agree with that – but at least I've got you to show some life. All I'm saying is that if you take these kids around the continent, you have to live with their limitations, and realise that things like living communally are their equivalent of your Party discipline – which in any case you've been able to do without. They are trying to overcome their limitations by courageous experiments. They aren't Marxists, and they're certainly not communists – and this is where your test comes in. I believe you still are: I think you're afraid that your gentleness prevents anyone from seeing your courage, or at least your obstinacy. When a twig is old enough, you can't tell if it's oak, or just gnarled.'

'But I'm certainly gnarled – thank you, duckie.' Leo was flattered, though.

'Why not get just a little drunk,' said Shirley, 'and tomorrow you can think more loosely. You've decided to stop giving directions and shouting warnings from the shore – you've decided to join the waves and the heads bobbing about in them. You have to start swimming, Leo, like the rest of us. I know you think we're open and shut people –when you look round this party, the guests are too drunk to know who the hosts are. I'm enough of a European to want some small emotional signposts through life, little bookmarkers at the exciting pages. "Here Leo was sad," "There Shirley was cheated and betrayed," and so on. But you can't blame the others, Leo. Their life is a nomad's trudge through the desert. When you look back there's pure duration and sandflies – occasionally a dry well or a clutch of broken cupolas, hatched a century ago. Sometimes you meet other nomads, and you carouse, or make love, or fight – then you plod on. It's a hard and demanding life, but there aren't many indulgences, or regrets, or much refinement.'

'Nomads don't live like that – I see your point, though. I think that psychologically you may be right. It's a kind of Augustinian world, with the good and the bad in an airless tumble before eternal bliss or eternal blister. But I can't like it – and I'll never be a nomad. I carry my little trinkets of recollection and emotion around with me, and when I unpack them, I don't care that there are some fakes among them.'

'But Leo, I trust your judgement. I'm fond of you, and fondness is rare – rarer than gratitude, which is the common coin of the desert soldier. And you must have had a prevision of this in your "difficult" room? But you I don't trust. We have to be under fire before I can do that. Now let's join the party. And not expect too much.'

aleya

'Will you please come in and see me?' the director asked Aleya. He emitted seriousness like a dust rising.

'They have written to you about my letter, then?'

'Just a moment. I have been reading a book about English literature, and, you know, I've been trying to understand you.'

'Me? Nothing to understand.'

'Ah yes, I think there is. People who live with intellectuals begin to ignore the difference between the poet and the critic. Do these intellectuals think we don't understand the demands of scholarship and the complexity of the tasks we are engaged in?'

'I don't know. I doubt if they give it much thought. Many intellectuals everywhere take up a negative and destructive attitude to the subjects they discuss – especially in fields where they cannot alter or influence the subject matter. It's easy to complain that something is difficult and obscure when you have the ability to expound those very obscurities – perhaps that is a critic-trap. But I don't understand you. I have respect for English literature and criticism. I live on a *sovkhoz*, not with intellectuals...'

The director stared at her, swaying slightly in his chair, like a boxer facing up to a kangaroo. He estimated other people's intelligence very low – and thought he could play his tricks convincingly. In fact, the workers found his simplicity childlike and tolerable, even at its most malicious. Or else they were overawed by his position, and the enormity of the claims he made for its responsibilities and demands. 'So, we are as hard to direct and control as that, are we? So there is so much involved in coordination and the organisation of others' work, then? A pity he's not more likable – we must avoid getting in his way ...'

Then, abruptly, 'What are your complaints? What must I do?'

'I don't want to give my complaints in detail. I hope you will take the opportunity to resign. I believe you have abused your position, and that this abuse is damaging to the technical and human operations on the farm.'

'Specific charges, please.'

'None to make at present. The mistakes in administration are just examples – they come from your attitude towards your duties, your concern to placate higher authorities by symbolic activity while ignoring the interests of production and of those who live here. In any case, to detailed charges you would promise restitution, make excuses. And I'd have to produce more and more charges – it's pointless.'

'Aha. I understand. It is a conspiracy. I have enemies on every committee in the republic. And you are their unwitting and unfortunate instrument.'

'You can't threaten and pity me simultaneously, you know. It is you who are the conspirator, you who resent competence in others, who drive away people you think of as rivals. You act like a landlord forced to manage his own farms – you do it badly and resentfully, and you hate us because we laugh at the mystery you make of ownership.'

'Ah, no, there I think you are wrong. There are not many laughing around here. Perhaps there are enemies of the success of the *sovkhoz*. There are backward elements – politically, morally. There are isolated people – and degenerates. There are people who use complaints against others to further their own huge ambitions.'

'And I am all these? Very well, if you want my declaration of war, you shall have it. I declare you *contra mundum*: it's you against the legion of the damned. Good luck, noble lord ...'

'Dear Aleya, I see I've annoyed you. Drama is so close to your nature!' he laughed. 'You see now my point about the critic and the poet. You're the poet who resents the critic, the organiser. The critic says – "But, Aleya, all your poems are about intellectuals – that is not a balance" and you reply, "Of course they are – I'm intelligent, and I like intelligent people." You won't see that you can't cast the world in your mould.'

The director thrashed about like a heavy grey fish snagged in the mouth. Aleya sat quietly, watching with increasing distaste as the director fought and thrashed against enemies breeding and crawling like armies of stinging flies. His passion was always thin, and now it is sour ... he uses our slogans as masks for his foxy faces. The only war he knows is civil war, to him the whole world is in latent conspiracy, and he remains correct – by organising a more active conspiracy. But it's a conspiracy of one – perhaps in a frightening league with thousands of individual conspiracies. You can only root them out one by one – they don't know each other's names – they just recognise each other by the air of listlessness, of activity at the end of its resources, of vigilance – and they suck at our vigour and goodwill, they breathe the smoke of our sacrificial charring ...

Aleya started to become restless – there seemed no reason why the director should not live out his life in self-justification before her, until he collapsed under the weight of crimes no one had committed.

Eventually he stopped – 'There will be a commission to investigate. Meanwhile I shall do nothing. Nothing at all.'

Every gamut seems to run from aesthetics to politics, and to die of repetition, thought Aleya. She stepped out into the sun – two shepherds stopped miming a game under the trees and waved to her.

A resident idler stopped looking merely busy as he passed her and winked. 'Work, work – that chiefly distinguishes us from the animals,' he said. 'And there will always be more men, like there'll be more sheep. And we'll always have to avoid the full heat of the sun...' He was the best singer in the district, and Aleya was happy.

aleya's diary

'Oh Alexei, Alexei – it is so hard to withhold pity, and pity is what you least need.'

I had gone to see him in his room, a room crammed with papers to the point of obsession.

'They look like magnolia leaves, don't they?' he said. 'Thinking about the human voice and its varieties, the need to imagine it stringed or struck – that is, as an instrument, able to imitate … I am working, you see, on a book of poems and jokes. Would you like to hear a joke?'

'Fine.'

'It seems there were two wolves who met up one day – one an atheist, and the other a most pious chap. They discussed the state of the scavenging, the best way for winter nests to face, movements of hunters and mutual acquaintances, and then the religious one said, "Brother, why don't you turn to God? I don't want to press you, or embarrass you, but I really can recommend it – the observances, the theology, everything." And the other wolf said, "I don't think I'm less pious than you, but I don't think our lifestyle is conducive to belief." And his friend replied, "There must be some compensation for being a wolf."'

On impulse I asked, 'Alexei, would you work more happily abroad?'

'In many ways I agree with you. Pity and gentleness and concern are no therapy for me. To go abroad would avoid the challenge of being ignored. But you see, I really am in trouble. I try to irritate my illness, like a soldier opening a wound to avoid being sent back to the front. But I have a wound. I exaggerate, I invent – but I am wounded. I had a bath this morning, and pretended the steam was stifling me – and then suddenly it was, and I had to lie on the floor like a fool, with my nose sticking under the door.'

'That's foolish,' I said. 'Like this stuff about magnolias, and tremulos of silence. I think I like the jokes. But you are simply rejecting seriousness, not getting protection. Is the trouble a political one?'

'My trouble is that I'm not clever enough to know what are the objective deformations and which the subjective. I'm too sensitive to be useful. Sometimes I feel like the boy who tells the emperor he's naked, and that the crowd shouts at me 'so are you', and I am. And that the palace issues a statement saying that despite slanders to the contrary, the emperor is always fully clothed, even when bathing, and there will be another procession to prove it tomorrow. And it all happens again ... And I too am always naked.'

'But you're not, Alexei. Everyone *is* wearing clothes. The problem is to criticise their design, not their absence!'

'This is not my kind of life. I can't make these bellowing public statements. If I was lucky, after a lifetime of work I might manage to express my own concerns and discontents. Even to encourage a few other people. But this is not what is wanted.'

'There are difficulties in being heard in every country. As your wolf says, there must be other compensations than simply doing what you have to do.'

'That certainly wasn't the point of the joke. But confidence is such a fragile thing. When I can't write, and sit here and smoke all day, I am so oppressed by uselessness, my "museum of one". And to think of this lasting for years – you remember Vera who went to the clinic for depression, and found they'd cured her of being a painter? There are jokes like that to look forward to, but that's all ...'

'You're making me feel absurd. Do you really see me as some heroic figure beating down difficulties and opposition with my fat red cheeks and solid shoulders?'

'No – that is what I wanted to make you feel. Because I really am sick – I have to pass it on.'

'Let's go out somewhere. If I stay I'll want to read all your manuscripts, and that would take too long ...'

Alexei wanted to look at the cheese in GUM, and speculate on the sheep and meadows it had come from, to see the stiff black fish, the people fingering clothes and casually pressing each other away from the most volatile parts of the queues. I was embarrassed by his exhibitionism. But he seemed after all rested and appeased, and perhaps he got some satisfaction from my uneasiness in face of his sensuous delight. Another one who's convinced of my innocence. Oh well ...

We had tea in a little buffet, the fan batting lazily at the flies like a sleepy cat twitching its tail tip. I felt contented. Alexei seems quite reconciled to his terminal condition, and he has the clearness, the precision and detail of the schizoid which gives to casual pleasures the permanence and poignancy of the epic. I enjoy my status as honorary artist, even though I'll never write anything more than my diary, and end up somewhere in the sun teaching collective farmers *King Lear*. Alexei would call my desire for a decent life escapism. But it's no more than self-preservation. I couldn't live in Alexei's chaos. I like his imagination, but I don't enjoy seeing him in labour.

I suppose I'm like all the little girls who romanticise the wildest literary fantasists – who think every poet spends the time between acceptances of his slim volumes being welcomed at airports. Instead, like Alexei, he's shaking away with the grippe, crammed full of snot and self-pity that his mistress has gone off and left behind only a knob of bread so stale he can't break it.

And when we get him home, 'Alexei, please don't cry. We all share it –

we all share you. When it is winter, it is winter for everyone. You're so distressed – and I share your fears of what distresses you ... But I can't give in to it. I don't want to be a part of your life. I can only help you by being separate, not by joining you.'

As I went away – down the street, I heard him singing – it was horrible, just as he said, like a voice being struck, scraped away at by some child fiddler. And I'm sure he know this, and is stronger than the torment he causes me. And I try very hard to draw warmth from the fondness I feel for him.. It is a silly notion that my affection for him, or for what he might be, could make me feel better. But just not deserting him warms me – an end of charcoal made to glow by a cold wind.

Sergei had bought me two peonies – I found them when I got home. There was a note, 'For the last of the incorruptibles'. They are so red and dark.

leo

Before they left, the police visited them. Leo was himself still trying to devise plays for the group, but though Shirley encouraged him, it was by saying, 'Why that's beautiful', or 'I never knew you could write like that – is it really yours?' Not the stuff to rock the bourgeoisie back on its heels. Nor audible or visible, thought Leo.

'The cops think we're raising money by pushing,' explained Peggy.

'I know the Trots do that,' said Leo, 'but we're not Trots,' and, defiantly, 'Opiates are the capitalism of the masses.'

'Who is *this* guy?' exclaimed the sergeant. 'You found the granny of the Mafia or something?'

'To me it's just like prohibition – just one of the modes of puritanism that North America puts itself through for excitement,' said Leo. 'If it's not religious ecstasy, it's putting wood alcohol in the booze. Something in everything for everyone – perfect. How boring! – all that biology and knowledge of legal systems – one might as well be an Albigensian.'

The police stood grinning round Leo: the cop said, 'So, what are you going to do?'

'Something we might call "speculative theatre": an experiment in guerilla tactics and political education ...'

'Look, if you're just trying to start a revolution – come on, say it. Everyone else does. Please don't think my tolerance repressive – still less contemptuous, but tell me perhaps where you're starting? Town or country? Plenty of space in the Prairies for manoeuvres – you could have a whole cavalry division galloping about there for weeks…'

And Leo thought that in the long night of rationalism, when one was more or less by definition disarmed, one might have to do what Shirley advised, find a warm body and snuggle up to it. As a fellow immigrant told him as they left the ship, 'Here we know nothing which is OK. So we just look with eyes round like so and say "My, how grand", "My, how fine."'

And Leo had replied softly, 'Faith is dead, long live God,' and the other winked.

Later he had tried to explain to Shirley how things could be right because they are almost right.

'Doesn't this lead to deformations, and deformation of deformation?'

'That's what we call evolution,' Leo replied, and was comforted to see her silent. But now he was not sure. For what then do we call deformation?

The sergeant asked, 'What plays are you doing?'

'I have in mind three versions of *Hamlet* – the first anti-capitalist. Claudius and Gertrude attempt to institute an isolationist and paternalistic regime – monopoly capitalism with plenty of support for arts' centres.

Hamlet is a naive and conservative nationalist, hooked on legitimacy, naive speculation on his own origins, viability and so forth. Able to use and exploit others, but not to develop an élan, forever brooding in his tent. Able to terrorise too – but essentially mythic and atavistic. And it is Fortinbras, militarist, barbarous, who comes to set up a frankly military and repressive regime.'

'Sounds a bit weak – and not much like Hamlet,' said the sergeant, 'But go on.'

'The second is a satire on neocolonialism – Claudius and Hamlet represent different modes of decolonialisation – and forms of neocolonialism. After a period of pseudo-independence Denmark suffers her period of civil war and dynastic confusion – the problem of a successor state, in fact. Claudius has killed the great white mother, as it were, and it is left to Fortinbras to terminate the psychological confusion by making Denmark a colony or semi-colony.'

'Better – but it should be called Fortinbras, emperor of Norway.'

'Finally, anti-imperialism. Claudius has staged a coup with American aid ('those defoliants, so bad for the ears' someone whispered), and uses CIA agents to dispose of Hamlet. Hamlet uses guerilla theatre to stake his – bourgeois nationalist – claim. I don't think I need tell you who Fortinbras is in this one?'

'It sounds like guerilla puppets to me,' said the sergeant. 'I thought guerilla theatre used people's own culture, used what they're familiar with. You've simplified the play – but people don't know that. It's still complicated to them – and you've added a new element of complication – the kind of Marxism that went out forty years ago. I wish you luck, but I can't see there'll be a rush for tickets.'

'Then the experiment will be over. But there is a fourth version – which is the whole point. These three playlets take only a few minutes – and they are puppet shows. The real play is the rise and fall – of the emperor Fortinbras. The man without history, without drama.'

The actors looked relieved at this small final rabbit pulled from Leo's hat. The police went out smiling – a young constable said, 'Gee, it's not often you meet up with your stereotype of a guy, but that guy sure was him ...'

Later, Leo said, 'Shirley, I know it's no good. I can't rise to necessity like a salmon leaping upstream. I'm basically an old eel swimming about in the estuary.'

'And you have your Sargasso Sea too? Away from the mud and up over the land, past the jaguar masks and the tequila bottles, for one final splash. Up to the mausoleum and there, alongside our Ilich, your wife like Snow White? Leo, I'm not a bitch. I know your intensity needs quietness and reflection. Perhaps in coming with you I'll be forced by the strangeness of the whole thing into a harshness, a lack of understanding. But I'm as convinced as you that the alternatives are worse – not in a tactical sense, of course. This theatre is probably nonsense – but I can't ignore the imperative of action. And I don't find your wariness of the word and its consequences a weakness. You are our human mask.'

'What I must do,' said Leo, 'is to think out the whole play thing again. To lose some of this despair. Because,' more cheerfully, 'I have survived, goddammit. It doesn't matter that no one looked for me with any great attention – there are millions of corpses with the same complaint! Do you remember Lenin saying of foreigners, "They must digest a good piece of Russian experience"? And going on, "How they will do this I do not know"? I think we forget that our lives are devoted to study, careful, precise study – breaking away whenever we can to "start learning from the beginning". And so, Shirley, shall we start learning together? From the beginning?'

'You make me feel awkward, and I don't know why. So – you're right. Whatever we learn, it must be from the beginning.' She smiled. He followed the progress of her smile, as if it had been a dolphin. 'Vassili, Vassili,' he said softly, 'That's what fishermen call their dolphins – or so someone told me.'

'Some day,' said Shirley, 'I'll tell you about my husband. That is where you will have to start studying me ...'

'I have always seen you as someone who had a divorce rather than a husband.'

'That's probably because you liked me more than you knew me, or wanted to know me. That too will have to change on the road. We must start now – look, it's thawing.'

'I hate this Canadian thaw – it's so ugly.'

'But warmer – so stop being dismal.'

feodor

'Listen, listen, listen,' said the loudspeaker. It fell silent. I was given my new beginning – I had had so many, always yielded on demand, now I must try to resolve my dilemma. Analysis without power – which would be no analysis, or power without analysis – which would be no power. One side of me – perverse – longs for the richness of dissent. To paint, let's say, an immense and bright yellow wall, and have some critic say, 'That's the most astonishing thing I've ever seen' – to be the wit and wizard of the most intelligent men of the universe, living or dead. Another side – which is not weak, I think – demands a caution and judgement, serious purposes, the strength to change things. Imagine these two battered old horses with Sophie as the third – pulling and cavorting like a shell-burst, or three bickering drunks pooling their roubles for the next bottle of the evening.

Back in Moscow I used to discuss the release of my potential dispassionately. Like the doves of peace let out at the start of international games – my schemes circled round disconsolately and perched about on the roof of the stadium, watching the professionals fight it out on the pitch. The girls, off to the southland: all the serious warriors, off to fight the States with their notebooks, heads lined with the battle-strain of ideological combat – none of them doubted my capacity. They all tried to release me from the tension as they would help a child imprisoned in its stammer. But the thing I have to do – I know how difficult and dangerous it is. I've spent my life in training for the moment when I have the choice, to speak or be silent.

Last night my old friend Mikhail came to see me. We were at the Institute together, but he left to become an engineer. He works hard at his ideas, but from nervousness or intimacy I always attack them, and it is exhausting for us to meet. He was too shy to ask about Sophie, but he scrutinised me for clues.

'You know about America,' he asked me. 'What will happen?'

'When Marx said the choice was one between socialism or barbarism, he probably meant it rhetorically. But it seems to me that intelligent people may coolly and intently choose barbarism in preference to socialism. Or because socialism is too demanding, or unsatisfying: or not profuse and exotic enough. A surfeit of inequality can lead people to desire only surfeits – not necessarily social equality!'

'Do you think, then,' asked Mikhail slowly, 'that we have had a coexistence of socialism and barbarism?'

'I don't think, if you're right, that the barbarism was the result of an intelligent choice. Expedient, perhaps: tired, frustrated, alarmist perhaps...'

'But you've no doubt that where choices were made, they were the almost correct ones? Barbarism was absence of mind!'

'If I did doubt, I'd obviously be useless. Doubting is one way of making it be true. But if I lived in America, I'd be frightened. They're so savage, so bitter – they plan their temper tantrums like they plan building bridges ...'

'Yes, it's true that things seem bleak – I feel we have to face a long period of reaction, and that we'll all be deeply affected.'

'Yes, deeply.'

'You're very sombre for a man with a new project. And I've asked Aleksandra to come round too – she's the new counsellor at the factory.'

When she arrived, I instinctively disliked her: but I have my instincts well subdued, and she is quite beautiful. I remember someone in the repair sheds calling her 'the great white weasel', but I couldn't see why, except for her quickness and the way she tests out the chair she sits in with her body, like a cat.

'I'm trying to cheer up Feodor here,' said Mikhail. 'I think he needs a little classicism in him – he's lost faith in straight lines and angles!'

'Well, I expect living in the provinces does that – one loses touch with excellence, I find – people find their paths don't cross so often, and one is forced into a slower pace against one's will.' She spoke briskly, and apparently without thought.

She turned to me. 'Grigor was saying how bad it was for someone active like you to have to waste his time, little bits of writing here and there. I hope you can put some order into the story of our lives.'

'Well, as yet I've no plans for the research.'

'Oh – imagination will do it all for you, I suppose? When I started counselling I thought that. Talking of classicism – I tried to shape my "cases" like a French novelist reworking his material. I thought that by intellectualising I could make people interested in their intellects instead of their problems. Didn't work. People live in their bodies like heat in a flame – they twist and writhe and can't get out ... But Mikhail tells me you know all about America, and the southland?'

And suddenly I thought of the agony of walking in the sun that afternoon, not so many months back, when I'd known Sophie only a few weeks: and of seeing the dead dog – two streams, one of blood, one of urine, both drying purple-brown – abandoned where the sun climbs the sky on two tigers' backs. And of the hawk circling in the cracked dome of the mosque, as if it were watching me running about on my doggy errands, trying to pretend that no limits encircled my necessity ...

'Can I come and see you at the factory?' I asked Aleksandra.

'Today there was a woman, crying and crying. Something about waste and the waste of regret. And in the end I said, "I'm sure you'll feel better in time – but why wait for time when a decision can be made now – to be objective?" And she stopped crying, and straightened up and said, "You bitch," and walked out looking as stiff and brave as anyone you can imagine.'

'I think you were right,' I said. 'Impatience is a great virtue. I'll see you tomorrow.'

When they had gone I saw the clouds round the moon had parted –and I remembered the line of poetry, about how in every true Russian there's a Decembrist, and of my own lonely conspiracy, and the need to spread it – perhaps to Aleksandra.

aleya

Aleya remembered, as she looked out over the low valley, the lines:

How happy might I still have mowed
Had not Love here his Thistles sowed!

The ground was matted with tall, sappy thistles almost to the stream's edge. Some geese stood about confusedly – flapping their wings as if for flights eternally postponed, gulping towards the thistles as if one day they would snap them down with their lumpy beaks. They were guarded by two little children, whose conquest of the fear of geese had turned them suddenly into sporty and malicious adults. An odd kind of love, though, Aleya thought – marked in real life, as in conceit, by technical difficulties. You could only feel love for the *sovkhoz* – otherwise you'd have left; but even so it was something of a forced marriage.

That day there was to be an open-air confrontation between Aleya and the director. 'It's insane,' she'd said. 'First because of the heat, second, because it looks like a wrestling match.'

'Aha,' said the director. 'We'll call out the guard dogs. No point in breaking into their leisure time – and wasteful to take them out of the fields. No one can conspire in the open air. The breeze will sort out the light from the heavy. This is the democratic way, no?'

'I've no idea,' said Aleya. 'It doesn't seem anything to me except inconvenient. I think everyone will be bemused – and tired.'

'Well, we'll see if it's just a matter of summer languor – the heat bubbling your brains in their shell!'

When the old Russian woman heard, she said, 'Fine. I remember we had the same thing once in Turkey. We all went out to the Sweet Waters of Asia. Plenty to eat, some excellent drumming: a bear to dance – so old he looked stuffed. By then, my dear, we'd become a sort of liberal Turkish aristocracy – the ragged frondeurs, they used to call us. We had a series of debating and wrestling matches – military and civilian, church and state, Great Russians and pan-Slavs, white-whites and red-whites. Great fun. I don't remember who won, but it was good entertainment. All started over some question of titles ... But you'll always find the grievances sound better – more generalised somehow – in the open air.'

'But I don't want to martyr – or be martyred! He's just got some plan, that's all. He wants to know who's making trouble so he can discredit them behind their backs.'

'If that's true, and even if he's believed – if he shows the authorities a huge conspiracy, he's lost. Everyone loves a successful plotter, my dear. No one has had more experience of that than I. My own life was a plot to rise to the gentry, and then in exile to sneak back over the wire. I came from humble origins and now I think I've done well for myself. My conspiracy is nearly over – you're just starting.'

'And,' she added, 'Don't overestimate the subtlety of the director. He will stake everything on the first throw – he thinks only in terms of apocalypse and transformation.'

There were two or three hundred people gathered. They stood and sat under a plume of trees by the water. Two Turcomen were playing 'Are you frightened?' on clarinets. A sheep had nearly finished its journey into hell, and was ready to be taken off the spit. Some men were dancing around it in anticipation. Men in caftans and leather hats which looked like sections of toadstool squatted in silence.

The director began, 'It seems that we are not happy – all of us – with our life here. There will shortly be a commission to ask us what is wrong. We must be honest with them, as we must also be comradely among ourselves. That, comrades, is democracy. But first we should hear from the one who finds our self-management deficient. Tell us, Aleya, about the quality of our life – what greater efforts we must make to improve ourselves, how much harder we must work, what firmer direction we require. Remember that we will all have to discuss these things again with the commission.'

Three men playing cards at the back shouted together, 'Tuz – ace' and many people laughed. An agronomist from the Ukraine said, 'Come on, I want my dinner. Talk and eat, or eat and talk, no speeches before the soup.'

Aleya said, 'Let us consider this travesty of democracy. For the first time we are asked all together – 'what complaints do you have?' With what – with wages, conditions, personalities – what? I believe, since our collective hunger makes us blunt, that the removal of the director, like the removal of capitalism, would solve many problems immediately. Just the big things – are we intimidated? Do we know what choices we can make when we lay down policy? Do we feel that our contribution is valued? Our advice considered? When new buildings are planned – do we want a few expensive ones or many temporary ones? These are simple but basic questions. If we are not satisfied – then we can discuss nothing, no restitution – we would have no democracy.'

One of the shepherds – we called him Sultan – said, 'We have thought about the question deeply. I find Aleya's incoherence encouraging. We do not know her well, but she is respected. We do not know the director well either, but he is not respected. We have a saying, "The sheep which leads the other sheep is not a leader – he's just terrified of being left behind!" I think the director is like that – and I'm not frightened to say it. The people who are afraid are the ones from the towns, from the professions. They deal in tiny perceptions, they have to make precise calculations – "Where does this man's personality end, and his job begin?", "Is this woman vicious because of her husband, or her job, or her neighbours?" – and we among ourselves are perhaps more used to judging people than these teachers and agronomists and medical orderlies and technicians.

'We are used to a democracy of judgement. I think Aleya means this too – you can't have confidence in a man by taking a vote, counting heads. If a man diminishes you – there can be no restitution but his removal – he oppresses you politically as well as personally, and the remedy must be political also. We are trying to play an instrument very delicately balanced – at one end is Soviet power, and at the other are ourselves, who are its subjects and objects, and also its players. This is a difficult notion, and a lapse of concentration, forgetting the metre – all is thrown out ...'

His friend Kulkul replied, 'Yes, but there may be immaturity in change too. We have grievances against the director: can grievance make a democracy?'

'Perhaps grievance removed may,' said Aleya, 'but we are not so immature. We have vast organisations for self-government. Are they not at present merely frustrated by one man and the information given to us?'

'Aren't you ignoring the whole basis of our labour here, which is to complement and compete with similar organisations? Our initiative is limited by our function and capacity – we are a link in the chain, and we can't decide to become a new chain,' said Gelderan. 'We must not exaggerate the effects which might be produced by a change of director. If the effects are not so great – then one is left only with small problems.'

'I agree,' said someone else. 'Democracy is misleading here: democracy is the universal form – it's the massive generality, and the massive banality. It doesn't help with questions of authority. Would we work better with a collective leadership – not simply in name, but in fact? For me – yes, certainly. You have only to see the production figures – they show how slack we are. It is hard to accommodate the freedom of others within the framework of one's own – but this the director has not tried to do.'

The director sat amazed. It was as if some guru had asked the standard meaningless question – 'What is a question?' or 'What is is?' and found the group of dim acolytes coming up with a variety of answers, and challenges to the propriety of the question. The saintlike curve of his body and neck ... reproduced from Novgorod to Sopoćani – showing concern at internments, virgin births, openings of tombs, plenums, coronations – was beginning to straighten and stiffen. The poet had strummed his lute and asked his questions of the burnished bird under the lilac tree once too often. The bird had criticised his rhyme scheme, and. produced its own slim lyrics and plump epics in revenge.

'Look here,' said the Ukrainian, 'I can't stand this painful attempt at sophistication any longer. Forced mental labour is out – it's worse than physical. Mental labour is mechanised too, you know. Write it all down if you're interested. If anyone will speak for the director besides himself, I'll hear him – if not, let's eat.'

'No, let's eat anyway,' said the director.

When the cause of asceticism is lost, bring on the mutton pilaff, thought Aleya.

The meeting adjourned, and the clarinets took over.

aleya's diary

This morning I told Larissa, 'You can't have a duty to immolate yourself: No one is helped by your wish to sacrifice yourself – it impoverishes, it's an insult. If you're afraid of living with regrets – that's better than regretting living!'

And Larissa said, 'If I marry Lev, I'll have to leave the theatre – that's all. It's not such a loss.'

'It's not a disaster. Do you want me to go on and say something ridiculously exaggerated? But you can't love someone who does not even understand what you are sacrificing. As the saying is, "In the country of the blind, Oedipus is a bon bourgeois." Why doesn't Lev sacrifice some of his volleyball, a few evenings carping and scratching in front of the television? Even if he thinks you are a promiscuous careerist – it won't hurt him. He's obviously beyond the reach of that kind of pain ...'

Larissa has always been a good friend. She carries her talent so modestly and surely, she never has to be harsh with herself – she is economical with her enthusiasm. When she is serious she commands attention, because she is suspending a good humour she obviously enjoys, and which fits her like a snake's second skin. But she wants to follow Lev into infantilism – teaching primitive ballet to little girls, making him supper, theatre tickets once a month for some glamorous revival he wants to see. 'Larissa, it's a kind of fossilised courtship – with a bit of bad temper thrown in. With that kind of peace and security you'll go stringy and acid in a year ...'

'Well, Aleya – and what will you have? You won't see there's a difference between tenderness and lyricism, between a sort of vulgar Marxist ethic in which privacy is an inessential – and my feelings for Lev. Those are creative, not schematic ... I don't want to be unkind, but you seem to he so busy loving everyone that you're deliberately avoiding specific creativities ...'

'Well, at least. I'm vulgar. And I'd rather be vulgar, than an interior decorator. I'd rather be public property than a young man's darling ... You're so hostile, so defensive.'

'And you're defenceless, Aleya. I don't resent your affection for me – only your clumsiness ...'

'But this is what some of the professors at the Institute say. One yesterday told us, "Delicacy of manners – a contradiction? Can one learn delicacy without learning manners? This is a central problem in English aesthetics – but not, I think in French, because the trick of learning there is always social, and imitation is always seen merely as parody."

'"I can't agree," I said, and then, "That seems what I'm always saying ..."

'He smiled and said, "Exactly. You are a good daughter of the Soviets – you have neither manners nor delicacy!"

'We all laughed, because he is habitually droll about categories, and our attempts to criticise him. But afterwards – I thought, well no, I don't know that I want either. I have both, I think, but they are always in my way ...' But I don't think Larissa was satisfied by this attempt to turn her flank.

I was still disturbed when I went to see Sergei. I said, 'Alexei has such capacity for bitterness. What can we do?'

'We all have such a capacity.'

'But his is a social bitterness which poisons his writing.'

'Correctly. But why do you think Alexei is such a special case? Do you think I'm so starry-eyed, then? Because I'm cool about things where Alexei is frenetic? Of course I'm often bitter and frustrated – but I don't believe this proves anything. Alexei assumes that his emotions and ambitions mirror the real world. I don't.'

'Sergei,' I said, 'why do you send me flowers? Convention? Are you touched by me? Does what you've said mean that you too despair?'

'No, only that I've the capacity for despair. Despair is what happens when you get tired of pushing forward – and I've a great deal of energy. That's why I like you – you don't cling. You're one of the best, the most independent people we've got at the Institute this year. I don't think you've a good mind, but you don't do any harm by that. One is interested in the success or failure of broad movements, tendencies: not by whether individuals are right or wrong, clever or foolish.'

'And you think I'll be successful?'

'If you work at it. I don't mean material or cerebral success, of course. You're not interested in those, probably not capable of them either. I mean, you intuit successfully. You can grasp the pressures and demands of living in a socialist society, and make something of yourself in this. People like Alexei don't have this power.'

'And you?'

'I think I can adjust to socialism well.'

'But you talk about socialism as if it's a suit of clothes and you can say, "Ho hum, this fits well – or it fits if I breathe in, or it used to fit but I'm too big for it now." It's not like that at all – if anything it's you that's the suit ...'

We watched the gardeners adjusting the sprinklers – the arms so exactly dropping their little receding rattle of water on the leaves, like a handful of peas tossed on a roof. It seemed as though this blue burning summer would last for ever – with me forever standing, looking through the railings, unable to find even a gate with a lock.

I said, 'Sergei, we're really not very close, are we? You're so sombre, so bleak. You'll go to the end of an idea or a suspicion till we're all left behind.

Inside, you're fearless: you don't need me.'

Sardonically, 'I don't know, Aleya. I've not been going very long. I am not afraid of my ideas: I'm not impulsive. I give others the benefit of my uncertainty. But I won't let anyone lie to me, or make me lie. I don't believe in endlessly suspended judgements, or permanent judiciousness. And if this makes me wrong – too bad.'

'Which takes us back to Alexei.'

'Alexei is beyond our help – really. He's still capable of making judgements. So long as he writes, he's in control. If he breaks down, it will be a reasonable decision on his part. We can't advise him.'

'But politically ...'

'Politically he's chosen to glamourise and generalise some wild and personal impressions. He may be right. But in any case, it's easy to see his position is inappropriate and unavailing. He doesn't hate injustice, he hates politics, and fears it.'

'Now I don't understand. You can't say "he may be right ..." and not wisely. Something deeper than that is called for:'

Sergei smiled. 'Cosmically, he may be right. But no resolution will be cosmic. In the detail, I think he underestimates the problems and the errors: in general, I think he exaggerates. That's all.'

'So meanwhile Alexei is permitted to shake himself to pieces?'

Sergei said coolly, 'I feel great loyalty. But not, I confess, great friendliness. People fascinate me, they don't often touch me.'

I felt hurt, abandoned. 'You analyse yourself out of existence. And me too.'

'No, Aleya, we all live in your shadow. Our darkness brings out your light.'

'That's cheap, Sergei.'

I went home. I could not bear to see his flowers.

feodor

As I went in to see Aleksandra, Grigor said, 'You're looking stronger these days – are you getting more meat in the soup?' What does he mean? Sophie – not Sophie? One of the pleasantries he throws out to everyone, like a child dropping stones in a lake to see the ripple of laughter return – part of the general bustle.

I am immediately attracted to Aleksandra – she is looking out of the window as I do, as if she'll never speak again, locked in the glass.

'Ah, Feodor – so you're to share my office, then.'

'No one told me – and won't it be inconvenient?'

'That's the point, Grigor thinks people will he coming for counselling every day – you're my deterrent to over-indulgence. He's afraid they'll criticise too much ...'

'So I'll have to interview in here too – analysis and cure, all in the same room. Why don't I start with you, and then you can carry out the therapy on yourself ...'

'No harm in that. I'm forthright, but I don't make demands – you'll see.'

'Forthright but not frank – I've had that one pulled on me.'

'You don't know me well enough to ask that question. When I was very young we used to have a dacha for the summer. Three cats rolling on the lawn. Everywhere pine shingles. Light broken up into gold and silver coins in its passage through the trees. Violin lessons in the kitchen.

'Talking to the workers in the collective – one old man used to tell me, "Eh, how different you look from my little grandchildren – what's that now?"

'"I don't know," I'd pipe back. "I don't *feel* different – really I don't. Will you tell them that, Please?"

'And he'd go on about his work on the farm, how he always spoke straight out, not like people from the cities, and how that's what the revolution had meant to him. "If I've an idea, I can speak about it. I'm master now in my own head. We don't always get what we need – the people who make the plan don't understand, you see – they've never worked on a farm, not like I have ..."

'I used to feel he was criticising my father who was always talking about some plans he had, which wasn't at all like the plans we had, to go and look in the stream or play with the dog. He always used to say, "Yes, Aleksandra, I used to work on a farm. I can stack sheaves now, or anything you want" and laugh, and I could never believe him.

'But mostly I remember the gold, grey, purple of the dark places in the forest where I took my books – and in the spring a lighter gold. In the forest I discovered my mind, while the old man's grandchildren were discovering their bodies. What a little prig I must have been – my white knee socks and a volume of Pushkin so big and heavy I could hardly push it through the grass.

'Can you imagine those brilliant summers, with the buzz of the harvesters, the golden dust from the broken corn-stalks, the shouts of the workers drifting in through the trees like big bright lost insects? I wonder if you'll find a study on the contemplation of collective labour – I assure you, until I was eighteen, contemplation was the only activity I knew. Even the Komsomol camps – the same old idyll.

'Then at university I met the man I thought would be the complement to these golden summers. But – how humiliating! I couldn't rise to his intensity. Should I have carried something more astringent to the thicket than Pushkin, perhaps? He talked of reconcilable and irreconcilable forces, of accents, of bird song, of Chernyshevsky – he was all of a piece, and none of it for me.

'"Can't you wait a little, give me some time to catch up?"

'But no, he wanted me to gobble everything down at once, so we'd start as equals. And I couldn't.

'One day I said, "I'm a drag on you, aren't I?"

'"Sometimes," he replied, and although this was only a passing impatience, I took the opportunity to free him.

'"How could you?" I said.

'And he told me, "What do you know of the hardness of our lives? You think I'm doing you a favour by trying to harden you – I'm not. It's necessary for you, it's inescapable. You're not liberating me – you're escaping from your deficiencies. And you think I'm repulsed by deficiencies! I'm your therapist ..."

'So here I am. We parted, and I decided, like you, to look and talk more responsibly.'

'But I'm not looking and talking. I have resolved, as they say, to devote myself to a life of action. The only problem ever is – which mode to use? What difficulties and inappropriateness lie in the mode we choose?'

'But Feodor, you make this sound a tiny question. It's the biggest you can ask.'

'Most people either live without asking it, or have the answer thrust on them. Ours is the first generation which could even begin to consider freely how large a contribution, how great an effort and in what direction, we were willing – and able – to make.'

She smiles sadly at me. We can hear an argument from the next office – 'Of course, of course that was my idea. I have to have ideas, don't I? No, I didn't think much of it – but someone has to have even bad ideas. No, I'm not surprised it hasn't worked out. It's not a disaster. We'll just do it the old way till some other idiot has an idea. Yes, I know, but procedures aren't ideas – of course I realise there are procedures, but if you can't change one part without changing all the others we'll rot of boredom!'

And from the yard outside came a voice – 'Yes, but today we must work, comrade, or tomorrow we'll die,' but we had not heard what had prompted this reply.

leo

At 'Fortinbras – emperor of the world' Leo's imagination flagged. A tug of the nostalgia Europeans have for Europe – for walking in the forest, picking mushrooms, clearing the hillsides of edible matter – silenced him. Was there a point in writing a play – undoubtedly becoming more convoluted and personal by every page – until instead of street theatre there emerged the usual magic epic, smelling of pines and cedars in sunshine rippling like silk?

'At least communists saved *their* intellectuals from hopelessness longer than the others,' he thought.

Shirley came to see him. 'Why exactly did you leave the Soviet Union?'

'So many of one's friends wanted to – it seemed a criticism of them to refuse when one's own chance came. But really – I think it was the impossibility of publication. It's a terrible thing for us not to be persecuted and censored on political grounds. My stuff was not good enough, that's all. I got tired, that was it. And my wife died. And a friend got into trouble over his categories – especially contradiction ...'

'Why didn't you persevere?'

'That's like saying, "but *someone* must be a virgin" – if no one got dismayed and discouraged in the search for recognition, we'd be submerged in rotten novels and film scripts. So many of us chose the hardest of modes – the most public, and the most: open to abuse. I went from writing plays to action – failing on the small stage, I decided to try the big one.'

'Why did you stop working with the steelmen here? You seem to feed on defeat, if I may say.'

'Not really. I don't understand these workers. I don't blame them for wanting a bite at any super-profits that are going. But their philistinism is so craven, so smug. You see, I'm something that is dying out. Until now, intellectuals have thought that in identifying problems, showing how the tricks are played, they were serving the proletariat – and it's true: they were serving them. But now – the problems are clear: any fool can tell you what they are. And now we've formulated them – we can't pretend that solutions will be worked out by us. They'll be resolved by forces over which we've no control – which may try to keep us alive and happy, but which show no deference, no liking, and certainly no admiration. We're occasionally feared, but not respected. There's no premium on declassed intellectuals anywhere.'

'That's why you're here, Leo, looking for a higher price – but no one's bidding.'

'No, Shirley – and I can be waspish too, you know. What more do you want of me – my guts are hanging like ribbons already.'

'So?'

'So, there is one last question I will not ask. Suppose I'm wholly right –

my analysis, my imperatives – so, let us say, without questioning too closely, I'm right. So what? So what for me? Am I to spend my life on the petty intellectual treadmill – "the role of the Leo in history" – when one knows the answer is "It doesn't matter – it doesn't matter much to anyone – it doesn't matter much to you yourself." I often feel it would be easy to write – subjectively or realistically – works of power and quality. Instead, one deliberately chooses the soldier's virtues.'

'But Leo, you have other choices. What of your need for someone young, alert, impressionable? Someone to whom this talk of treason, intellectual struggle, is not the common coin of the unsuccessful, but brilliant – like a hoard of archaic gold ornaments taken from the earth.'

'Your trouble, Shirley, is that you can't see the pain and the tragedy in all this without trying to add to it. And you can't add a thing – the forces which produced me and my condition are massive and serious. The question is: how to stay public and to concern oneself only with major things, how to be an intellectual, that is, not merely a critical intelligence – when no one is listening? Your remarks are of no more significance to this – than insect bites. You have to stand back in order to see the magnitude of the disaster you may be watching.

'That's why Fortinbras is the man who conquers introspection, who can't be brought down by poison or trickery, or human madness or error. He plays in the open, there's no stage trickery for him: he talks on equal terms with magnates and managers, technicians and generals. He has this power to homogenise life – to unite – only stylistically, perhaps – the variety, the intricacy of life. He's too big for me – because in a sense I'm his victim. He's a man who casts no shadow, because of the intensity of his own internal luminosity. He's like the real police siren that makes one's knees prickle in the *Dies Irae*, and he's the real cops that carry you out of the concert hall and beat you so you bleed real blood ...'

'Leo, I think we're fumbling towards each other, and always missing. I don't want to be cruel. Even when you're most irritating you have this poignancy, this guiltless complicity in the lyricism and awfulness of the movement and its moments. I mean – you fly your wife at half-mast, like a flag. Did you like her? The same with your politics – I'm not big enough to answer your giant question – and you know this. So my concern must be in a minor key. Your delight is the delight you have in writing where you're posing and answering your own problematic ...'

Leo thought of his wife, sleeping in the next room, curled up in indifference or bafflement, while he and his friends argued. He remembered someone asking the very question he had feared to ask: who ever had anything but dissatisfaction from history? A pointless question, but it had brought them all together. In the early fifties in Moscow personal satisfaction was coming to seem equivalent to cosmic deliverance.

'And your husband, Shirley?'

'We really didn't like each other. This gave us tenderness. But everything became routine very quickly. When I see you sitting there – in control at the typewriter, like a pilot – you have a delight, as I say, which love might let me share. With my husband – there were no private qualities, there was nothing to be discovered – the water ran fast and turbulently – but you could always see the bottom ... With you, I'm afraid of drowning, both in the darkness, and in the nests of tricky river-monsters. You see, Leo, to me you're the magician. You're like a very small creature living in a big shell, twisted like an ear. Nothing large enough to want to prey on you can follow you round all those bone pillars. And all you'll say impatiently – as if really all you want is to stand firm and be eaten – is "Here I am, here, here."'

'You pay a mean compliment!'

'You leave one no choice – you have this habit of intimidating by never discussing my problems. Just seeing them as permanent limitations. But back to Fortinbras ...'

'The man without a shadow. I see him as intelligent, rather good-humoured: perhaps a charming man. And with a wife who has all these qualities and so is rather boring. I see him as someone who is constantly nauseated by his own blandness, the comforts of deference. He's a Mongol general who can't shake off the air-conditioning and the bourbon before dinner. I think he does dream of scaffolds – producing neat piles of skulls like the ones in the battle room in the Tretyakov. He's a triumph of cerebration – wholly unsentimental about human existence, modes of production and so on. He's a despot of the consensus, a discriminating mass murderer. He supports capitalism because it provides him with corrupt versions of himself: he's not interested in skinning the ox twice – only in killing it efficiently in the first place.'

'What happens in the play?'

'We put it on in a square, a plaza. There are three themes – of internal dissolution, a kind of crapular degeneration, too much Volnay and blood pudding. Not a loss of will, but the realisation that Fortinbras is the acme of the unconcerned individual. He doesn't calculate interests – his interest stops when he's asleep. Selfishness can go no further, and people realise that what serves his selfishness does not serve theirs. Then there's the theme of colonial revolt, and finally, the rebellion of the mercenaries.'

'And what happens?'

'I don't know. You see, we start with the stage piled high with corpses. Clearly, we finish in the same way. In a sense, Fortinbras is not only a professional soldier, he's avid for drama. He doesn't want to hire players, though, he wants to play everything himself. Deliver the funeral orations on everyone. I think in the play, he may even win: temporarily – but his strength is out of proportion to his vulnerability. You can't get rid of him by a quick switch of weapons. So perhaps – we're looking again for a party of a new type.'

'And an end to sects?'

'Yes.'

'But Leo, the group is so far from you on this. They're so like Peggy, all of them. She regards anyone who calls themself a socialist as a freak. Her life is a religion of discomfort – of doing unpleasant things with people she doesn't know or like. It's an asceticism so extreme that it just might produce some crude artefacts in a generation, and a little simple food. It's a notion entirely like Fortinbras – of collective selfishness. She thinks you're Moses – for her it's not the East but the Sea that's Red! It's a humble and isolated existence and its notion of what constitutes simplicity and purity is pretty vapid. I've no idea what they'll make of the play – but nothing of comfort to you.'

'But I'm the magician, remember?'

aleya

Over on a low hill a single black buzzard, like a scout for his horde. Well, thought Aleya – we seem to have tamed this desert. And really – I'm not inelegant. When all this is over, perhaps I'll turn to poetry, like an English bureaucrat. We're running from politics into picnics. It is after all a sweet life – easy to become soft and discontented.

The buzzard lifted off the slope like a scrap of charred paper, dwindling to lark size. Aleya walked through the raspberry plot. Things chirred to each other. Insects so bizarre they must spend a lifetime looking for approximate mates went about their small household tasks. There was a scent of pomegranate, damp clay, warm flesh – a dangerous subtlety which flared at times into a wild aphrodisiac intensity. Aleya envied the women who worked in these fields – their total immersion in the aroma of legend. Now the director had forbidden the gangs to have musicians with them at work, there was nothing between your own work rhythm and burning thoughts ...

How many strange armies, thought Aleya, must have come bursting through these hot stones. And how different this heat from Moscow's. It's eight years, isn't it, since Alexei wrote that parody for me – a parody of my girlishness. Always look on the nasty side as a matter of principle, he said – it's amazing how often you'll find something. He called it Visit – and it was my visit –

The long tongue bubbles in the pot
and granny prods it, chats to it:
ah, now I see you, duckie, new dress and all –
at the corner pause to rouse the cat –
up the stair; burst in
on the peonies I have for you
heads heavy with blood.

How absurd, she thought, to worry about this before our confrontation. The old Russian woman had said, 'My dear – you're doing very well. I know you don't want to, but this once you can't help it – so enjoy the experience. Who can stand up to objective scrutiny? I doubt if you can, Aleya, even though you've had practice. The director can't.

'I remember someone in Istanbul – he was always saying, "Tell me your criticisms, what are my faults, what can I do to help you?" Until I told him, "You're always trying to do things wrong so that other people have to sweat to get them right – and also to forgive you. Your fault is you've faults like a geyser. Every hour or so you make some totally predictable mistake! It's no good blocking one vent – you're turbid with error – you'll only cool off when you're extinct."

'My! how he shouted at me then! "Forgive? Forgive?" he screamed. "It's you I've to forgive all the time, it's worn me out."

'So I said, "Why not try a little quiet recrimination all round – so much better for the heart – than criticism and atonement?"

'He actually stamped a hole in the floor – easy enough to do in those days – and you know Turkish workmen? He could never seem to get it mended – they would suggest instead turning closets into fireplaces, or blocking off half the room, but never manage to bring themselves and a piece of sawn wood on the same day. But you must think my stories are like the man's who is always the last across before the frontier closes, or the man who liberates Bucharest a day before the rest arrive ...'

The Ukrainian started the discussion: 'It seems to me we can choose between loyalty – which in this case means familiarity – and potential, which in this case means doing the moderately unsettling thing and being moderately successful at it. If there has been intimidation, there has been slackness. Now there can be no more intimidation – but the danger of slackness remains.'

The director said, 'No! The question of motive is paramount. Suppose our enemies discovered all this – I call a meeting to discuss, and it turns into a trial!'

'But,' said Aleya, 'we're all used to trials like this – just for once it's happening to you, in a mannerly way.'

'Aha – so it is a matter of charges,' said the director. 'What of my counter-charges? That you, Aleya, retain feelings of contempt for us, the *sovkhoz* workers? That you look down on our enterprise. And you despise my origins. In the war our bread was so hard frozen we had to urinate on it to melt it. That leaves a mark on a man, you know. You lack charity, Aleya.'

Sultan said, 'That is really irrelevant. We are not discussing moral sensibility and delicacy in what anyway seems to have been a question of necessity or technique: You choose to remember that element in your past – but what do you want of us – that we should all produce some *cochonnerie* to match yours? For you to call a meeting – that is a good way for the old regime to end, if you ask me. All our origins – all of us here – we're Soviet originals! Aleya can't despise me, even if she wants to. We do our work: we are polite. Sometimes we discuss what we have read, or drink tea together. It's not an ideal social relation – it doesn't have to be. But there is no chink for contempt.'

And all round there were voices – 'How can she despise me?' 'What is the discussion about – *Sovkhoz* matters or war memoirs?' 'Is the sheep cooked – we've had enough of bickering ...' 'Vote and let's be done.'

Aleya said, 'I love the farm. If I didn't, I should leave. If I don't seem very warm – it's because it really doesn't seem necessary. I live and work here, I have my concerns and my pride. But I am wholly content.'

Someone said, 'This business about criticism being harmful – I've not heard that for twenty years. In any case, criticism isn't a luxury – we don't have to buy it with our labour. There's a story about one of the emirs. He was very arrogant, very cruel: and he had some kind of talking bird – a raven, I believe. And the only criticism he would tolerate was from the raven which he taught himself. Anyone else was tossed in with the snakes and lizards. And one day the raven said, "Look, your magnificence, I'm getting tired of my critical role. You've done very well by me all this time, and I'd like to tell people of your kindness towards me. I know they think you're a cruel tyrant out there – but believe me, with no desire to flatter, I find you wholly tolerable."

'At first the emir wouldn't hear of it – he taught the raven ever more ferocious critical comments, and the raven almost split himself mouthing these phrases, while really he wanted to hop on the balcony and praise the emir. Well, in the end the emir relented. The raven made a special appearance: everyone went away with the words of the raven in their ears – "Your emir is a man of great, if potential, saintliness. He has lavished his care and protection on me – though I am, as you see, only a stunted and shabby raven."

'But when they got home, everyone said – "This is too much. Not even the raven can criticise that tyrant now." And a huge mob stormed the palace, and threw the emir to his comeuppance off the tower of death,' he paused. 'And they threw the raven off with him. But he fluttered away, of course, being only – and exactly – a bird ...'

'I don't understand,' said the director, clutching at straws as if they had been raven feathers.

'Now we're on this,' said Kulkul. 'Even "our enemies" have some intelligence. We have, surely, every intention to recast the whole organisation. When we've discussed this privately, this has been our conclusion and recommendation. No damage can result from this. No one is to benefit or to be punished. It's our decision.'

'Let's at least have a bit of music,' said a young mechanic. 'The question's settled – the commission's reported?'

'No – only a commission of our own organisation ...'

'Well, anyway, there's a song going round:

'Our throats hurt with the dust and the singing,
Our fingers too with playing the komuz and holding the reins – Galloping across our rich valleys, through our rivers –
Spray like the pearls on a warm white neck ...

Hope's like a fledgling, and every morning
We ride, young eagles, plucking happiness
Like ripe peaches for our lovers in the sovkhoz ...'

'Rather self-regarding,' said the Ukrainian, 'but short and clear.'

And Aleya felt the pressure of the pleasure which comes from living in an environment which many people working together have adapted to their convenience without spoiling it. The director continued to protest.

'You pass through moods like a fly going through a rainbow,' the Ukrainian told him. 'Try to be a man, take some pleasure in the shape of the argument, not your own metamorphoses. You've marked so many of us down for execution you'll need to replace us with sheep.'

'*Je rêve la tête sur la pointe de mon couteau le Pérou,*' whispered the old Russian lady.

'Who will speak for me now?' exclaimed the director. 'You talk of intimidation – now some tiny group has to intimidate you – no one has a word of gratitude for me. What's to become of me, then?'

'He is struggling to emerge from bathos into tragedy,' whispered the old lady, louder.

'I am several kinds of Hero, you know,' said the director.

'Then add one more – Hero of comradely silence,' said a shepherd.

'It's not that I mind going,' said the director. 'But who here has any experience?'

'Your fault if none of us has. We have experience of our jobs, of political work – we have many types of experience,' said Aleya.

'Lenin said he expected the level of sophistication to fall when the mass tried to operate democracy,' said the director. 'He said it would be simpler and more direct – which was fine then, but now we're too complex. The amount of work I myself had to deal with – incredible. No cooperation from above – single-handed I toiled ...'

'But we've always been here!' shouted a labourer. 'You make me sick with this talk of Lenin. Of course there is a difference in the level of consciousness of different strata. But that's not at stake here – through action you become wiser. You never trusted us – to talk of Lenin is not appropriate ...'

Aleya thought, as the meeting once more broke up and the men and women went back to meadow, field, plantation, or office, of the English poet's –

'... now I all the day complain
Joining my Labour to my Pain;
And with my Scythe cut down the Grass,
Yet still my Grief is where it was: ...'

She had certainly, like the mower, expanded the possibilities of action. There was more labour, more pain: and the intensity of this labour did, up to a point, discipline her subjectivism. But the discipline smarted, and the grief remained, a grief which could not be connected with the director, certainly, and not even with Alexei, or Sergei. But, she thought, one victory a day is enough. The buzzard was flapping away, back to the mountains.

aleya's diary

Alexei is dead.

We have a lifetime to make up for it.

I cling to Sergei's saying – 'but he intended it. He was quite wrong – but he wanted it, he wanted to end the pain.' But in fact my feeling is closer to Dimitri's – fear.

Dimitri said, 'Was he afraid of something in himself – or of something which we cannot see, which menaces all of us?'

And Sergei said, simply, 'Suicide as a form of praxis – I don't think so. One has one's thoughts and opinions, and if they're unpopular one tries to withstand pressure for as long as resistance is justified. Suicide is a subjective response to an objective situation – that's to say, it can only in this case be subjective.'

'But that's why we're terrified!' I shouted.

'Look, Aleya – Alexei might have been a good poet. At present he was ragged and undisciplined. He'd no idea how to write for an audience, or how to project a personality through his work. He killed himself for one of three reasons – because he felt his talent was too slender and had come to an end. Or because he felt he would never be a popular and respected poet – however much he developed, and was prepared to accept the responsibility and strain of writing in isolation from an audience. Or because the people he admired had also committed suicide – for many reasons, but together making up a style of life. Or death.

'Politically, as I've always said, Alexei lacked originality. He alludes wildly to all kinds of deficiencies – to crimes against *joie de vivre*, to woolly speculation about the mental equipment and character of Soviet man – the whole thing done with neither humour, or understanding, or analysis. I'm sure to the normal run of anti-Soviet readers the poems will say one thing only – there is something deeply troubled in Soviet society. I say only – well, that may be: but I see in the poems only that there's something troubled in Alexei. They don't say anything about our problems negatively or positively – he just spots problems and wrings his hands over them.'

'What about "Dzerzhinsky Square"?' Dimitri asked. 'Who has seen it?'

No one had. 'Do you remember,' I said, 'how Alexei always used to quote that conversation he overheard between an American and a Russian? The Russian complimented the tourist on his accent. "How do you do it?" "Aha, you just heard me ordering breakfast – and I always have the same thing. So in this area my accent is perfect."

'And to test him the Russian said, "In order to travel in Russia, it is necessary to speak Russian," and the tourist, misunderstanding or smartly, said, "In order to travel in Russia it is necessary to speak, and to see, in the

Russian manner." His poetry is full of just such insights, which he worked over – rejecting the false or the over-literary.'

'But that's it exactly,' said Sergei. 'I don't want to destroy a reputation before it exists. But essentially the insights are all literary – he wasn't getting away from Gogol. When his characters take a walk you can hear the quails calling, even if they're on Kalinin Prospekt – and in every factory canteen, people can choose between six flavours and colours of mushroom. People are always breaking off in the middle of profound discussions to comment on the quality of the light, to get drunk, or to listen to men singing three blocks away, or smell some old-style Ukrainian cooking which just happens to be wafting by. He's a sensationalist but he borrows sensations ...'

The police called us, and we had all gone over to his room. The ambulance had taken his body, and his suicide had become an affair of flesh and blood, not poetry. His room was covered with cheap paper – most pieces blank, but some with scraps of poems, phrases. He had been working on a wolf joke before his death.

'It seems there were two wolves – a husband and a wife. And the wife was complaining about the size of their nest. And the husband said, "Why do you want a bigger one – this is snug." And the wife said, "It's so small – you're always bumping into me." And the other wolf said, "I do that on purpose – I like the feel of your fur. Very sexy." And the wife said, "Well, if you promise not to do that any more, I won't ask you to get a bigger nest ..."'

Dimitri was reading this with me – he said, 'He encouraged bitterness in himself. It's as though he's saying that to be happy is to stand accused – even in human relations. Unless one picks at the flaws, like lifting off scabs to see the infection below, one is deluded.'

But I am still not able to accept his death – and the arguments about his poetry do not refer to the man I knew. I suppose there is an element of the heroic temper in me – though I feel awkward even writing that.

I remember the photograph of the professors sent just after the Revolution to start a university in Tashkent. They are standing outside the railway station in Moscow in the snow. Serious, non-committal. But as though they had been ordered to walk through thick fog for the rest of their lives – to lose touch entirely with the world of rational expectation, the world of reasonable aspiration. I feel like them.

In a way, I'd always half thought that I had the choice to make – marriage to Alexei; marriage to Sergei; or rejection of both. There was no urgency. But now, Alexei's death has, as it were, sent me to the railway station. It would be as impossible for me now to marry Sergei – if he wanted – as it always was to marry Alexei. Alexei would have exhausted me – he was insatiable for the loyalty and reassurance of his friends, but himself unchangingly sardonic. Obsessively, he demanded disillusion. The excitement you got from relations with him was the testing of the fencer's nerve. You were always parrying, defending, watching every finger and toe for a surprise attack.

I couldn't have lived with his poetry, wondering what cruelty and bitterness I'd read there – a life to which I could only bring some petty order, some minimal discipline. Living with a writer – you can't affect the inner structure of his life and work. That, he has to build and develop in isolation and independence. I would be devoting my maturity to his immaturity and his brilliance. I'm not ready for that – and it offends my sense of justice.

And Sergei – an inner life and response not developed, but concealed. Sergei is capable of the greatest fortitude, everything he does is based on decision. What he plans he executes unsentimentally. If he fails, he doesn't take it personally: the plan has failed, that's all. But attack when he hasn't failed – and he'll fight.

But there's another side to this. This lack of sentimentality, this lack of concern with himself, can hide a withering away of integrity. A man who uses his integrity only to defend mistakes or successes of the intellect is not, after all, a deeply engaged man. He's incapable of judging himself, or listening to the judgements of others – intellectual arrogance becomes a shabby isolation.

I can see Sergei in ten years carrying out some task with dedication, but with profound unconcern about its effect on himself or others. He has a capacity for becoming engrossed in the petty. And I know that he'd soon poison my enthusiasms – 'This thirst for life and vividness – rather self-indulgent, rather breathless, don't you think? Struggle and enthusiasm are fine – but not always appropriate, eh?' That's what he'd say. And I've no reason, no need, which forces me to take the chance.

Larissa came to see me this evening. 'You complain about my loss of intensity,' she said, 'but what of yours? You look quite dispassionate to me – and you were always so fond of Alexei.'

I said, 'Whatever Alexei meant, whatever he dreaded – this was a big wide public gesture. He didn't collapse slowly. He died as a man of action, and he killed himself because he saw himself in a war. I don't know who it was against – perhaps he killed himself to provide a concrete victim in place of those who may not even exist. He had a peaceful nature. And he was tormented – I know this, because he said to me once, "Aleya, these crimes of the cult of personality – am I guilty of the same cult, and by neglect and omission, of the same crimes?"

'And I said, "Alexei – I can't comfort you over crimes you've not committed. Suppose there is a similarity – it's a similarity of paranoia. But with you, it's your own little paranoia – it doesn't spread outside. It can easily be treated – it's a genuine, non-infectious disease."

'But he had a terror that he'd be cured of his talent. His trouble was that he couldn't distinguish politics from poetry. I'm not trying to analyse the similarity – but yes there was in Alexei the troubling duality of what he called *l'âme bolchévique*. I think, you see, he thought of himself as some kind of spoiled Bolshevik, with the qualities and strengths exaggerated and perverse. He idealised and fantasised the whole thing, of course.

'He knew nothing of politics – he did talk about souls, spirits, guilt – poetry was for him a kind of religious mania. He saw in the history of our Party a marriage of terror and innocence. And in himself the hysteria, the hypersensitivity of the victim turned executioner, the executioner turned victim. And in place of innocence, an innocence perverted by the knowledge of things one does not wish to string together, actions from whose consequences one turns one's head.

'I think he was afraid that he was made like the people he hated and feared. But really, he wasn't. He was totally unfitted to understand either dedication or vigilance. He wasn't one of us because he wasn't one of anyone. I loved him but now he's dead, there's no gap. He couldn't fill a gap in anyone's life.'

'But do you think he was right?'

'He was a dangerous man. He felt things very deeply. He had no judgement. My concern for him was all personal. He said to me one day, "Aleya, I don't know if anyone anywhere is constructing anything to last. All I know is that my poetry dies with me, I can't give it life. I'm inventive, not creative. I so want my work to have autonomy, to breathe." And he felt he'd never succeeded.'

'It still seems to me that you don't care that he's dead.'

Alexei couldn't breathe life into me. I was living already: because he couldn't create me, he didn't want me. He ended by not wanting himself either. I can see the morning sky now – blue as the sky over Nishapur, blue as a blue bowl, with a hard line of moon setting. There's a cat patrolling. Everywhere seems deserted. A wisp of scent from the syringa rises to me, like the last smoke from a candle pinched out. Alexei is dead.

feodor

Aleksandra continues: 'It's so easy to be young for ever. To make this a land of eternal childhood – bleakness is not growing up. I see now how bleak my childhood was. A decision to live unopened.'

'You're so sad,' I say, 'and about such little things. Sad because you don't want hardship. Would you really like to live in New York – your friends making bombs, or money? Every day a physical adventure – even sitting in those little bars with the weak beer, the big cat stirring the ice cubes in its scotch and soda with a dusty paw. Men coming in and talking of Carnera and wife-beating ...?'

'You really believe it's like that? You'd hate to travel?'

'Travel means acquiring a seamless and unchanging reverie. I don't know that that would be good for me.'

But Aleksandra still seems interested. We should start work. Reminiscence is fine – but as Yuri says, it is time to stop when you hear someone saying, 'Do you remember when we began to reminisce?'

She says, 'How firmly my grandmother impressed me with a life lived in defiance of history. The ways of plaiting hair, times when one could gather quails' eggs. All as if the world were a garden – the birds all and for always singing the same song. One just gathered goodies, dried them or stewed them.'

'And then? The princess awoke? The dragon ate a poisonous mushroom and died?'

'Yes, I know it makes me sound flabby. Certainly granny died. You know how people who've lived through every awkwardness and privation resent their internal cooling and waning. She struggled against death so much it weakened her. She was afraid. How deeply she loved those summer days, when the heat struck through her – piercing through black stained glass. She – quick as a gnome in the grass – sorting the edible from the inedible.'

'You're a funny girl, Aleksandra. Life here is very different, you know. It's an abrasive life – but not exactly stimulating. I confess – I spend the winters dreaming of the south – music and storytelling in the open air, what keener pleasure than that? The little cubes of melon, thin wine; crowds round the try-your-strength machine; people carrying in weird things from the desert, and inventing legends about them. And I think about America too – little boys sticky with orange soda pop; youths in cowboy hats driving recklessly round small towns on Sunday afternoon; millions of the poor and lonely going to the corner store for wieners and cigarettes, and lingering – to hear a voice that will speak to them.'

'So what do you do here?'

'Drink amateurishly. Music, the theatre. Whatever one can do in the provinces. It's as if one were studying for some great metropolitan exam, some urban fantasy. The life of big cities is the only one I understand – rural life the only one I enjoy.'

We sit and look at each other, like two strange animals in the same cage – are we there to mate or entertain the crowds?

Aleksandra does not understand me – she is so determined to get used to the unpleasant that I'm just another challenge, another bitter medicine to be swallowed quickly.

But we have a client this morning – Andrei, who says 'Well, the history of my life. Well, not much history. First, the fighting, then the holocaust, and now another bit of a rest, praise God. I remember at first: you'd be walking along the streets, and you'd see people eyeing your shoes – seeing if they'd go well in the pot. And thieving – well, we had to. I stayed on here working – lots of lads from my village were in the army. But the rest of us didn't get fat, I'll tell you.

'And then it was hard again – when they were putting in the factories. I've seen men work themselves to death in a few months: we were frantic to get the thing finished. We were almost crazy here, It seemed like the one chance to secure ourselves. And the engineers used to weep when they saw what we had – we had nothing! We'd build things three or four times – the cement would be too weak, or the foundations too shallow. Some got discouraged, some took to thieving.

'But I always used to say, "It's the only way: if it kills us, it's the only way. Someone'll survive. Look at us – we're survivors, aren't we?" I gave two families – my brothers and sisters, and then my own wife and children. And none of them died pretty and silently. I'm lucky to be here – to see the parks and the flags and the cars. And the tools we have now – when I started here, there were men coming in as mechanics who'd never seen a whole truck. They'd learned their trade on the pieces!

'But I don't begrudge the effort – I used to say, "I'm carrying you fellows, but I don't care. There's some of you as are lazy, and some discouraged – but just think, what if we succeed? We've to get the whole thing moving that's for sure. We're all making mistakes right and left – who needs sabotage? But there's not much we can do about any mistakes apart from our own."'

'Andrei, won't you come again, and we'll write you up?' I ask. 'And Aleksandra will have questions.'

Aleksandra still looks vacant. She says, 'Yours has been a life of great privation and sacrifice – and danger.'

Andrei says, 'Yes, in a way I've been lucky to have seen so much. No one here will ever see this again. I'm what you might call a founding father

– a sort of collective grandfather, and it's only right: you should come to me for my story.

'And you mustn't think we were savages then – we studied, how we read and studied. We just needed to get into the rhythm of things, learn how to do things in the proper way. Learn to trust the other men on the line, and show the engineers and all them we knew what we were talking about. It took a long time – but now it's done, isn't it? We didn't have much to start with. We didn't do it brilliantly, but we did it. It was a hard slog, and a lot of us didn't make it.

'But as my wife used to say, "There's only the future, Andrei. The past has gone, the present is going. Only the future's coming." It sounds silly, but there's sense in it. Now, I'd be quite different. These days, I'd be an engineer myself – at any rate, I'd be able to lift my head off the job and my face from the soup as they say. But I'll be back.'

I too have to leave – a day in the country with Ilich. Trundling out into the birch trees, the train busy with improvised meals, cloths full of fish and pasties, cards, singing, vodka, accordions. How can people play so coherently when they're too drunk to stand? The conductress running from naughtiness to naughtiness with round threats. Now, no one cares if they get thrown out on their heads. Ilich and I are drinking quietly – and a man comes up and tells us a legend about a bear who had a paw cut off by one of the princes of Moscow, and raised an army of bears to avenge him. But the prince cut off his own right hand and sent it to the bear general, who promptly retreated.

'That's very odd,' says Ilich. 'One doesn't expect to find such a sense of honour in a prince of Moscow.'

In the distance, as we leave the station, we see domes like blue dough, with gold stars painted on them. There is a smell of new logs. It is warm enough to lie in the grass and watch the clouds breaking up like smoke. The grass is so thick, you can't see the soil.

'How good to be a beetle,' Ilich says, 'a built-in helicopter on your back.'

And I think of Andrei, working to stay alive so that I can stay alive. And we lie out in the meadow till the last bird falls silent.

leo

Leo told Shirley, 'I'm not a dilettante, I'm not a charlatan. But I grow to distrust passion. You can call my play a *tour de faiblesse* if you like – but it warns, it doesn't maim. Do you remember that passage where old Karl – I don't myself remember exactly – is discussing philosophy. He says theory is never realised in a people except insofar as it is a realisation of their needs. Will theoretical needs be directly practical ones? It is not enough that thought seeks realisation, reality must also seek out thought ... Just as philosophy finds in the proletariat its material forces, the proletariat finds in philosophy its intellectual weapons ... The emancipation of – he said Germany – is the emancipation of man. Philosophy is the head of this emancipation. The proletariat is the heart. Philosophy cannot be realised except by the suppression of the proletariat and the proletariat cannot be realised without the realisation of philosophy.

'I think that's close; and from idleness or optimism, one awaits the working out of the process. I see from your face you don't understand me – but I'm sure underneath there is a question?'

'What did you do when you knew of the extent of the purges?'

'At first I felt like a driver, intently whipping up his horses through the snow. "Faster, faster – we're gaining on the wolves" – and the horses try magnificently, and we do indeed go faster. And then the danger is over, you look back cheerfully, and your passengers – a family of sixteen – have disappeared. Gobbled one by one. You almost laugh, because of the tiredness, and because you're the survivor, and because you were the father or the brother of those children. And so you think: next time it will be different. More horses, guns to shoot the wolves. Meanwhile, you look for decency where there might be despair, potential instead of slaughter. I think you just sweat it out – we who did not really leave, who didn't desert. But these actors we have here – without fear or reproach – I doubt their ability to survive. You may think I'm at the end of my rope, that I'm a walking shadow. But it's always easy to personalise answers to personal questions. I exist as long as I keep going. I won my existence the hard way, and I don't believe in surrendering it easily.'

'But you defend this existence against those who want to share it.'

'There are big gaps between us, Shirley. There's no point in cutting down trees indiscriminately to see if they'll reach across. One should always be economical in one's gestures, especially when holding an axe.'

Leo had just presented the play to the group. Lloyd said, 'No rehearsals, man.'

'I thought we'd all just pick it up as we go along,' Peggy said, 'we're not real actors, you know.'

Does anyone like the play?' Leo asked.

Some said it was too complicated: others, too baroque.

'What happens in the end?' asked Shirley.

'I think we must make it clear that there is a difference between the way in which people are actually fighting Fortinbras, and the effort we ask of the audience – to choose sides, to work out strategies. The play simply shows us Fortinbras exists ...' said Leo.

Later, he said to Shirley, 'There comes a point at which simplification becomes just simple. It seems to me there were three reactions in the group. One element wants the theatre to be simply an emanation of group life. This would be "our" play – personal and proselytising – "be different, imitate us". These want something sad and lyrical – arousing pity through suffering. To others, the theatre is just a way of moving around – they enjoy not understanding the play, since that makes so few demands. The others want something less cool, something full of rage and despair. Everyone believes he lives in the eye of the apocalypse: this is not just *a* play – it must be *the* play – they want David and Goliath, not Fortinbras and the masses.'

'And they're wrong?'

'Wishful thinking is deeply addictive. But you always put me in the position of negative critic. I like speculation and argument – not movement and agreement. At the same time I don't want to start a commune – to me there is a coarsening in that life. I don't want to buy friendship at the expense of impoverishing myself, intellectually and physically. But there's no general significance in all this.'

'But there is,' said Shirley, 'since you see this as symptom, not therapy. You see it as a path to disillusion.'

'Well, I've been often enough and rightly disillusioned.'

'But,' Shirley went on, 'don't you feel you could be accused of fighting the movement?'

'My dear, where can you be more private than in conversation? If I put my reservations always tête à tête – what conceivable harm? Can one make mistakes talking to a friend? It is for you to correct me.'

'But you know I can't. You've had a lifetime of winning arguments and losing battles. You remind me of a man I met in the war-history museum in Vienna, who said, "Patriotism sealed in defeats – especially defeats as complete and humiliating as these – is far superior to the opportunist enthusiasms of the perpetual victors. There's nothing like a string of military defeats for awakening interest and pride in the arts." You're my Austrian, Leo. You're well on the road back to cream cakes.'

'And wine, I hope. Let's stop picking at each other's feathers like two vultures in a cage. You never know when there'll be a corpse, and you'll need all your energy then ...'

They drank in a bar where the electric candles flickered three times to the right and twice to the left. A few miles away, moose lifted their sad old noses as they tramped through the swamps. Six men in uniform watched a cartoon on television – the mother of invention being pounded by her technology.

'I find that coyote more moving than the book of Job,' said one. 'At least Job grew older and wiser – but what can you do if you're a hungry animal? Chastening experiences don't fill your belly.'

Leo thought of his wife saying, 'With you, everything seems secure. I lived my life to find you.' And he corrected her. 'You lived your life and found me.' And his wife had cried, because in his correction there always lay a distancing, pedantry for the sake of punishment.

'I wouldn't punish you,' he told Shirley.

'I wouldn't let you.'

'Tell me about your husband.'

'I was deeply fond of him – but it didn't grow into anything. We were very young, and the poignancy grew and grew. He, I think, was ashamed, and I was desperate because I didn't know what were problems in his head, and what were problems between us. We kept off the delicate areas, until everything was delicate. I can't remember now how we spent all the time. He seemed very active at first, like young people do.

'But really he just did the same things with lots of people. He'd known, for instance, a lot of women – but only the same thing about them. When he'd taught me what he knew – that was it. He'd no inner tension. He only ever thought of what he could do next – he never concentrated on anything – just practised it. He was a teacher, and that too was just a game – he popped subjects into his students' heads as he popped golfballs into the holes. He was normal and decent to the point of insanity. If you desired him, it was an admission of promiscuity, he was so blandly efficient. He was as well-rounded as a well-cover. He tried everything – drama, pot, lechery, radicalism – he walked round life as though it was a department store, and he only picked up bargains. Nothing troubled him except the void he poured all this experience down. If, just once, he'd heard a thud at the bottom, he'd have been happy. In the end, he threw me down – but I never hit anything solid – just screamed at the sensation of falling.'

'Ho hum, yes. Seems to have been a bad choice. But then, you seem demanding yourself.'

'Well yes. Why not?'

They sat quietly together, and Leo wished that someone would bring some flowers to sell. Dark blue, smelling of water, these would be best. After all, Fortinbras did not like plays, only musicals. Somewhere a man was singing, 'I went down on Shannon Street, now to buy some alcohol', and Leo relaxed, ‘drinking my conscience’ as he put it.

aleya

Aleya waited impatiently for the commission. Each morning now the shepherds called to her as they rode off. People seemed to feel a lightening in her presence – without discussing matters with her, they talked more freely of their own affairs, as though they were aware of a courage that was osmotic. The Russian woman was amused by the impatience – 'early awake – all day to worry in, as we used to say'. She told Aleya the story of the bowl.

'When I was making my way through Iran, they told the story of a bowl-maker, somewhere in the south of the country. A man commissioned him to produce a bowl. But nothing happened. After a long time the patron went to the artisan's house. After much delay he brought out a beautiful bowl, needing just one feather on a bird, or berry on a bush – I forget which.

'"Fine," said the patron, "just finish that, and I'll be back tomorrow."

'The next day, the design was changed. Perhaps it was the bowl itself that had been switched. A new set of glazes was being made ready. The bowl was beautiful again, but this time the wing of a bat, or one character in a poem, was not quite ready. Again the patron accepted the bowl on condition it was finished the next day. But the next day and the next – and so on – something was always missing: the eye of a hawk, the toe of a beetle, a plume in a turban.

'Finally, the patron said, "All right – you must tell me what is wrong. If you don't wish me to possess a bowl, tell me, and I'll give you restitution for what I've done wrong."

'And the artist said, "You've done nothing wrong. Jut as there's an art in making an unfinished bowl, so too there's an art in contemplating the unfinished work of art. And it's this art I've been trying so painstakingly to teach you all these months." No need to say more.'

As, finally, she waited for the commission, she could hear a man strumming and singing over and over the two lines:

'My horse's mane reminds me of my darling's hair –
But now they've brought tractors to our sovkhoz ...'

Through a heavy heat haze, almost white, she saw the director coming. These days he affected a limp, and occasionally from his fierce mask of concentration a smile would ooze, like a sorcerer remembering at last where he'd hidden all the serpents in the world. He and Aleya waited silently – though he greeted her with 'aha'.

Aleya was struck by how unimpressed the members of the commission looked. They were the eagles scanning the steppe – from so high, it was hard to see when anything moved, and what things were – voles or petals. The Party secretaries of the district and the region – Asan and Yevgeny – were the most significant.

'We came here to show we've no intention of castigating anyone,' said Yevgeny. 'These matters should be settled without bitterness. We have Aleya's letter, and reports of your meetings. We will try to reach a decision in private – but if there is no agreement, we can do nothing, we can only recommend.'

Yevgeny summarised the arguments: the other members sighed and sweated – the director glaring at the lazy fan as though it were an artificial lung. Aleya thought of the softening of her sense of isolation: perhaps it was no more than a certain restlessness, a fastidiousness, of regret for choices made and made correctly. Perhaps it was only a refusal to accept security – a fire burning hotter because no flame is allowed to show. How good, she thought, not to be married to Sergei, not to wake to hear him creeping to bed from his books – both dressing intently and silently next morning.

She thought, perhaps I should be more attached to my body and the history of my life. But it was so good to stand in the sun and feel the last northern dampness, the last corner of swamp and marsh burn off into the burnished sky. Physical intimacy is, after all, she thought, the least precious. On a collective like this one lives a man's life anyway – one's not put out to graze through department stores, to goggle at the meat and the hats and the matrioshkas in the main street. One can sustain one's own moods and enthusiasms without the furtive selfishness that marriage encourages.

Asan said, 'As I see it, the matter is simple. Aleya, and many others, Party and non-Party, see the issue as this: here we have socialism for the people, but not by the people. Aleya claims the initiative of the mass of the workers is not allowed to develop, that the management of the *sovkhoz* produces arbitrary decisions, some good, some bad, by means of favouritism, misleading advice – or at least partial advice – and even by maintaining a set of numbing traditions. She does not say that, if this is true, we also must bear the blame – but it would be true that we must.'

The director said: 'Of course the workers support her. She is essentially anarchic, a wrecker. Discipline hurts. It is hard to enforce – I work by the hour to enforce it. Our record is good. The incompetent are ruthlessly identified. Where is the gratitude? This is an ideological struggle – Aleya is a saboteur, she undermines morale. Her contacts are with politically backward elements. We cannot co-exist in the same community.'

Yevgeny said, 'Crimes against production are serious. But I often think that a crime against the political development of the mass – instilling feelings of helplessness, of deference and inferiority, is worse. It leads to economic crimes – it's regressive. I remember an officer in the early days of the war said, "Don't blame me if we've no tank support – you may blame me, however, if you're scared." Perhaps we're a people to whom effort does not come easily, perhaps we're too easily impressed by what we've done, too lenient with mistakes. We like looking back at the ground we've covered – look at the potholes and puddles, look how high the mountains are, how primitive the villages. And we don't realise that the effort of constructing the way ahead and over the horizon will take ever more effect.

'Aleya, now – a girl of determination. You know how we've used the "link" system? In industry we can set targets by using workgroups of Party members, or new machines, or incentives. Not so easy out here. Hard to organise. Mixed results. You know all this. We've been thinking – and I know the director disagrees – about a little experiment. To organise a "link" of active people. Even living away from the main *sovkhoz* compound – organising their own work, taking their own decisions – and reporting back, of course. A little acting and thinking collective: not people who want private property or the easy life – but people who will find out more for us if they fail than many who succeed.

'It would be a hard life. You could draw on the machinery and so on – but on the basis of a plan that you'd draw up. Our guess is, you see, that these things fail for many reasons, but that inexperience and poor coordination are the main ones. You would be able to choose personnel – within reason. Say thirty-five people.'

Aleya asked, 'But what would we produce? How should we be organised?'

'That is for you to decide. You may find farming is all about politics, or all about sheep. We'd like to know.'

The director said, 'That's irresponsible. Too vague. And she's no experience. It's too hard. And it's too easy – she'll be a parasite.'

'Well, that's our other problem raised,' said Asan. 'Frankly, I feel we've gone beyond what you can give us. If you're the only one who can run the enterprise, then either it's run oddly, or else everyone else is incompetent. That too we must know. I don't know if you're temperamentally fitted for bureaucracy – I find you unfitted for collective work.'

'You're very bold, suddenly,' said the director.

'Yes, Aleya woke a lot of people from their sleep. She's not a conspirator – I think that's why you dislike her so much. We had to support you to avoid the appearance of conspiracy. She's like the girl who killed the dragon with a ladle when all the warriors had failed to pierce its skin with their swords.'

'Well, Aleya. Will you do this?' asked Yevgeny. 'We expect you to fail, but to fail nobly. But we have to try.'

'You're asking me to destroy myself to explore a blind alley – because you don't expect me to get out, but want to record my death agonies.'

'Yes, or even worse, to see how many people you can take with you,' said Asan.

'But really, what are you being asked to sacrifice? Only effort, and there is only ever effort! And think of the gain in consciousness!' Yevgeny smiled.

Later, when Aleya had accepted, and the director was still trying to disgorge hook after hook that he'd swallowed over the years, she said to the Russian woman, 'Katya, are they insane? They are supposed to dispose scientifically of our resources. What do I know?'

And Katya said 'That's your great alibi! But as for experiment – why not? If you lose money by conservatism – why not lose it instead by radicalism?'

'Will you come with us?'

'Certainly – every vanguard needs its granny to look after the children. If we sleep in mud huts, it'll be like Turkey again. Don't forget – a good part of the old regime ended up under newspaper blankets in Paris – by comparison the stars over the Bosphorus were cosy little nightlights.'

So, thought Aleya, this is where it's all been leading. On the anvil all these years and finally about to be used.

So much to be done – so much that she walked to the vineyard and watched the women tugging the long pale grapes – like fingernails. She sat and drank wine as snatches of song and laughter lifted the dark leaves.

John Fraser

aleya's diary

Alexei's absence is beginning to haunt us. I was talking to Dimitri last night. He had been complaining that boasting about one's achievements was a kind of philistinism – too much Taras Bulba, he called it. Suddenly he said, 'Aleya, you must quieten down. You're so tense, I can hardly sit in the same room with you. You think you're unaffected by Alexei's death, but you're almost terminal with tension.' He looked at me with such pity.

I said, 'Dimitri, I never knew what my feelings for him were. That's the problem. Feelings are irrelevant now.'

'Can't you discover what his feelings were for you?'

'Not easily. Despite one's impressions, he was a very taut writer. There's a roughness, a derivativeness which he'd probably cut out. But he's aware of writing in a tradition, and he doesn't give too much away.'

I showed Dimitri the last poem – Alexei had called it 'Last Poem':

I draw my trees freehand –
Sometimes their boughs don't join
Casually I botch my work, playing at it.
Someone is guarding our frontiers –
Sorry for you, lad, but thanks.
While you watch, cherry trees
Are springing everywhere from the ink ...
I don't want to hurt you – how could I?
Anyway, you are all I have to love.

You grind my colours – grind them hard,
They have to last. Remember, though,
Cobalt is poisonous.
Drop by and see me –
Good black bread, tart cucumbers,
Plenty of bottles.
Ah, the door's blown open –
In comes free goose and blinis –
Thank you breeze, and thank you cherry trees.
A light diet leaves more for the kids,
Fumbling shoulder to shoulder for the fruit
I hid under the greenest leaves ...
So many fruitpickers and in the stream
A few branches going under, that's all.

Shyly, taking the microphone –
Snortling down it – 'You see –
Carving a komuz, making a bowl or poem,
Even grinding a cobalt,
Brings us together.'
Or not us exactly, but people
And the microphone which today
I hold. Please don't applaud,
The mike is louder – and can't hear.
Anyway, you'll later wonder –
Was I the bowl you broke? –
Silly question.

not the best bowl
or the best poem.

'So Alexei really did not fear losing his talent,' said Dimitri. 'Yes, it's really too dense – rapprochements with the world, with poetry, and at once a precise re-distancing. I find the irony marred by the bitterness – the frontier guard who is "all I have to love", who handles the poison. And poetry itself – so insubstantial, so incapable of making a human contact. Except in the voice of the master, perhaps, and Alexei wasn't that. I'd say he didn't have much time for individuals, not because he was cold, but because the task of defining his own function was so desperately important for him. And of course, he changed with the definition.'

'But however desperate, why kill himself?'

'I think it may have been a sort of ennui. He may have realised his technique would present problems virtually beyond resolution. His was not a loud public voice. He felt he had to be a public poet – but he was disenchanted by the public style. One needs huge courage to be a perfectionist. And rather than continue to falter, or even worse to stop writing, he killed himself.'

'Do you think he would have done better in another society, another country?'

'He might have felt more settled, because more commonplace. But he wanted, you know, to be alone, to be unique, to walk very high up, so the crowds would hold their breath and see him surrounded by cloud. If he's bitter, he's not cynical.'

In class that day we were reading the lines:

Beyond the rocks, the sea lies still
But in my heart a heavier swell
Heaves to be free – and drowns me – for
It never can, it never will.

The professor said, 'Well, that's pretty weak. That doesn't make any kind of sense.' And I told him – 'No, I don't agree. But that's rather like a doctor saying "I've never seen this illness before – it can't be serious." I've had a friend die of that stanza! I know we're supposed to be precise, and that precision of meaning alone can deepen our understanding and all that. But that's too cerebral for me. If we study the limitation of people's understanding – these limitations are vitally significant.'

'You mean "the world rounds upon error"? I only half understand.'

We discussed my little idea for a time. And then he said – 'Aleya, it seems to me you gain insensitivity at the expense of what we should all know. That sensitivity is a privilege which we use to acquire further privileges, and exemptions. You must not forget that there are many grey and unpleasant people in the world. You think only about the kind and the courageous, and this is a fault. You don't see how difficult it is to live alongside cruel and selfish people. This is a kind of bourgeois vice – you're blind to ethical poverty as once you might be blind to material poverty, And I am one of the cruel and selfish – I don't belong in your world. It is too hard to meet your demands. You're someone whose perfectionism lies in admitting faults. It's just too uncomfortable.'

And now Dimitri is sitting beside me silently, privately. He is thinking about his first symphony – looking out over its expanses, like a swimmer who stands on the beach waiting for dawn to start, even though he knows he'll have to swim through several nights. Summer lightning reflects in his deep brown eyes like white veins cracking open. I wish I could leave all these things that trouble me so.

feodor

A strange thing this morning – 'Have you forgotten your little wolf, then?' It was Sophie as she passed, disappeared. Perhaps, after all, she is simple, rather sad. My bitterness is just a reproach for her inconstancy – but does she want inconstancy? I remember too when I outlined my project to Grigor he smiled, and said, 'Your view of the Soviet Union is somewhat fanciful.'

It seems to me that where we differ from my America is that we all have a plan for escape. Our secrecy brings us together. In America they will have to escape together, but here we sharply differentiate our public lives from our fantasies. And yet, I confess I am afraid. For I *really* want to know the truth. If here philosophy has become reality, then indeed I understand why theory needs only to be adapted to reality – and why, frankly, I find it boring. But I don't know if I believe that! Suppose in my work here I find only noncommittal statements, reminiscence? They know themselves much better than they know me.

Or again, suppose I can't distinguish between socialist labour and a quite specific way of organising work I'd hate to do myself? If only I could make a film – little nodes of coloured thread which turn out to be stylised trees with real thrushes in them, the plains of Moldavia counterpointed with tanks, the Paris where they talk of China and eat brioches ... And in Paris, would they find me comic – or inappropriate – and how long can we stand outside the European zoo, silently watching the animals chatter to each other?

I remember going to a reptile house, the toad's eye so glossy, the lizards, blue, green, puce-spotted. Sophie was with me, and she said, 'Suppose they escape?' And I told her, 'All they'd do is look for someone like them. Or quite like them. Just someone who'd not sting them or crush them. One can't begrudge them their food, and willingly concedes them friendship.' She stared at me as though I'd told her the truth. And now Andrei is here.

'What was the worst time you remember?'

He's laughing. 'Well, the worst time's easy – they took my card, and there I was, carpentering in a camp. One thing I've never been able to do – the wood's never friendly to me, it's perverse and bad-tempered.'

'Why were you sent?'

'Some joker with a grudge. When you pay people to tell tales, they'll always overproduce.'

'Did you lose faith that you were living in a socialist society?'

'I didn't expect it to be all roses. Any kind of struggle finds out the weaklings – and a lot of strong ones were the first to go. It's easy to be scared when things are hard. We were scared in the camp – there wasn't much to go round. You never knew what the authorities were doing next. So people learnt to thieve and bribe. Those that wouldn't – got pushed aside, got the worst work. What do you expect? Those of us who did their best to keep straight – we knew we weren't socialists in the same way as the others, or the authorities. So – there were three kinds of socialists, that's all. And some of each kind got through.'

'And the conflict between them goes on?'

'Look, Feodor – you must know all this. I'm not saying that what they call deformations are permanent. But of course I've struggled all my life. I don't believe other men's versions of the good life just because they're written down. I've learnt to obey – but not to acquiesce. I can still judge men. I'm not a fool, I'm not complacent because I'm grateful for the chance to keep struggling. We have a huge potential: I believe I'm part of it. I still think I'm part of the future: I believe communism is indeed the society of the future, and that is why to keep struggling I must be a communist. But like everyone else, I get bored and tired – and when that happens I want some other comrade to come along and talk me out of it. And sometimes they do.'

'I don't doubt your willingness to make sacrifices – have you wondered if you ought so willingly to make them?'

'I think I've nearly finished making mine. It's very hard and dangerous for individuals to generalise about a whole society, millions of people all holding cards in secret. Only when the last card falls are you certain you made the wrong discard way back. You want a preciseness of answer I can't give. It's too soon to say. You want me to say that this factory is socialist as it strikes me every moment. I'll just say – if work doesn't make me happy, it's still more important, it's essential. Being needed makes you hard, and austere. In the evenings, I can enjoy myself, I can think about being a socialist, or whatever else I want to be. These notions are not always useful during the day.

'You see, I'm someone who's had to keep going while others have had a much easier life. In the camp, when we had the materials we'd sometimes made a success of some project. They'd keep us five minutes while we cheered ourselves, all wanting to get some rest. So the biggest successes got the least cheering – because we were most tired then. Someone like you – perhaps you're enjoying the fruits of my efforts already. Perhaps you can enjoy being in socialist society, and I'm pleased for you.

'But I can't stop. I have to work to keep you going. I expect you have to do the same for me. But I don't expect to be able to comment on your work, or tell you and your colleagues how to go about it. That's why I used to laugh when I read what the Americans said about us – they guessed about us as though we were animals on another planet, fetching mosses for our nests and living in herds. And then suddenly they said – no, after all, they're quite like us …'

'What do you think about my notion of escape – that everyone has a private bolthole?'

Andrei smiles: 'I think I'll stick it out, Feodor. It was hard to keep dignity when we had to congratulate ourselves, but I tried. Can you imagine that – hundreds of us, covered in cement dust, standing in the icy wind, the brief, hoarse shouts – we'd beaten the snow by twelve hours. No, I don't believe in escaping. It's as easy to talk of escape as to talk of revolution. It's not so hard to try either. But socialism – that means succeeding, not congratulating yourself.'

Aleksandra has heard the end of this. She looks so white and shy, the full poignancy of someone pleading to be awakened, to be disillusioned. I've acted this part myself. She says, 'I'm so angry. We were waiting for the bus, for the driver to come and drive it – and all the time he was sleeping on the floor, where we couldn't see him. People are so lazy. He came blinking out to us like a cat that's been hunting all night. "Well, citizens, in a hurry to get to work again? Keep the wheels turning, that's right." So, I'm late.'

I can sleep with my eyes open – Aleksandra is right, only from idleness and rumination can come the finer perceptions. But she's disproportionately angry. When Andrei has left, she'll tell me.

'Feodor, I'm so concerned. I want so deeply to experience everything my family hid from me, but it's so demanding. Yet, Grigor has been so kind to me. He's an attractive man, you know, his eyes are so sad. He's courteous too.'

'Aleksandra – I don't know his motives or his sincerity. Or anyone's. He's done this before – but I don't know if he's different from anyone else. Only, I myself am very fond of you. When we know each other better, I thought we might spend time together – discuss your problems, whatever they are.'

'That's just it, Feodor. I don't want time and reflection. I'm tired of my problems. I don't want to know anyone except in the most immediate way. I want strong and competent people around me – people like Andrei. I want to feel an interaction of forceful personalities. I'm tired of this tiptoeing around practice, these endless debates on theory, all the stuff you talk about faith and dignity. That's not life, movement. I like you, I enjoy you, Feodor. But my time with you is one of constant irritation and frustration. You live in failure because you don't strive. You're like the driver today – we're all waiting outside for you to come and show us where we're to go – and all along you've been curled up somewhere. I hate to tell you this, but you're passive like a mushroom in the field, which thinks – ha, when they pick me I'll poison them. But who'd pick a poisonous mushroom rotting away there?'

'Aleksandra – suppose I come up with a new theory – suppose my research is really useful. What then?'

'I don't think it's possible for you. We'd have to wait and see, but not for too long.'

I think the best thing would be drink at this time. Running away to Samarkand, sneaking some little pots of spiced meat and drinking in the shade. Let all the black dogs in Asia twinkle away to their destruction on the square, I'll be the patient one. But tomorrow we are all on *subbotnik*. Grigor has devised petty things for us all to do. So the donkeys will have to stand another day, twitching grey dust from grey ears, eyes closed against the sun, without me. Here it is getting colder, and there is an edge of snow in the air.

leo

'My friends,' said Leo, 'I call you friends because comradeship takes so long. We have not yet begun to experience even the intellectual hardships of comradeship. That is why we must begin to define our joint aims. Living here on the periphery we must remember we are also a frontier – and that the iron heel mutilates wherever it treads. We must show concern for each others' wounds. Living as we do in a system we have not constructed, to which we do not wish to lend our support, we face a strange mixture of regularity, even cooperation, and persecution. Our situation is strictly transitional. To live, as it were, in a state of perpetual transition, is highly confusing. We are not yet at war, we are not even in much physical danger. We may stay employed, we have legal status. This ambiguity is deeply disturbing – disturbing for everyone, and that is why one needs strength to operate under these conditions, and not simply to escape completely. There is, of course only the merest shadow of escape – but because this is a world of illusion and tactic, it is comforting and encouraging to live in the shadow.'

'That seems to me profoundly mistaken. I have written Fortinbras as an exercise in comprehension. An exercise in 'how to destroy the tyranny' it shows us the full size and shape of the monster. The audience is not permitted to make its analysis – the invitation to suggest ways of overthrowing Fortinbras is a concession, a pedagogic device.'

Someone said 'horseshit'. Peggy said, 'You sound very condescending. We're not in Moscow now, you know, this is a free country. You're treating actors as though they were servants.'

'Peggy, if you want, discuss the play. You aren't actors or servants. You are pedagogues.'

'Leo,' Shirley said, 'I think you're either too far ahead of us, or too simple. Are you saying that the theatre is just a political gymnastic?'

'It's just a part of a many-sided political activity, it cannot be a total politics. But because Fortinbras is what he is, all we can do is produce the kind of entertainment Hamlet patronised in his day – perhaps to stir the memory of the courtiers.'

'So you reject all other political means?' asked Lloyd. 'Everything is premature until it succeeds, is that it? You. ride around the country saying how backward everyone is, carefully avoiding every large centre, every established movement?'

'Well, Lloyd. There's subjectivism and subjectivism. To know when to immerse oneself in a movement and when to make one's own contribution – that's a fine judgement. Are we so far from a movement now? It seems to me that the kind of stirring of which we are a part does not yet demand immersion, has more the character of a stream bursting up through the earth in hundreds of rivulets than a river determined to plunge off to the sea.'

Leo remembered an afternoon near the Caspian, an area of rocky forts, rocks clenched like fists, salty plains. The surprise of just such a break in the ground, water cooing and chirring as it wreathed through the outcrops. And his wife saying, 'Leo, I try so hard to understand you, do what you want. But you seem made only for tragedy. My needs are so simple – a little affection, a little sympathy. And you won't tell me what you want. You have to accomplish so much, and everything tastes bitter to you. It's killing me – your sense of my inadequacy. I live only for you, and you don't even live for yourself.'

And he'd been able to say only, 'Look at the water – who'd have expected it to break through here – the rocks must have weakened but there's nowhere for the water to run – or do you think it will make it to the sea before the sun does for it?'

Later he sat alone in a pub. On television someone was cutting up a large fish, tossing sections like logs into a pot. At the next table a blond student was saying to his girl, 'Aha, a little too much to drink, I'm afraid. Don't take your eyes off me, such lovely eyes, such a strong focus. Would you say you were virtuous? Funny things, virtues. Hard to find. What say we have a little hunt round for yours later?'

I don't have a sweet tooth where sex is at issue, thought Leo. He could hear some people nearby talking about Shirley.

'She grunted when I had her,' said one.

'Probably trying to speak your language, Harry,' said another.

'Bullshit,' said the first.

Aiieee, thought Leo. What better to come and drink and have one's lover-to-be discussed by the lovers-that-were! Life's biggest surprises were always that there are no surprises. A good time to drink. Apotheosis and fall on the same day. At least one's small tragedies don't get in the way of the major ones. Even so, fastidiousness is a considerable virtue – as from one dumb ox to another – and I think Shirley could have spent a little longer looking around. Still, one has achieved one's own moments of grossness. Time to try for another with some of this beer.

Go down, drink, thought Leo, and draw me a map of all the streams bubbling to the Caspian, and show me and my wife sitting under a thorn tree. No eyes around but the eyes of sheep and thrushes. Sweet red wine with. a prickle of freshness, and cheese. Sun from Iran to warm us, a double line of script round the rim, which, by tilting my head this way and that I can just begin to decipher. 'Drink while the sun is hot, so you can sweat it out during the hours of darkness.'

aleya

'New world, new peace,' thought Aleya. 'I think not, I hope not.' Every morning a new song:

> *'The plains full of sheep as a rug with threads,*
> *A rug with birds in the sweet trees, a shepherd beneath each tree ...'*

Aleya thought of the adolescent days in Moscow. 'Yet didn't the generalities seem larger, abstractions more freely used? We were, after all, being trained as intellectuals – as Dimitri said, learning the world is not only round but spinning. Do we avoid the big issues now, with our openness and liberality towards our own world of action, miss the big problems in everyday life, come to act indifferently to them?'

She remembered a dream – of bowls, heavily, stickily glazed, like panther-skins flecked with blueberries, or the backs of halibut. Outside, the trees swayed in the heat, the flags hung slack like pelts from their poles. Perhaps, though, the morning was cooler. Today she had to start picking the members of the experiment. This involved an awareness of her own purposes she did not have, and had no time to acquire.

'What will be the future of the director do you think?' she said to Katya.

'Aha, here's what they'll do to him,' said Katya. She showed Aleya a newspaper article. 'The candidature – did not proceed.' A regional committee of popular control had overcome its hesitancy and rejected the application for a managership from some arrogant embezzler.

'They'll call your experiment a reorganisation of the *sovkhoz* – call for new candidates and not consider the former director. My husband had the same thing with the Cossacks. They said they were only used to electing officers when they were drunk. Once they elected a general who was so drunk that not only everyone else but he too forgot he'd been appointed. The committees here are so slow they have the same meetings ten times over, till everyone forgets who is to vote for what.'

'But,' said Aleya, 'how could they impose someone unknown on us after all this? They simply recognised what was obvious, and now they claim the power to give us some director by fiat, as though we were illiterates, incapable of assessing the man. What kind of method is it which allows us our moment of protest and then steals away our initiative again?'

'My dear,' said Katya, 'it's your Party. If there's backwardness, it's your Party which takes the burden of remedying it, if there are shortages, your Party takes on the job of stirring up the state authorities. If there's centralisation, dictates from above – well, after all, you've done a little of what you wanted. A lot more than if you'd been in exile like me. If you want to be in on what's done, you should move more in the right circles...'

'I recognise how various my deficiencies are, Katya. Am I to be prevented from making mistakes by all of us here, or is it simply assumed I'd be making mistakes?'

'I don't think that's a good question. People get tired of asking for initiatives and hearing nothing. I think if things were more exciting, you'd start asking the right questions – producing interesting or even correct answers. But you know, your own vigour seems very synthetic. It takes something very big for people to be vigorous outside themselves, their own concerns.'

'Katya, everything you say dismays me. You've only to look out over this valley – we're like sculptors who can shatter the whole thing with one blow, or spend years on its contours ...'

'And the mountains too? What will you do with them? It takes more than a blow to break them up, I assure you.'

'Perhaps we'll find questions for your answers as the weeks pass, Katya.'

Sultan and Kulkul came to see Aleya later in the morning. 'We feel,' said Sultan, 'we owe you our support. We are not asking to be chosen. But if you want to choose us, we will go, that's all.'

'I don't think I should choose anyone,' said Aleya. 'It should not be done in this way. It compromises me, and the whole experiment.'

'Remember this,' said Sultan. 'My father lived under the emir. He was an illiterate brigand, and he lived a tribal existence when he was not escaping the many cruel things most people wanted to do to him. To me, this life is very strange. To have the whole world given to me, to be told, these are your valleys (of course they are), to discuss democracy and the proletariat ... I find all this curious. I want to live in this new world, to learn all these new languages, make critical distinctions in them. I don't want to think all day of singing songs and sleeping under thorn trees. I enjoy working with things that come easily to me. But deep down I am very puzzled. Sometimes things are soft, and sometimes hard. And I don't know why. I want to make my choices, and know what and why I'm choosing. If you choose me – I understand that choice. I appreciate your position, I want you to understand mine. I don't want to feel you're condescending to my wonder, because you too should wonder.'

Kulkul said: 'I remember many years ago, my brother said, "Look at this area – where there were a few poor families, now roads, buildings. Springing where we weren't aware of planting anything. Well, we can either pull them down, or try to build more." He was not a clever man, my brother. He had no specialist knowledge of what happened in all these buildings, how you could have chosen to have better sheep, for instance. I too keep quiet about many things. But there is no virtue in always keeping quiet.'

Later the Ukrainian dropped by. 'There's a legend they tell here,' he said, 'that there was once a sheep wiser than all the others. And he said, "Why do we live in this way, the property of the humans? We should organise and stop this exploitation." And the other sheep thought this a fine idea, and said, "How should we begin?"

'And the wise sheep said, "Well, humans usually start with an emir." And of course the other sheep immediately appointed him emir. The emir of the humans recognised him, and let him live in a palace, and keep a harem. But the sheep were annoyed at all this, because they seemed no nearer emancipation. The stronger sheep simply sold the weaker ones to the humans, even though the emir said there was a divine law against this. Eventually, the sheep organised and threw the sheep emir off his balcony. And as he fell, the sheep emir thought, "Well, at least I've taught them how to organise against tyranny." And the human emir said, "That's what happens when you give sheep an emir. Only humans are fit to be ruled by emirs." Pungent story, don't you think?'

'And that's a legend?'

'As good as. Am I to be sent off to the desert to build the new world?'

'Do you want to be?'

'In a way, yes. It gets boring doing the things one can do. A chance for a massive failure doesn't come along so often as it used to.'

'I think that all we volunteers should meet to discuss the procedures for selecting the rest.' She could see Gelderan in some fine new boots coming towards her office door, carrying a pheasant.

'There are already enough of us, meeting under the trees. I even found this bird there – a good sign on the whole. It was not right that you should choose us, but we should choose each other,' he said.

As she went to join them, Aleya thought, 'Is it politics or agriculture we're learning? The first problem is to rely on other people, even when they're not strong.'

The pheasant broke free and skimmed in front of them to the meeting.

aleya's diary

Dimitri threw himself into a chair. 'How impossible to work at being a socialist! They've gone and had a scientific-technical revolution, not even asking if I'd like to join! How can the gap between my physical and mental labour be narrowing? Can I sit and think publication? Can I scribble and come out quartets?'

I said, 'Dimitri, Larissa said a disturbing thing today: "Suppose Alexei were misjudged. Suppose he really wanted to be left alone. Where do you really think this dualism he sees everywhere comes from? He gives it a political origin, the conflict: between purity and connivance. But in his own life – isn't the conflict between bitterness and dedication close enough an analogy?" What do you think, Dimitri?'

'Same as usual. But my news is better. I've found one of the sequences of Dzerzhinski Square. It shows Larissa is partly correct, but completely mistaken. He clearly recognises himself as an effect, not a passive and unconscious victim. He calls it, "An Appeal to Sonya, far away":

How distant we can be in this country,
You so far east – you've used the sun for half a day
Before we see it, cold. Withered in exile
We live our private misunderstandings, free from the telephone,
From any injustice but our own.

How bitterly we struggle, enemy twins,
Locked in our collusion, our dependency.
Felix still watchful, and you too Sonya,
Jealous and grudging. Can't you remember
'Eisenstein made me do it' – widen the eyes
All over my body. And Sonya replies
'You hurt me always – suspicion breaks my heart.
Your gifts destroy me, I don't trust your thoughts.
Deep down I know how deeply you betray me.'

Let me alone, my love,
Let me abandon hope in you,
And you, I beg, in me.

'Yes,' I said. 'I remember Alexei showing me – some Indian film director it was – he made the remark about Eisenstein. He hates Dzerzhinski for sometimes being right, that's the trouble. Alexei was so simple, just wanted to be left to his acrid images. Yet in fact, do you see how rough, how uneasy he is? This poem is like a splintered door – botched by some craftsman, in resentment. He wants to pour so much in – but is always saying, "Who cares about my bourgeois fastidiousness, to hell with you, I'll be a bourgeois, anyway." Why is it so hard to be sensitive without being so exclusive?'

'I don't think it is,' said Dimitri. 'I've no trouble living a life so rich it's like eating éclairs a yard long. One looks ridiculous, that's all. But there's something very autonomous about music. I've no trouble In leaving the little chicks to fend for themselves long before the first performance – musicians are such good wet-nurses – they positively adore a healthy feeder. Saw the Moscow Philharmonic do Shostakovich's *Hamlet* last night – and they just beamed to see such a determined infant.'

'And the book of wolf jokes?' I asked. 'This was one he told me recently: 'There was an old wolf and a young one. They'd just come through a winter together. A terrible time they had: the beetles frozen like buttons, squirrels like hanks of twine. So bad, they took to hunting together, half crazy for a good warm, a good stew and a nice solitary howl. But the young wolf retained his sensibility: "How despicable – how much opposed to the individual wolf's better nature, this ganging up and roistering about.' And the old wolf sighed and said, "Well, my son, you've got a point. My own view is that we wolves have a great capacity for noble deed. But – hunting in packs is better than cannibalism."'

Sergei came in as Dimitri was saying, 'I'd not mind being remembered for a book of jokes ...'

'I was in class today,' Sergei said. 'And the professor was telling us about an evening walk he once took. Old wooden churches – all the ways of going to hell and making one's way through, scratched in the pine by the priest. Mushrooms, scarlet berries, furry ears enough to make a quilt. And suddenly he came on an old man with a gun – moustaches oblivious to two wars at least, a fine red nose with a good way of tilting. There he was, bottle and all, sitting on a stump. The professor thought, "Aha, a little chat about pickled mushrooms, and which foxes are chirpy tonight, a shot of vodka – and I'll be on my way."

'But no. The old man was fascinated by the idea of language: whether you could properly say that animals had one, in particular. Did the formalists – if they'd stopped to think about it – believe they did? If they had a language – did they also have a poetry, if so, did it rhyme? In fact, the. old man speculated and systematised till the professor's ears froze numb on his head. And the motto – don't enter into conversations with strangers if you're in a hurry.'

'Sergei,' I laughed – for he can never destroy one's fondness for him, 'we'll be your strangers tonight. Let us talk you to sleep. I'm tired of going early to bed. Let's make our talk last: see, how soft it is tonight! Look out, my friends, smell how sweet and dark it all is. Let's make a living monument to Alexei – to Alexei, who'd little enough from my thin selfish love ...'

Too late I remembered Sergei and Dimitri, who spoke of love as one might speak of friendship or rose-grafting. I felt angry towards everyone. 'You sit there so sombrely, you two. Alexei has at least achieved his cosmic indifference. He doesn't have to worry now, he's got what he wanted. He's a nice happy memory, and we can all warm our toes at his embers. Alexei's big joke – to leave three little jokes behind.' Perhaps I was crying by this time. 'I cared so little for him. As little as I care for myself, much less than I care for you ...'

And Sergei said gently, 'Yes, I know. Aleya, it's all difficult for you. Being courageous can be an obsession too. But we have trust in you. We have to adjust now – Alexei is no more now than his wolf jokes and what we can find of Dzerzhinski Square. He chose this, and we can understand his choice. When I criticise him, I do so as I would when he was alive. But my regret lies in his inability to answer back, to say, "Sergei, stop trying to make me like the unlikely and the unlikeable – some people like to eat raw snake, and others are forced to. Excuse me, I prefer cheese pancakes."'

We sat and watched the little late girls flash by half-concealed in the gladioli. And as my eyes throbbed, I could feel the tenderness he never wanted pouring from me, pouring out over the sickly white jasmine in the garden below, perfuming our soft Moscow dusks till your throat aches with it … Oh Alexei, what an idiot you were, and what a challenge you've left me!

feodor

I remember one of Andrei's stories. In his camp, a group once caught a gang leader unprotected. They said, 'Isn't it bad enough here without you persecuting us?' It was by a pond, frogs creaking the doors of all the secret cupboards in the world, red and yellow flowers straining their silent throats. He says the criminal looked at them calmly: 'We understand each other. You may kill me – but remember, you had to be alive for me to exploit you. I kept you alive.'

'But if we let you live – what could you do for us? What use would you be?'

'I could be the first of your prisoners. And help to persecute your enemies in their turn ...'

Andrei seems so different from anything he has been made to be. Patient, sardonic – I seem to buzz round him with three childish questions to the minute, while he smilingly reduces me to the landscape. 'Andrei – these subbotniks – do you think they accomplish anything?'

'Well, so. It's just a day. It's a taste of what it would be like if work were a little more voluntary. But Feodor – remember the synthesis. You'll never have rest till you do. Don't get so involved with an aggressive position that you miss out on the synthesis. No contribution is ever without its effect, you know. You don't have to worry about making an impact: wherever there's an impact – there you are, like it or not.'

But disturbing things are happening. Aleksandra says, 'Feodor, you're so relativist, it disturbs me. You're like a drinker with his fish. He nibbles it down speculatively, tail first, until only the eyes are left outside – and then he sees them and says, "Damnation! I'm being eaten alive!" I wanted abrasive professional company, not a sentimental friendship.'

'Aleksandra, these attempts at toughness won't work. You can't sit in an office all day and tell me about the cats you dragged in wild from the fields, remembering the shade of every berry you picked – and then pretend you want to break hearts. If, as you say, Grigor is a sad man – leave him be. There are always other sad men. The only thing wrong with you is there's nothing wrong with you. You are placid and untroubled, but want to be racked with pain. No doubt it will come.'

'Feodor, I can imagine you in Moscow so vividly. Joining the crowds around the ministries as though you were struggling up the profession, but really only with a drooping sentimentality. There's no such thing as equidistance or free thought, but you carry these about hidden like slogans on an embroidered handkerchief. Your concession to the modern world was to walk in the city instead of the countryside – to patronise the workers instead of the peasants.

'What possible value does your sensitivity have when you compare it with my father's life? Imagine – sweeping in on Kiev in his tank – again and again into battle. Waking for weeks and seeing the mist burn off, as though his life were the last smoke from a lamp in some cellar. Only afterwards does one remember this as heroism: but at the time – how much of a radical abstraction from all ends! From survival certainly. Here was an existence which drove out idle speculation, which forced him every evening to examine himself all over for wounds. And what of the shock-workers ...'

'Yes, of course, Aleksandra. These things now have a solidity, a permanence, to which I'd only seek to add. I'm very aware of the justice and injustice of what you're saying. I don't find it easy to sit down and say, "What am I doing exactly, what precisely am I thinking?" This is because it is only at the moment of praxis that one really requires theory. Only when the barricades are up do you realise that it is the long mental gymnastic which can keep the muscles and the blood going. At such points, theory transcends muscular limitation. Speculation is not vain – but it is not always applicable.'

Shall I tell Aleksandra? That I now really have my chance: to decide on silence, or exposure? Just how shabby the origins of the factory are, I'll never know. It should not have been built here – in a sense it was stolen from itself. There's a huge story of theft and corruption, even exploitation, which went into the early years of my history.

Most of the older workers know about it – some of the younger. They're watchful now, but survivors have a loyalty which we, who have yet to survive, lack. Well, so here's a surprise. All the years Aleksandra was reading Pushkin and sucking her thumb, the years I was gawking at the trees on Gorky Prospect, streams of workers were coming through those gates, to work for a few of the locals – perhaps three, four hours a day – to pay off the debts and kindnesses, the fears and promises of these sharks. When did it stop? Who was implicated?

Of course one expects to find entrepreneurial banditry here and there in the thirties. It doesn't smudge the general picture. Besides, there were the saboteurs in the camp with Andrei. But when my task is to comment on one tiny detail of the picture – and it's decidedly smudgy – what then? Do I make a scandal? Who is interested in this old history? There's no doubt the exploitation is over.

But what of the men who lived through it? Who organised it? Perhaps it was the only way of managing the enterprise, it became a spontaneous custom, as it were, a biological, rather than an economic, deformity. An eccentricity. But not something to be viewed with pride. Can one install on this a mechanical system of socialist relations? I don't know. How can I tell if the struggles have been fierce enough? How many heads should roll? Can one really assure everyone that in the end the guilty are punished? – remember Andrei on synthesis.

The assurance would come in the form of a threat to some, a revelation to others, a release for still more – so who is left to do the rooting out of the villains? Me? If I go to the Party – what then? A huge historical examination, with no doubt men long dead failing to testify. Possibly there is and never was any evidence – only a sour memory. One of the engineers, Ivan, comes in.

'How do you find working relations these days?'

'Fine. Not the work, but the company. We'll have a car in five years – we count off the days like the plan.'

'I'm conducting research on socialism.'

'Oh yes. Pretty tough, I should think. We keep ourselves to ourselves, me and my wife. Theft and politics – keep out of those, I tell her. Nasty to get caught out in either.'

Impossible to dislike such an idiot. Yet.

He goes on, 'You see, to me socialism is being left alone. Not having to worry what the next man is doing. Perhaps it's what he should be doing, perhaps not. But it's not your concern. It's the concern of everybody, right? All of us, we do our job ordinarily. Then, the higher you get, the more the fiddle begins. I don't mean like some tools – that's just a nuisance. No, the really big stuff. But I've been modest. Some of them complain about politics – always looking for foreigners to tell them what I'm sure they could find out anyway. It's just bleating.'

When he had gone, Aleksandra said, 'I'm really sorry for you, Feodor. You ask such difficult questions. And you've so little chance of answering them. And of overcoming the difficulties. And you won't realise that it's your subjectivism I like.'

Yes, It's true. She really does want to like me. All this nonsense about Grigor – some signal too abstruse to read. 'But Aleksandra –I've discovered something!'

'And I've discovered you, so we're both lucky!'

'Today has been unusually full of ambiguities – so why not, after all, end it with an idyll?'

'But really you are fond of me,' she asks, and looks away.

'Why, yes. Actually, evidently.'

We are smiling at each other like fools. The lights are flashing on in the dusk like a salute from a heavy battery, all the way into the city. A breeze, heavy with quince and almond from the south stirs and dies into the room. It is dark where we are sitting.

leo

'Leo, you're so quiet, you're in danger of effacing yourself completely. We must have. a little talk,' said Shirley. 'You're visibly breaking up – you look like someone from the Confessions. Instead of imitating nature you're trying to become a part of it. I want to make no demands on you, I realise this Fortinbras business is fraying you – and I can't understand why you don't just write it and be finished with it all. You may think the achievement would be minor. I know how important the conditions you write under are to you. But it's so many years since you stopped writing. Things develop – even in latency. You can't tolerate me until you've taken delight in your power to create ...'

And Leo answered through a terminal hangover, 'Why do women find drama so seductive. What is that quote?

'The metre of my darling's feet, the rhyming of her thighs
Cripples my verse, frightens my owl – away it flies ...'

'How odd that writers should once have owned owls.'

'Leo, I don't understand you. Of course if you judge yourself by the standards of history, you're not of general interest. But it seems to me that you're frozen, choked up. This kind of refinement and attention – it leaves me hurt and bewildered. I'm used to grossness and philistinism. My husband was born bourgeois. He had kept all his college textbooks – here, that's a mark that education has temporarily suspended greed or need. But in pubs, when he was drunk, he'd offer me to the men at the next table, then hit them when they lurched over to me. Gentleness, melancholy – I have to be educated in these modes.'

'Shall I tell you the truth?' asked Leo. 'Not, by the way, that the concept of grossness or boorishness has any part to play in the bedroom ('how European,' thought Shirley) – I think of myself like this: I'm like one of those that you call transients. I'm slowly and painfully trekking over the whole country, trying to find something to make me stop – that would be like stopping in the desert a hundred miles from water. I can't give sweetness, Shirley, only light, and not much of that. We should need to commence with a physical relationship so that intimacy might grow and I fear there would be four in the bed. And I think your husband would terrify my wife. I'm afraid of you too, for being able to marry a man like that. Frankly, it seems perverse.

'I am, you see, very precise in my relationships. You find this a mark of dryness, pedantry. You can't, as they say, relate to me. You're in love with the distance between us. But this preciseness is what we used to call friendship, something you don't understand in the same way over here. I have had to struggle to keep on, and I've done so in isolation. Marxist exiles don't expect to be swamped with kindnesses, or interest. But I'm wholly lacking in self-contempt. I have lived in the Soviet Union, where there is perhaps a difficulty in conveying the complex excitement, the multiformity of the most ordinary things. This is a nation not yet accustomed to injustice, not resigned to comfort and disillusion. You can still live there like the Italian intellectuals sometimes do – living in communes where there is an expertise to the cooperation, where there is a chance of mental enrichment – not, as over here, simply material impoverishment.

'I know you think I despise you over here. I don't. But I shudder for you. You have so far to go. Transformations will be so shattering, so many pure and noble souls will destroy themselves for necessary but brutal deviations. Noble and pure souls are as hard to chum up with as the grunting and misshapen ones. I see you all, striding into the abyss like Faust – so human, so experienced, such a fine engineer – but, alas, damned forever. And one does not lightly make friends with Faust.

'More lightly – I do not find Canadians like intimate friends. Intimacy is not confession, nor is it sitting drunk over the big roast – like Polynesians without the flowers. I'm withered from lack of human contact.'

Shirley said, 'I wonder why you can't adjust? And what of socialism in Canada?'

'I think if it came it would be very efficient, very communal, very correct. One might fight for it, but would not want to live under it. You have here the life of urbanised peasants: you rush to the country – and find only isolated cottages. In the pubs the other peasants are always all unfamiliar. You need wedding music, but there's only moose in the freezer and Schumann's Greatest Hits on the hifi.'

'A despair so dense I can't even sink in it? But you see, I agree with most of this. But why can't we work together?'

'Perhaps we can. But at least you know now why I'm not too warm and wide-eyed.'

And Leo thought of all the men he'd met who had spoken of torture and imprisonment with a kind of grim horror – walking so seriously in the Moscow streets, like a huge school on the way to its next history class, only the smallest girls giggling.

They were sitting on a bench in a shopping plaza.

'Why bother to live in communes,' thought Leo, 'when we already do? After all, nothing is more exclusive than this deep social silence.'

'So, then, you'll finish Fortinbras? And not worry too much about the others?'

'Yes, we'll play it my way. The idea was lame from the start – as the

Kazakhs say, "I am the crooked-footed goose, I am the puddle the geese use to wade in, I am the cornflower withered on the stalk." But Fortinbras will be a good play. Aesthetically. It pays to work as hard at your failures as at your successes.'

'It wasn't a bad idea. But you were the wrong person to try and run it.'

'Shirley, that's like drawing the sting before the bee has left the hive. We have all tomorrow to live through. The playing of the play.'

Later, he said, 'My wife was a very gentle person. Provocatively so. My temperament is like boiling tar – it looks quiet and solid, but wiser people don't go near for fear they'll fall in and be cooked like eggs. She suffered with me – and I expect people to rage against suffering. She didn't, just became sweeter, softer.'

He remembered her saying 'Am I your little pheasant,' and the shame of his replying 'yes, no, perhaps'. They would sit by a stream, under the fretting of the cicadas. Watching the husks of beetle, and the green crickets bounding, resting, bounding. And he had been that cricket, restless for ever to make those impossible jumps. Seemingly resting, resting, resting.

aleya

Aleya thought, 'I really live in the modern world,' looking amazedly over the yellow grass, here and there a blue cornflower shrivelled with the heat. 'Adjusting to the people here who are adjusting to me. And how fortunate, and irresponsible, to be used so experimentally and amateurishly. How good that we should be able to satisfy demands qualitatively different from the capitalists' political needs. But how comfortable the *sovkhoz* is. How closely we live together – a nest of warm bodies, needing no communication beyond proximity. On the point of leaving, how clear the figure becomes.' A man was singing:

'When the auls were huddled together,
yellow grass turned to sand, came the Russian thief
dressed in black like a stick – where was our falcon,
where the talking white armour, come to give back our lands,
cover the invader's face with the wings of a crow?'

Another man took it up:

'Bitter it was
tasting the dust like a goose,
bowed under the brigands' burden,
lower than the belly of a horse.
Where was Tarlan, the faithful horse –
where the clever wife? Our jawbones
twisted like thorn trees, horses and women
stolen – our lives a desert, and the children dying.
We will make a new life – we will use
Soviet power to regain our homelands,
make the plains alive with auls:
driving the foxes back to the hills ...'

And seeing Aleya, one of them sang:

'Your hair pleases me well,
It is dark as barley.
Your voice pleases me well,
It is like a stream that rushes sometimes,
and at times lingers in deep pools.

Your skin pleases me well,
it is like the fleece of the tiniest lambs,
it is alive with snow petals.
When you came, you were full of pride,
with eyes shocked open like a foal.
For five years we trained you with silk ropes,
But you were silent.
Your eyes please me –
they have the pride and silence of a horse.
After five years you said, 'Have courage –
the training served me well.
I have a spine like a mountain ridge –
See, your enemies tremble at the sound of my voice.'
You please me well.
The Russians came as thieves, but you,
you leave as a hero.
When you are away
nothing pleases me well.'

Later, Katya said, 'My dear, what a capacity you have for ignoring the drama in your life! When I left Istanbul for Paris – it was as if the sun and the moon were leaving for good. You've never seen so many dignitaries! Of course, they were selling evil-eye charms, sweets, even each other – but a ragged army of generals is still something. My husband said, "It always helps to regard one's adventures as mere deviations from one's normal life – an additional bonus laid over the respectable herringbone. It is always better to have come down in life than have wild ambitions to make it to the top – the fallen angels want only a minimum of effort, which is not so hard to acquire!" And so – we went west with a suitcase and some drill manuals. Can you imagine destitution in Paris – amid a perpetual smell of wine and sweetbreads? How hard to assert one's bourgeois skills when someone in the next room is slicing mushrooms ...'

The group to leave for the experiment had been picked. Sultan said, 'Everything's ready. We are about to write the first sentence. Only now do I realise what socialism means – trustfulness of one's friends. How good, without fear or suspicion, to attempt all one can. Even failure is no longer disaster.'

'I'm not sure,' said Kulkul. 'We have physical hardship to face. But after all, what is ice and heat? That passes, but servility doesn't. I often wish we could have had more movement – "stagnation under a red banner" my brother called it. We have been so cautious, and sometimes so brutal in building our base – and what then? Until the Russians came we had always satisfied our needs for food and clothing – there's no problem there. The big problems have always been those of mourning, heroism, trust, devotion, independence, These are the real needs.'

Aleya said, 'This politics leaves me confused. In Moscow we met many foreign students who found us so placid, "But you're supposed to be revolutionaries," they'd shout. "What do you know of the world of street fighting, arrests, sectarian polemics? All your intellectuals are interested in is foreign currency, bourgeois publishers, imported whisky, and meeting people as craven and petty as themselves. They despise their political work yet all they want is to write exposures – of their own cowardice."

'Imagine these people, their frightening intensity. You'd read later in the papers that they'd been killed, arrested, denounced. They certainly were struggling against monstrous, vicious forces. There was no communication between us – they wanted to talk of China, of the Agitprop, the Proletkult, they saw us as ruins fit for the archaeologist. The lives of most of them must be so lonely, so bitter. Yet at times I felt we were the only young people who could speculate and create. Seeing these generations of students leaving our airports for the front, as it were, seeing the blurry photographs of them and their banners in all the demonstrations of the world – one's own discontents seemed luxurious. Will we ever meet them again? I think not – their experience has been so savage, so highly spiced with every kind of intellectual explosive ... Perhaps it takes someone more like them to carry out experiments.'

As soon as the trucks moved off, the dust hung over them like arches of sandy trees. Sheep ran grudgingly a few steps off the hot track. The group climbed towards the end of the valley, and some birds which looked like falcons stood high up in the corn-yellow sky. The heat haze turned the mountains into waterfalls. Like exiles, they stopped singing as soon as they left the gates of the *sovkhoz* – the dust clogged their throats with clay. Only Katya met the eyes of the others with a smile:

'I once knew the finest tailor in the whole of Turkey. He had a son who was a great lump – hands and feet like hooves, and a face on him like a kitchen stove. But his father was spiteful and fierce, and this son was the sweetest-natured boy you could find. And one day the tailor said to his son, "The government should feed you, clumsy – go and be a thief and get caught: prison food will do for you."

'And the boy said, "Father, why are you so bitter against me? I know I'm not efficient but I have other qualities."

'And the tailor said, "Efficiency is virtue – how can there be virtue in slackness?"

'And the boy said, "But father, my big bones can wear out your best trousers in two months. You have to start over again."'

'We are going to suffer,' said Gelderan. 'And not just for the sake of efficiency. We are moving from the world of legality and technical responsibility back to the world of primitive democracy. We are going back to our origins, back to the dictatorship of each over all. It is a moment that calls for deep understanding and silence. We will not be aware of these things while we are living through them. We should not look for deep lessons – but as an experience, it is unusual, it seems to me.'

And Aleya saw the falcons rise, getting a better grip with their wings, or caught in a spiral. Some horsemen galloped alongside them, joking like centaurs. She thought, 'I could begin to feel frightened,' and remembered the people who had taken the hard way out from fear, Alexei by suicide, Dimitri by silence. 'And yet, how beautiful, how ruminative all this is. This is my home, where I feel free.' The falcons followed them until everyone could see the huts and shacks of the temporary settlement.

aleya's diary

My mother said suddenly, 'Your father was obsessed by virginity – but where he looked there was precious little of it ...' She is always ready with some such statement in the midst of placid conversation of her own invention. She had made one of Sergei's visits official by coming and sitting with us, offering some of the sweet liqueur which, rationed out in this way, will outlast the most determined body of suitors.

'Is your friend an alcoholic?' she asked when Sergei came in. It was genuinely to put people at their ease.

'Ah,' she said, 'so this is Sergei, the striver and organiser,' to welcome him. Sergei is exactly right for this treatment – he will rise above embarrassment to patronise her. We had been discussing Dimitri. My mother distrusts talent – she believes she has a great fund of talent herself, and that is what is making her unhappy. But really, she is a born spectator – pushing me to take part in what she only watches.

Sergei said, 'Dimitri will quickly go through music into silence. He distrusts his own technical mastery too much. He won't make big statements because he really wants to invent a new language, not use an established one. It's the great fallacy of our century, that you can devise new men to listen to unintelligible diction.'

'It's the great philistine fallacy,' I replied. 'Dimitri wants to make important statements, but he's modest enough to have doubts. It's easy enough to address a circle or a coterie – but to tell a hundred million people something? That requires thought.'

My mother asked 'Do you really think there's that much to be said? Life is very various, and no one sees more than his own.'

'Yes, of course,' I said, so vehemently that I stood up. I suppose I stood there irresolute, wondering if I could hide what I'd done by getting more drinks. Sergei and my mother laughed at me. My mother said, 'She's got so much vigour – she'll burn herself right out.'

I said, 'There was a joke Alexei used to tell. There were, as usual, these two wolves. And one said, ruminating, "Why do these humans give us such a terrible reputation? I know we scavenge and generally rootle about in the forest. But how would they get on – out in all weathers, nothing to build decent nests with ... I mean, what are we supposed to do?"

'And the other wolf said, "Of course, we know they would die out if they had to live under these conditions. But still they vent their malice and criticism on us. I don't understand."

'Alexei once said to me, "You and I – we're wolves in this society. They're afraid of us both – but it's me they'll hunt and shoot."

'And remember when I told you, mother, you said, "Yes, there is something a little yellow round his eye, but not you Aleya, your eyes are so blue." You're like Sergei. You're so literal-minded both of you – you won't acknowledge the poetry of other people's existence. Prose or nothing.'

'Yes,' said my mother. 'Poor Alexei. Such a waste – talent again, I fear. Tell us some of his poetry, dear.'

One should celebrate one's friends whenever possible, even in circumstances like these – when I can feel Sergei's hostility as keenly as though a cat charged with static had clicked its way under my hand. 'Do you know "Waiting for the train to Vladimir"? It goes:

The right way to travel – knobbly sack,
Vodka, and no wristwatch. Ladies, don't scold –
The militiamen know enough to look away –
The craftiness of rural life can't heal your tutting.
I love our failures – they play the accordion
Wonderfully.'

'Alexei had such a lively feeling for entertainers of all kinds – I think he saw peasants singing in the train as the most munificent of benefactors. I don't understand how you can be so threatened by him. I can sense your revulsion from him, as though you are relieved by his death. He loved the detail of our life – in its set pieces and informalities. He loved to see those little ceremonies by the Kremlin wall – cavalcade, some children, those brilliant flowers. The whole thing stiff yet noble. A few more dead remembered, a daily acceptance of mortality and comradeship. And at the same time he enjoyed the life of the courtyards – someone whittling away at the beans, a dog panting and the radio chiming away the long hot days.'

Sergei said, 'I find Alexei's criticism irresponsible, that's all. He doesn't understand his subject – so, of course, he lacks control.'

And my mother said, 'Yes, you two lacked discipline. You were like brother and sister. But there was wildness in him. He had such passion and such coldness, such restraint.'

'But mother,' I said, 'we were none of us alike – it's just you who wants to be like everyone, so you make them seem the same. I think Sergei is crazy. Alexei lived as a socialist – he was devoted to his work, and his work was for anyone who wanted. About his gifts he was wholly unselfish. He wanted to talk to people, not remove himself from them by becoming famous. And you, mother: you can't imagine how vibrant, how moved, he could be. I've seen him cry because he found his own work so touching. Even Dzerzhinski – he found poignancy in his divided nature, and hated himself for the inappropriateness of this pity.'

'Exactly,' said Sergei. 'He was a lyricist who had no business trying his hand at epics. In that he was like Dimitri – public themes were not for them.'

'But surely you see,' I said. 'Lyricism for them was the language, the vehicle only. Alexei was only less vulnerable than Dimitri because he'd gained confidence from being so often wounded! And as for his criticism – at worst he was following the path of all our best writers, forever discussing public issues from the point of view of the most highly developed sensibility. At best, he was looking for a way of using his sensibility to account for his alienation.'

Sergei said, 'In this judgement, at best he was totally sensitive and totally alienated. Which is true. He didn't talk about dualism, but fatal flaws. That, by extension, was his judgement of you, and of me: that our historical existence oppressed him. Why should I feel attracted to that?'

'But Sergei,' I said. 'You surely don't believe society will collapse because Alexei swims against the tide? You surely don't believe he would have damaged the people he lived with? He wasn't struggling to be a propagandist, but a better poet. I don't feel the misery he felt. Perhaps I don't know as much, or think as deeply. To me, these problems – Dzerzhinski's ruthlessness, the psychology of unity and struggle – it's something I live with. I'm conscious only of making my own way. I'm very simple – to me every experience is new, every problem is appearing for the first time. The schematic approach – I don't find it helpful to me.'

'But dear,' my mother said, 'unless we're going to lose all judgement, Alexei's problems were his own. You can't let the question become one of aesthetics. Either he was mistaken, and generalised his mistake, or he was a serious critic, and must be taken seriously.'

'But what society is it,' I said, 'which so freely admits past and present errors – and then takes a perfectionist attitude to Alexei?'

'Because, Aleya, there are errors and errors. And Alexei only concentrated on errors – ineradicable ones.'

'But he didn't. He concentrated on human and transitory successes. Sergei – I've devoted my life to struggle against cruelty and waste. Alexei was my ally, not my enemy. What is your life dedicated to? The same as my mother's? – the reduction of the large to the petty, the complex to the manageable. You want the pace of all to be the pace of the slowest because it takes you less and less effort to keep up. You'd really feel happier if we could stop Dimitri composing?'

Suddenly the two of them seemed horrible, repulsive. I had to get out. If I could I'd have got drunk – but I'd just have looked pitiful, and surrendered myself. There are so many like me, I'm sure, placating my mother's moods and her intimacies, deferring to Sergei on technical matters. And I can't do it. It's no way to spend a life.

I ran out into the street – past the dried fish in the shop windows like bundles of liquorice, the benches where the drunks lay like Roman emperors in their vomit. Four cats, their tails standing up straight, sniffing at the same barrel. An Uzbek shaped like a pear so seriously carrying two nectarines in a string bag ...

I'll forgive Sergei. The evening is again so heavily scented, it makes me prickle with desire – but not for Sergei. That's why I'll forgive him. It's an intellectual decision. I didn't want to live with Alexei, but I wanted to hold him, to feel him as something firm and solid, to show him he had a physical presence, that he was not pure spirit, that he could feel delight. He was so sensuous – I think I felt worried that I would not please him, for he was so sensitive, so delicate – even when I looked at him, I could see the tremors run through him like a breeze through barley. We seemed just out of phase – the day he cried at the Institute – how could we make love when all I'd offered was therapy? And yet – I see now I would not have disappointed him. Just a taste of sweetness – like the last nectarine – sent all the way perhaps from a lover in Samarkand, 'to cure your bitterness …'

Alexei, you're dead, I can't move you. There's no sweetness for you now. And none for me. Tears lodge like a stone in my throat. The evening reminds me of your delicacy, your tiny controlled ecstasies, but now you can send me nothing. And I long to sit quietly by your mind, as it curves away into the distance like a river – seeing its inventions, listening to it rustling away the softer stone until it has two firm and rocky banks. I can't move you, but one word from you, by you, on paper or in my memory, can move me to the point of physical weakness. How deeply your silence wounds me. How I long for your strangeness.

feodor

I remember the French students had a slogan, 'to ripen is to rot'. So much to do today, I can scarcely enjoy my idyll. Discovering Aleksandra requires that I suspend my belief in mortality. 'I know how this ends,' I tell her. 'I've looked at the last chapter.' And she says, 'Nonsense, we're spinning out to sea looking for the wise fish,' and laughs.

'Aleksandra, I'm twenty-eight. I have several unshakeable convictions already – that New York is uniform and blasted. I should hate to go there. I am already so old, I have to soak in all the sun there is, like a leopard on a branch. I have a full set of memories and images – covering our history and philosophy, the heat of the south, drinking tea where charcoal smoke and silver leaves merge into sun and dust. I'm too wily to become a captive, still less surrender ...'

But as I speak, I feel like the last cake on the tray, sitting back to enjoy the argument as to who will eat me. Sophie was never like this – she hated waiting as she hated politics. She said the forest frightened her, but really she disliked walking. But Aleksandra – what can she want of me? Probably nothing more than a recognisable image of myself – some kind of consistency and good humour. The things which come so hard to me – a few lines of prose, the figure which might some day be worked into a poem – these she takes for granted. The dilemma I have about the factory – this too is a technical matter. For her too, politics and imagination are dead, and because I'm concerned with them, they are simply my concern, not hers.

But see her in her white dress, running down the path before me, ungainly, something almost of the goose in her stresses and rushing forward; I'm drawn along like a performing animal. And half amazed, half irritated, hearing my wit roar out when we're together with Yuri and Ilich, who are used only to dourness and incoherence from me. Her strength lies in her ability to resist intellectual curiosity, her weakness – inability to comprehend obsession. And she says, 'Stay close to me, so I can learn about you ...' – how silly, and totally endearing.

Grigor came to see me today. 'Well, well, my volleyball watcher. Perhaps we should play it like the Mongols – if someone should donate their head.' He smiles, and looks unaware of the menace and obscurity. 'Have you uncovered any surprises? Socialist labour is rather noisy routine, I'm afraid you'll find. Problems of finding the right work for the specialists, and a deal of letting things take their course. Knowing when to do nothing is the problem. Turning oneself into the wallpaper.'

'Grigor, I once heard a story. Some time during the Civil War – in a Cossack village there was a party of peasants leaving – some to join the reds, some the whites. The sky was purple with smoke, foxes and wolves running in terror through the villages. Women burying the family treasures so frantically they forgot where the holes were an hour later.

'The white leader came to the red, and said, "This is a terrible time, the worst I can remember. We're all going off to be killed, and we're leaving our homes and families at the mercy of anyone who comes along. Let's get well away from the village before we start killing each other. After all, we'll still be peasants whoever wins."

'The red leader said, "I agree, that so many will die, where they die is of little importance. Why kill each other when there are so many others willing to do it for us? But then again, why not?"

'And the white said, "If we start fighting here, whoever wins – our numbers will be depleted. Even the victors will lower the morale of the main army by being so few."

'And the red said, "Silence and complicity are even worse for morale."

'And so they started firing. Who do you think was right?'

'Feodor, I think you're trying to tell me something. I see I'll have to ask someone – Andrei, perhaps, what you mean.'

Is that a threat, or a lucky roll of the dice? 'The trouble with history,' says Grigor, 'is that it's never finished with. For those that make their living at it, that's good – but for those that want to close the files, tidy up the correspondence – it's a frustrating job.'

Now I've to go to a meeting of the Komsomol group. 'Comrades,' I say. 'I should like to receive guidance from the group. When errors have been exposed, we always have to consider how widely these errors have been publicised. In some cases both the error and its resolution can be secret. Publicity would, as one says, help the enemies of the movement. But how to know how widely known the error is? Isn't secrecy not only a bad thing, but an imprudent one too? We are told it takes courage to keep silent when conscience urges us to speak, but in the nature of things, errors are committed by the top against the bottom. Doesn't our democracy demand exposure?'

Someone is making a point about the 'literature of exposure', and how without our Party nothing came of it.

'That's inappropriate,' I say.

How seldom these meetings catch fire. You teach people a little history, and they fling it back to you at every occasion. Some of these sessions have seen fifty years of deviation thrown back and forth over some phrase in the factory paper. I suppose we're livelier than most – but although I find this all rather tedious, I've gained a reputation for unpopularity. Today has been a dry day – I can almost feel my toes crack like sticks as I walk about on them. It's not a great ambition to want to sit in the sun and drink wine and write poetry, but just now it's very pressing.

A lad whose name I forget stands up: 'Comrades, the history of the world is the history of men working and making love and building and making things. The history of capitalism is the history of how men were prevented from doing those things as they wanted. That's all.' So, to speak or be silent? He goes on, 'I don't think we need theory until we're in the midst of praxis. Correcting errors always involves, requires, fresh errors. That, comrade, is dialectics.'

'You mean – I take the decision and you criticise? Some collective principle that!'

'But mostly we're not interested in questions like this – they're not a part of our life,' says someone else. 'If you tell us the problem, we'll help you.'

'But will you help the problem?' I ask. 'I don't want to sound selfish about "my" problem. But if I tell you, it becomes a bigger problem. Perhaps you think my scruples silly or premature. I've decided, however, that the problem – the original and the subsequent question of exposure, cannot be ignored.'

'So you don't trust us, comrade?' asks the secretary. 'We can't force you to tell us, of course, but we can censure your attitude. You come to us for help and advice, and then contrive to put us in the wrong. I don't question your loyalty – only your judgement. I know you think I'm unnecessarily rigid. But here is a case quite clear – you have become our problem. If there are questions concerning the Party, or the operations of economic or democratic organisations – then you can't pretend these are your personal property.

'You talk of conscience – don't forget your conscience is formed by your consciousness of duty towards your comrades. They too have consciences. Withholding problems is a part of the problem! Here is just the secrecy you talk of, the committing of errors by the higher – in your case, the better informed – against the lower – in this case those you choose to keep in ignorance.'

'Yes,' I say. 'You're absolutely right.' We are all silent.

The Georgian girl says, 'I really don't know what is at issue. But Feodor suffers in his political work from a distrust of human contact in solving intellectual puzzles. But these puzzles are really human ones, in which intuition and impulse are as much a part of their solution as their cause. Feodor doesn't trust us because of the depth of his engagement. It is a great virtue, but a frightening one. We are here to help each other, not tear ourselves to pieces in vain regrets and longings, we are not concerned with intellectual absolutism, but the condition of our daily existence. Only after mastering these can we see what else we have accomplished. Feodor, it seems to me – and I speak with all kindness – has not mastered these conditions, and consequently his struggles and his criticism reflect this disorder, this discomfort, discontent.'

I must say something. Tell them about Sophie?

'I accept the comrades' strictures. But perhaps we all have these subjective reservations which are only resolved over a long period. At least mine is not a personal selfishness. Or is it? It is shot through with a wish to put myself right with the aid of you all, in addition to my efforts.'

Outside two crows are standing shipwrecked on a tree, watching the leaves flick away. A little comfort that all over the world comrades are being taken apart by other comrades, before going off together to sing the old songs, drink the cheap courageous wine. And what will Aleksandra say? Not to worry. There are worse than you, who are not so sweet either. And more about her childhood, the untroubled effort to understand, and to stop caring when she doesn't.

I say, 'I should like to raise the matter again when I have more evidence. But I thank the comrades for showing me the perspective of my dilemma as it concerns them, and the whole collective.'

People are smiling and whispering. 'In addition, I must say that the problems I face are concerned with historical interpretations of allegations for which the evidence can never be conclusive.' So much for loyalty to Andrei. The secretary charges me to report at the next meeting, and they will decide whether to conduct their own investigation.

Aleksandra is waiting for me, but I walk out into the rain alone. I try to avoid Ilich, but here he is: 'Feodor, when are you coming for an evening out?' Streams of workers are hurrying home to parties and vodka. We are in the estuary where two shifts meet. Ilich notices my distress. 'These meetings are the devil,' he says. 'More trouble than they're worth. Condemnations, denunciations – some chaps resent them, some are scared – what good do they expect them to do? We work in the place – that's all. Let's not turn it into a circus ...'

I can only nod. I'm blasted with desperation. I remember Herzen talking somewhere of some Roman philosopher, 'in his dialectics there is a kind of irony that is enough to drive one mad ... but man is not so easily reconciled to mistrust of himself, to the certainty that his mind is not absolute ... Laughter is not always an expression of gaiety...'

So, I'll go for some beer with Ilich. And laugh.

leo

They played the play in a big shopping plaza. It was a bad day to choose – cholera in the Caucasus gave the more cosmopolitan in the audience a stick to flail about with. From the first metallic cry of 'Fortinbras – emperor of the world', Leo was convinced he was making a fool of himself. That morning he thought of the lines he'd learned so long ago:

> *'Shall we awake, and not be taken for players?*
> *Never – the actors' mask is fleshed out with our flesh!'*

and he understood the private fear which prompted this. Mechanically, 'Fortinbras' worked magnificently. The padded heads of the cast fell correctly between the awesome and the grotesque. High above them floated a huge expanding fish, engorging strings of smaller, more brilliant fish. The banners of the International and of Fortinbras' court floated above them. The red pulses of police cruisers twinkled on the periphery.

Before the play began, they passed – symbolically – resolutions for countries their audience had not heard of.

'I feel,' said Leo, 'that intellectual rigour is not highly esteemed here. It's like going into the Chinese countryside a generation ago, and before telling the peasants a revolution had succeeded having to break the news that there was no more emperor.'

He remembered seeing *Hamlet* by the sea, in a night hot with maraschino and tramcars, the trailing flowers still busy with insects well past midnight. The artificial darkness they had designed for the plaza did not work.

Fortinbras said: 'I've no intention of speaking in blank verse. That was a foible of my predecessors. You've no idea the trouble of clearing up Hamlet's mess. But I don't complain – all that's past. We are not prisoners of the past, we are trying to capture the future ...'

Gradually, Fortinbras spread his net over the whole world. His mercenaries pressed forward, engulfing the audience. When the question, 'Will you help us to fight Fortinbras? Will you think of a way to defeat him?' – was asked, Leo hurried away. He had not lost his power to irritate, he noticed. A section of the audience – dreaming of scaffolds again – wanted arrests.

A sergeant said, 'Well now. Obstructing traffic. But almost any activity blocks traffic, as you might say.'

'You'd do better to root it out before it starts,' said an American tourist.

Others in the crowd admired the clean-cut mercenaries.

'Shirley,' said Leo, 'I've a feeling we went above their heads. I always assume that to be rich you have to be drilled in your education to make a solid foundation for later philistinism, but I guess I was wrong again.'

'Leo,' said Shirley, 'it's true there's an element of the ridiculous about this. But it was beautifully done – the conception and the mechanics of the fish, the checkering of the plaza, the banners – the artificial darkness if it had worked. It was a work of art. You're a talented and imaginative man.'

'And selfish? And self-obsessed?'

'Sufficiently, certainly. But what did you expect to accomplish with Fortinbras? Even there I think you made too many concessions.

'You're just not a populariser ... I could have done it more effectively, but less beautifully than you. I don't want to pretend that I care much about artists' dilemmas. I knew an author once – he'd say in the evening, "Aha, I'm just ready to do the reconciliation scene tomorrow," and then he'd be pleased and drink. And in the morning he'd have such a hangover he'd just grind the stuff out like marble dust.

'And I'd say, "I've no sympathy. You can't have the same pleasure twice. Think yourself lucky. You just reach into your head, and out come friends, trips abroad, witty conversation. I have to pay for that – but for you it's free. And then you complain about publishers! They're just jealous, that's all.'

'I feel we're getting nowhere. I realise that my work before this was grossly self-indulgent. Groups will come with bombs – I know this. There are two racks – one is for lack of conviction. One is stretched on that one. The other is for the cosmopolitans, the eclectics – one is compressed on that one. The pain, I imagine, is about the same.'

'When were you ever on the lack of convictions one?'

'Oh, I go on once in a while, for practice, you know. I think lack of efficacy is a great failing. But convictions – well, there was my wife. I'm someone who resents being asked too little. She always said, "But Leo, I ask so little of you" – and I'd say, "Raise your price a little, my dear, perhaps there'll be more buyers." But she never did. I don't even feel guilt. She was so loving – that's a hard thing to recover from. I always feel I'm lucky to be a selfish bastard – it saves me from perfection.'

Peggy came over to them. 'The others want to know: what's the next play? How do we get more response?'

'I'm ready to accept improvisation,' said Leo.

Lloyd said, 'What a frost this was. They thought we were insane. They went away puzzled, and I don't blame them. "Incitement to frigging poetry," one of the police called it.'

'Don't be so scathing,' said Peggy. 'It was our first try. Next time we'll know better.'

Later, Shirley said, 'Will you do this again?'

'I don't know. I feel Peggy's probably right. You have to raid a few stores before the public grasps the drama.'

'Leo, you're so inturned. Can't you even accept my sympathy? You seem to take that as part of the punishment. You can't be that independent. You have this desire to be needed – how can I long for someone who's all back, whichever side you look at?'

'Shirley, things *are* becoming very difficult. I'm not a young man, or a happy one. I've travelled most of the roads you're describing to me. This tentative relationship we have – it's so replete with speculation, we've passed beyond passion to tranquillity. That is why we are almost able to talk about politics together. Don't you see – I'm desperate to have you cuddled up all round me. But that would be the final defeat, the private solution to a public question. You choose, as you can, the arena on which you'll bleed. You don't complain then about the colour of the sand, the smallness of the crowd.'

'Or the pain?'

'Not if you can avoid it. That's why I almost resent you – you're coaxing these confessions out of me which frankly I find boring. At least Peggy sees me as something almost inanimate – an old dog who's to be congratulated for not peeing on the guests.'

'Leo, you have the most incredible images of yourself—'

'And you, Shirley, believe in magic. You believe if I transfer from politics all these emotions, this fixation, it'll all fall on you! But it can't be transplanted like that. I'm too old a fox to be covered in parasites.'

'But suppose you wrote instead. You're not a man of action – you're forced into it because no one else will do it.'

'Yes. Writing. I suppose there's always that when the rest fails. Really enshrining one's particularity. Able to enjoy to the full the dilemmas of the western artists. Ho hum – who shall I write for today? Why don't the workers read my pretty novels? Shirley, if I'm ridiculous, you're sensible, which is worse. Who needs sensible people at a time like this?'

'I just want you to do what you can do, and I want you to be happy.'

'Two assurances where one uncertainty will do?'

Outside, two children ran past shouting, 'Fortinbras is dead.'

'So, Shirley, the rot's begun. The play is dead, long live the author and the actors – someone always has to survive to write the criticism. Probably you're correct – writing would keep me quiet. But don't efface yourself in the effort.'

Shirley left, saying, 'I've no more patience with you. Walk your own way to hell, I don't care.'

Well, thought Leo, if you go on tormenting someone for answers, you mustn't be surprised if they're not the ones you want. But she tries so hard, and so tenderly. Who needs sentiment, though, when one has so many memories?

The big fish slowly reversed its digestion, and the plaza started to fill with smaller and smaller bright fish.

aleya

Aleya thought, 'Now, really, nothing frightens me. And the *sovkhoz* was small enough to split – yes, obviously. How strange everything is becoming. As if we didn't live in the world of economic reform, of directors asking for more initiative, but were back to the huddle on railway stations, waiting to be sent out to Central Asia for the first time. And I too am changed. I always used to think of Alexei as being immature. But now – was his not a completed position, and myself too simple in accepting him and his work as all of a piece? His youth saved him from a savagery of development, a stridency, which would offend against gentleness and formality. Wasn't it savagery which led him to conquer his fear and loneliness with suicide? There's so little time to form our opinions of ourselves, so little inclination to check them against the record. Better to think only of the parties we shared at the street corners, the concerts, the evenings musky with the smell of flowers beaten into the wet earth ...'

A man was singing:

'Forge the links into a chain
To bind all the horses, all the auls –
A chain thick as a man's neck,
Joining together all who hear my song ...'

Strange too, she thought, that my only real friend here is Katya. I will live in Kazakhstan all my life – why do I think of this time as merely a prelude?

Outside, small bulldozers were burrowing like beetles, shaking the temporary huts. Two truck drivers were talking, and one said, 'Yes, this is the way to see our country. I have seen so many odd things. I was once caught in a duststorm – like being smelted into a copper bowl it was. And the man I was with said he had been, as a little boy, taken to Tolstoy's funeral. He could have been, too – he was old as a thorn tree. And he said he remembers thinking, "How long can this go on – this dying and solemnity?" and his grandfather said, "Now that Tolstoy is dead, we can get down to business."

'But I don't know if I should believe him... Our job's still very individual, you know, and very abstract – just a few levers, and time and space.'

And the other answered, 'What a rambler you are, Nikolai Timofeyevich. And talking of duststorms – I was sitting one afternoon in an orchard – just me and a length of fine sausage. We were just getting acquainted when this storm comes, and I couldn't find my truck. Suddenly, someone said, "Quick, in here" – a tiny old man led me into a wooden box – I had to lie down in it. It was like being in a coffin, and this little old chap told me he just guarded the orchard. And he caught moths and things. Huge trembling dead things they were – I'd have thought he was inventing them. Wings like shale and mica. Eyes like beads of caviar – but some with yellow eyes. I'll bet you never heard of butterflies with eyes that colour?'

They moved away, and Aleya turned back to the plans they had drawn up. Katya asked, 'How's the bureaucratic deformation going this morning? I don't want to bore you with local legends, but there is a story about one of the "Chinese begs" they still tell around here. It seems he was collecting money to build a mosque, and he hired an architect to draw up the plans. And the architect turned against the "beg", and decided to make the mosque with insecure foundations, so that the first tremors, or even heavy rain, would weaken the whole thing. And that's what happened – the people were taxed, the builders built, the mosque was completed and the architect left. In a month, the cupola started to crack.

'At first the "beg" was furious, but soon he realised that here was a fine pretext for taxing the people to save an obviously faulty building. This went on until people cursed the architect so loudly that he heard them.

'"Only I can save the mosque," he said. "I'll come back and put an end to the whole matter."

'And so he did – only the "beg" was so annoyed with him, that he put him to death, and secretly stuffed his body in the foundations of the building. And this so weakened it – the tunnelling, I mean – that the whole thing collapsed a few days later. And they had to start everything again.

'But Aleya, Sultan and Kulkul are disturbed about something. They feel the plan has taken over from them. You should speak to them. As we said in Istanbul, "If you take someone's humanity from them, you should do so in a manly fashion, tell them face to face that it's just a personal matter."'

Aleya could see the cornflowers and here and there a flower yellow as corn – a huge sweep of them into the hills. 'It is beautiful here,' said Kulkul. 'But our problem is this. The machines are busy working: we will soon have buildings. Living like nomads is our life – we are not too concerned about our comfort: a little shade, enough food – the best singer from the *sovkhoz*.

'What concerns us is this only – that there is nothing here that is different from the former life. We are like bees – when we make another swarm, we are only able to make the same kind of cell we always did. We are asked to experiment. But we can think of nothing new. We don't want money. What then? Not another plan. As they say – this is a bureaucratic deformation. We should all meet and discuss what more it is that we want.'

Sultan said, 'No, I think there is a genuine problem here. We have reached a point at which everything becomes very difficult. It is difficult to move forward. We are like the khan's army which fused the sand to make a glaze for its armour – in the battles under the sun, the glaze melted, or turned back into sand, and the warriors were caught in the molten desert like trees in the ground. As for us – the machines run from dawn: a man can't make a song, take a sleep. The animals are numbed with the noise. We are eating into the hills and the plain, we will soon be using the river, jostling and nudging it.

'So, this is efficient. Everyone knows what is expected of him. But – we start with a plan which already is stifling us ...'

'That's true,' said the Ukrainian. 'But we spend more time revising the plan than carrying it out. The experts and specialists spend their time trying to fit what they have to do into what they've agreed to do. We know we have to have a plan, and to change the plan. But the committees on the plan – they've become an army of directors. We all wait for them.'

'What do you suggest?' asked Aleya. 'The general meeting is very cumbersome and slow.'

'I think we have simply to struggle,' said Sultan. 'Struggle against the bureaucracy. Struggle against the noise. Struggle to make the plan and to carry on despite it.'

Katya said, 'Now we are here at last, we are thrown onto resources which do not exist. We have no doubt: we can come through, that we can achieve all we want. But we must do everything ourselves – as the poet says, "Knowing what has to be done / As the goose knows the number of its feathers / We have only to count each step / And muzzle the hedonists."'

'Do you think we're hedonistic, then?' asked Aleya. 'I should think the opposite. All night the insects in my room held a plenum and a victory march. I've never seen such loyalty and unanimity between beetles and mosquitoes.'

The Ukrainian said, 'Of course, these problems are not just accidental. We're living through the mistakes of setting up all such enterprises. In a compressed way, of course. I think we should forget that courage is a weapon, and say merely, consciousness should help us regulate the distortions. We must stop the more active, or the luckier, fulfilling their section of the plan by unofficial means – or by driving the workers. That is initiative, but it leaves us with a lame development. Collectively we have to ensure collective success.'

'You mean – even here ambition and partiality flourish?' asked Katya. 'Well, of course – what could be more ambitious than to want to build a new world? And retain one's comradely virtues in the process. You have to combine so much. It reminds me of the old dancing bears crossing the Bosphorus – they were so shambly, they'd seen so much and had so much to remember, they could hardly think how to stand. They were traded and trained so often – life to them was a revolutionary technology. Sometimes in the middle of an antique dance, they'd forget who they belonged to, and start boxing, or playing the cornet. Their expertise was indistinguishable from senility ...'

Aleya thought, 'Poor Alexei. How he'd be furiously bored with all this. Sheep, cotton – the long-term fruit trees. Zoo-technology, soil samples, irrigation: control over wages, capital funds – takes longer than he ever had to find the dualism there. And yet, how much more keenly can one enjoy – without nostalgia, or even hedonism – the tired and lazy fellowflow of chatter in the evenings. Men breaking off their jokes with a sad song. To see the shepherds squatting in the dust, rolling bone dice, smiling, but never laughing aloud ... Life in Moscow was an obscure training for an existence which gave only apologetic compensations. No one, none of my teachers, for instance, expected that with so little I would be happy and satisfied.

And yet – apart from reviving the dead, which perhaps I don't want to do – I can do everything I want. There are no vampires or images here. No literary fancies, pushing me where I don't want to go. Just making a life with these people, learning with such difficulty what makes them sad. Katya, so cheerful despite burying a husband and an empire. The pride and relaxation of men who can feel free from fear.

'It will take so long, this discovery. Long after I'm dead, there will be people like me – still firmer, harder. Coming from the institutes and discovering "the history of the transformation of the uplands of Kazakhstan". Instead of a bowl, a komuz – I'll leave the grandsons of sheep, fruit trees so old there's nothing to be done with them, but sit in their shade, and rest from the sun ...'

They passed a resolution later that day – condemning excessive bureaucracy. And that evening – a concert: everyone, it seemed had an instrument, a song, a comic dance. The trees around were full of owls, flying and tootling like soft ocarinas. When the concert broke up, it was nearly dawn. How sad, to have to sleep at all, thought Aleya.

aleya's diary

How shocked they will all be when I leave. We have been so close, Sergei, Dimitri and I – and yet about us all there is a kind of reserve. How little time there seems to be to order our lives, to make firm and open commitments. How can I explain to myself?

Dimitri said to me today, 'I try to make my music as inexpressive as possible. And the professors say, "Try to communicate something simple and human."

"Well, yes,' I tell them. 'That's one kind of music, or so they tell me. But what are emotions to music? What do I know of your emotions – what do you care of mine? It is surely the formality of the design which should concern us. When we discuss life, it is not its meaning that concerns us, but its interrelationships and interdependencies.

'It is not its human qualities which have to be established – those are self-evident. Nor its niceness, certainly. It is absurd to suppose that music can itself be the framework for a new ethic of labour – it is a formal reflection of frameworks, of networks of human relationships – but it is an arrangement, not a vehicle for self-indulgence.'

I said, 'I can see how they dislike you, Dimitri – can't you? This sounds to them very cool and arrogant. They don't know how much of yourself you give in what may be not only mistaken but destructive activity.'

Dimitri smiled a little strained smile: 'I think I need a new definition of socialism, that's my problem. Or not a new definition, so much as a new reality, a freshly constituted province of reality. Look at your own life, Aleya. What kind of shape does it have? You can give it a shape by inventing a consistent sensibility – or by marrying, immolating yourself, like Larissa. But in a few months, Larissa will find the marriage pyre is getting hotter than the marriage bed. She'll start wriggling till she gets to a cooler spot. The things for which one feels intensely, for which one can sacrifice – these are bigger, perhaps more bitter things than one finds in academic music. At least, I think so.'

'Dimitri – tell me, they've rejected something of yours again? They're so blind! They never talk to you. They want lyricism – but they sit all year in their black suits in front of a metronome! They want dedication, but they escape to their dachas as though they were dogs taking a rat home to chew! Anything but music – they resent your refusal to compromise. That's what I admire about Alexei – he's wholly unsentimental about himself. And I speak of him as though he were alive, because he was that unsentimental ... You remember "Theatre"?

'I'd drunk so much

I saw two Cherry Orchards,
One sour, and one sweet,
And wept one sweet tear, and one sour.'

'And a wolf joke, which I feel is the essence of them all. There were two wolves, and they were lovers. The male wolf brought a nectarine for his girl. "See," he said. "It's nearly round." The girl pouted and said, "If you weren't such a dilettante, you'd find one that was completely round." The other – perhaps because he was a dilettante – searched and searched for one that was round.

'He said, "No, I looked and looked. That's the only kind there is." And the other wolf was very discontented. "Always nature spoils itself," she said, eating it.'

Dimitri said, 'I have the same problem with Sergei. Sergei is extremely simple, in a highly selective way. Without any real concern for what he's rejecting, Sergei has always refined his perception. He doesn't see much – but what he does see, he sees with a clarity that's rather shocking. As for you, Aleya, he condemned today what he calls your "emotional radicalism". He has a capacity for speculation which he distrusts. When the camp stories came out, you remember there were some people that were profoundly moved. It was a kind of tenderness, not anger, that they felt. And there were others who said it had been so long ago, that everyone had forgotten, been rehabilitated, or been guilty anyway.

'And Sergei said he could have sympathy with either view – but that what repelled him were those who said, "Ah, but even here, we see the qualities of man shining through." He said that formula was the most cowardly – it was the mark of a deformed sensibility. And I think he resents and envies your radicalism. He resents being so sparing of himself. He's afraid when the time comes to speak out – he'll have nothing but footnotes to add.'

'Dimitri,' I said, 'you know I'm leaving Moscow in two weeks? They'll take me as an economist in Kazakhstan. I feel I must get away from Alexei's city ...'

'Voluntary exile? It always amuses me when you say you're an economist ...'

'Or a demon lover – Dimitri, I expected a fuller response than that.'

'I'm not used to the idea. I won't be till you've gone. We'll never see each other again, I'm sure of that – and we'll always wonder why not. We've lived in a kind of intimacy which can't nourish itself in the banality of domestic life. Sergei says of you, Aleya, that you are too lively to have relationships. You crush everyone to you so tightly, they have to struggle against you to survive!'

'Aha, so we're to talk about love, not departure?'

'Aleya, you're leaving because you don't love us. There was Alexei – but you realised there was no hope there. He had this deep urge to self-destruction, you have this fear of losing yourself in individuals, in partial relationships. Our trouble, the three of us, is that none of us will compromise. So, what future is there for us? For Sergei to be competent – to work always at the limits of the possible. For me – just chance. Either a tough-minded composer or an idiosyncratic failure.

'You're the puzzle, Aleya. I can see you weighing peaches or whatever you do, so seriously entering the results. Thinking, "How can we get all this moving faster?" – glinting your eyes at the fruit like a big eagle. And inside? I don't know. I wish I could forecast happiness for you, Aleya. Not that you'd want it. You long for challenge, for an exoticism to arouse and extend you personality. And yet again – you are going away because you've lost something ...'

I was angry. 'Dimitri – you sound like the professor I heard today – talking about literature as though it was a kind of quadrille between moral failings. "Elsie's fatal flaw is that she gives more to Nature than to Spirit" – some such nonsense.

'And I said, "These people spend their lives as if they were family fortunes! What kind of morality is it which is crowned by success – who are these authors who make the patterns and award the prizes? Life is not a joint-stock company, declaring dividends for the intelligent and cultivated ..."

'And the professor – we've clashed before – said, "There are more lives to be lived than yours. If you would ask questions more, you would come to see the reason for other people's answers." Dimitri, what will happen to me?'

'Aleya, I want so much to be able to tell you.'

We looked out across the ponds at the blocks of apartments. A man with a crafty face snuffed the evening breeze while his dog ran about impatiently. There was a patch of sunflowers almost hiding a wooden house – sagging with outhouses. Dimitri must have been thinking the same as me, for he said, 'How different Kazakhstan will be.' And then, 'Aleya, I'm not being unkind to you. I'm protecting myself. I'm not sorry you're going, because you're rejecting me. I've to look after myself first.'

'But Dimitri,' I said, taking his hand, 'don't you see how disturbed I am too? How odd that people so articulate should be so incoherent. Alexei's death – can only be worked out in practice. To recover from his death – I must make my life, as well as I can.'

'Without us?'

'Dimitri, don't be naive. Sergei disappeared when Alexei died. I. needed

Sergei to help me put Alexei into perspective. But in the end, Alexei did that himself. I respect many of the strengths of Sergei: when I'm with him, I even admire him. But there is a tentativeness in him – he won't step up to things and outface them.'

'Will I? Do I?'

'Oh yes, Dimitri. You've the strongest stare at the Institute!'

'Laugh then.'

'And be glad that I can.'

'Aleya, you seem able to divorce the physical and the emotional. You're too much for any one man ...'

'You make me sound very schizoid. I'm not very sentimental about my body – and it's certainly not sentimental about me. It gives me no thought at all.'

'Aleya, I shall miss you so deeply. All your convictions are so unshakeable, I can't even ask you to stay.'

'Dimitri, I'm not a very settled person at present. I'm so impatient with the life of training and waiting. I couldn't live with the life you lead. Waiting, polishing, revising, rehearsing.'

'For you, it must be life on the grand scale?'

'For the present, life on my own.' Dimitri kissed me, and I tried to forget all other mouths but his. How can I bear to leave him – except by leaving him. I am escaping responsibility because to live with Dimitri should not be a responsibility at all – but I know that it would be. And yet – I am so concerned he should not think me cold. These warm evenings, with the bodies of Alexei's wolves – stiff carrion in the forest – how desperately I have to struggle with nostalgia! How bitter this discipline is. To hurt and puzzle Dimitri – someone to whom I feel so close, in whom such a desperate interest ... When will this summer end? When will the faces of those I love so deeply cease to hurt me?

feodor

'You are very far from us,' said the Komsomol secretary. We are sitting alone in my office. The winter which has so long been nibbling at us has at last closed its jaws. It is snowing – the roofs and yards are abandoned to the snow, only flagpoles and cupolas are holding out.

'I don't feel far from you, Timofei Vassilievich. On the contrary, I feel I'm wrestling for a stick, with you on the other end of it. If we let it down together, release our jaw-hold on it, perhaps we can talk?'

'Don't forget, Feodor, that our central experience is class struggle. This is a struggle which can still kill you, you know – and it's absurd to deny it or forget it. You're too intelligent to need me to talk about deviation, disloyalty. But, frankly, yours is the nature which actually does deviate, becomes disloyal. And this disloyalty is not to me, or to our Party, but disloyalty to the masses of people over the world – still locked in battle. This is an immense and very complex movement. Of course it is often difficult to be loyal to our Party – perhaps that is our little part of the struggle.

'We are in a privileged position – after fifty years we can enjoy a portion of what we've fought for. Possibly you think "too small a portion" – but I'd warn you, avoid eclecticism. If you concentrate to the point of obsession with your problem, concentrate on your responsibilities so intensely – then the problem must become a limited, personal one. That is, *you* may collapse under the strain – the problem doesn't. How can I convince you – the problem doesn't belong to you: its resolution cannot and must not belong to you alone: even the discussion of it cannot take place in your head!'

'If I say "but" – I stand condemned. If I suggest that the workers involved in this affair may rely on me to make the decision – I'm disloyal. If I say it's too early to speak – I'm disloyal. You are simply demanding me to yield my personal judgement – in a case which bears on our total development. The Party can judge me, of course. But can I judge the Party?'

'Feodor, you're inflating things. You're talking about people who do not generally believe that what they read in newspapers is a transforming force. History is for them not something which can be constantly reused to make a point, a reinterpretation – it's the memory and experience of every worker in the country. Proletarian history is made by everyone, and only an outsider would believe there was concealment, or that there could be – in this process. I'm not talking about events or mistakes: these can be concealed or unnoticed. But as regards consciousness of where we are – this I believe we have.

'Don't imagine I want to hide your information because it might be embarrassing. I don't deny that every injustice has its victims. But any process of judgement involves the possibility of injustice. Here I am – twenty-one. The reason you stayed close to us in the Komsomol was to educate people like me. But perhaps you've forgotten how the people who work here pass their lives. If you are convinced that you have a complete and mature understanding of them – then make your own choices. They will be as ours. But if not, if you understand only yourself, only the tensions of a formal dialectic – then whatever you have discovered, you have not earned the right to be heard.'

'Timofei, I think the problem is tougher even than you say. Of course, to intellectuals in placid situations, or to people who believe the exposure of any injustice is obligatory – issues like mine are vitally important. I'm not talking of abstract freedoms, but what is to be done about quite self-evident waste and brutality! I'm not sure I even deserve your criticism. I know to you I may seem a dilettante. But my struggle is as real as any you can imagine – and it affects you, vitally. The question of how the proletariat makes history is surely the central one for us all …'

'Exactly. That is why we must discuss it together.'

'Very well, I'll try.'

I have to see Andrei now. What a dry day this is! The early shift is going off through the snow, bandy like dismounted cavalrymen, hatted like tank crews. All the hollows Sophie and I made in the fields will have deep drifts. Aleksandra and I haven't had time to make any – perhaps we never will. All the lucky cherries which hid all through the summer will he black with frost now.

'Andrei, they want me to tell the whole story, to produce evidence. And – at present, you're my evidence.'

Andrei suddenly smiles at me. 'No, it's not much, is it. In the war, in the camp – one's daily life required courage, while facing death was very easy, almost a self-indulgence. You thought – "I must come through this – someone must hear what I've to say." And then, when you come out – you find millions of people to tell you, "But that's exactly what happened to me!" – or "It was worse at Yaroslavl," or "But I was the first into Kiev – imagine that!" Feodor – I'm an old man telling a story. It's all true, all unremarkable, widely known and prehistoric. It would be like going back and saying to Stalin or Ordzhonikidze or Dzerzhinski, "Haha – just a minute there: it seems to me you're starting this thing off in the wrong way." And now, of course, we can't speak to them at all.'

'So you're saying we can only concentrate on the moment – eternity is the instant? Is that what you mean? Groping forward like a blind giant?'

'You concentrate on what you like, Feodor. It just seems to me that this episode is closed. The factory has now materialised – it is where it is. The error has been rectified. The human victims have been patched up, have had their apology.'

'But how do I write a history of an error?'

'I'm not an error. Write the history of the rectification. But that's your problem. I remember my grandfather saying to me once, "People's lives go on together like instruments in an orchestra. Not everyone has the melody, or even the same music. You have to try to get everyone in tune – but at the same time, you have to listen. The orchestra is playing all the time, with you in it. You have to get your notes in at the right time – and the music is all there is. When you are hearing it – it's already gone. Of course, we hope to become better and more inventive musicians. There's some that say we should be able to play without music written down at all. But we write the music anyway!"

'And I argued with him – driving the poor old chap nearly mad, wishing he'd never started that illustration. But I'm in his position, now. I don't want to go back. If you do – well, good luck. I just told you what I knew. I don't expect anything to come of it.'

As Andrei leaves, Aleksandra enters, shaking her head and feet like a cat. I feel like the foolish prince who calls all the wise men in the world to cure his foolishness, and they all say, 'Ho hum, your trouble is, you don't know enough.'

'Aleksandra, may we talk over my problem for a while?'

'It's always your problem. You discuss it so much – and then ask "Should I discuss it?" You're crazy. You want the luxury of making decisions after the event.'

'I believe in everything in moderation, even – no, especially – moderation.'

'You believe immoderately in everything. You're enormously gullible, you know. You look like a little boy, pretending to be a tormented intellectual – I can almost hear your brow creaking from the furrows! Feodor – give it a rest.'

'Don't tell me you're another one like Sophie, who thinks conversation is the fruit of boredom, and politics of ennui? Do you think humans should just couple up and sleep together like squirrels in a hole, nose to tail? Even squirrels must have to discuss which one is to throw the excrement out of the tree!'

She's angry – but she would have been angry anyway. She finds me so irritating – I satisfy her demands for a challenging life. My girls seem to mature fast – often to the point of senility. But how wearisome – to have to convince people of things – like sincerity – they can never be sure of: you can only do it by reiteration, but in the end, what does it matter? Aleksandra could give me the advice I'll now have to coax out of her, on the spot. If I don't take her advice she'll think I was playing with her.

Instead, frowning over her work, 'I'm not angry, you know. I'm always very fair to my friends. I give them my attention. I'm just not fitted to give you advice. It's too big and too personal a decision. I'll help you follow it through once you've made it. And how many intellectuals are so lucky? Your decision matters.'

'Aleksandra – what kind of intellectual is that? I'm editor of the factory paper, I run induction and orientation courses for young workers – and yet you persist in inflating me like a balloon for no more pleasure than to bear the air rasp out.'

'Feodor – you have this capacity for making any conversation centre on you – you're so open and strange. Yes, you're like the sea – whatever you drop in, you never get back, and everything you take from it has a different shape from the things which resemble it on land. But, poor little Feodor, little wide-eyed wide-awake, I love you.' As though that matters. As that matters. She has her arms round me to protect me from things I should deal with on my own. Things I do deal with ... I feel in myself there is a harshness, an indifference which I do not sufficiently resist. Like the sea! – obviously she's right ...

Tonight I'll find Yuri and Ilich, we'll go for some drinks. They won't play volleyball now for five months. Aleksandra will soon get used to being in love, she'll start counselling the others now. Until one day she thinks, 'What the hell – I've lived through the whole episode, and come out the other side. I don't need Feodor any longer.' She'll have traversed me like a liner crossing the Atlantic – sighting the occasional iceberg, but at the end, only Liberty. Liberty corroded at the knees. The torch full of penny bubblegum. The young refugees, escaping half-demented, looking at the world with such big eyes, my America, becoming just – empty. Empty and smelling of cordite.

If only Aleksandra and I could go South. She's smiling at me, and I feel awkward because no one should smile at me like that. Why can't I admit my excitement, my passion? Because of the snow, perhaps. Because of the sting of the vodka, pricking me like the pitchfork entering the first warm hay of the harvest. Because of the questions about our life which I ask in such way they can't be answered. It is dark with snow outside, and I can't look at Aleksandra, the girl I almost love, and who fills me with such loneliness.

leo

Someone had painted 'Don't Husserl me' on one of the buildings round the square. The group was to improvise 'The day of the Tiger', and Leo noticed one of the mercurial shifts of police policy had hemmed them about with cruisers.

'Don't you know there's a by-law against improvisation?' asked a sergeant.

'Even in a political cause?'

'On any pretext: we must have a script.'

'Suppose they all forget their lines?'

'Then we have a scale of fines.'

The sergeant grinned sourly: 'Look, feller, do you really think we're letting you long-hairs rant out anything that comes into your head? I know that's a set speech, but I for one never tire of it. If you think the law's harsh – well, we've a scale of fines for leaving keys in unattended cars, interrupting funerals – you name it.'

Leo walked away to talk to Shirley. The police were covered with accoutrements which could be used to scratch or club – even on casual contact. Some wore black leather leggings, as though they feared attack by leeches.

'I feel foolish to say this, Shirley, but I'm more interested in the play than the scuffling. I've always felt the police have so much more time than we for studying the niceties of brawling. We, after all, have problems of recruitment and studying – I've always found the undercover cop makes a poor theoretician. Apart from the usual infantile disorders, there's a tendency to eclecticism, even to fantasy. Interesting that in Canada where class struggle and national liberation are so often fought out in booze there should be more laws for liquor control than gun control – there's sublimation for you!'

'Leo, I feel you're more out of place than me here,' said Shirley. 'I don't enjoy being hurt, even as a gymnastic! I often think the anarchists are right – sometimes you break the law, sometimes it breaks you. I can guess which way it will be today.'

'I don't have your resentment,' said Leo. 'This seems a clinical, a formal, procedure. One is relieved to be able to read the signs. We at least will not be shot – and it would be foolish to regret the possibility!'

'Leo, I guess we're no longer with the group?'

'Are you saying I've lost contact, Shirley?'

'Not with me – but if I say you're incongruous here, it's not an aesthetic judgement. You can't use the group, and they can't use you. You can't improvise, because you intuitively reject spontaneity. You know yourself too well to value your instincts. It's not being old – it's being an old dog.'

And Leo remembered somewhere in the Caucasus, looking down a hillside blurry with the life of lizards, apricot and almond trees straggling among the rocks, until far down like a ribbon of blue sky inverted between mountains, he could make out a hazy blue river. Mist burning off like charcoal smoke, children selling wild cherries and windfall apricots – and someone saying, 'On this rock the princes of Gori lived waterless for eighty years. They loved the view, but even though they built a temple they could never get closer to the river down there.' And his wife had seen his happiness, his absorption in the liveliness of the people, the vigour of the princes' old eyes which had swept the valley like kestrels' – or perhaps they'd simply drunk wine? But to Leo it was a reproach that she should get her pleasures at second hand, from him.

'Don't look at me,' he said. 'Look at the river – that has to last: another thousand years!'

But it hadn't lasted her two. Who can get pleasure from nostalgia when the immediate need is for ice-cream. He remembered some poetry:

'How dismaying is your need for me –
Demanding that I be
Balm for your wounds
For I give only wounds.'

'The day of the Tiger' began. The people had built a huge tiger to govern them – 'tired of the governments of men, individual tyrants, the fine print in contracts we have never read – tired of cannibalism – we do here this day set up our tiger. Let him adjudicate and rule, let him decide our fates. Let the tiger govern with his plaster paws. We set him up in the image of our indifference, our hopelessness. Let no man try to seize the tiger, for his paws are impartial ...'

The huge tiger was wheeled in – its paws indeed dispensing summary justice, as the citizens went about their business of selling each other under the sign of the tiger.

'Let there be no pope but the tiger, and no god; let the police, let the army, serve the tiger. Only in this way will we be free from the domination of man: gladly we submit to the rule of the tiger.'

The tiger became the property of the nation: he funded loans, he appeared on the currency. He became a trinity, and criminals rushed gladly to self-immolation with shouts of 'For tiger, tiger, and tiger.' The only question forbidden was 'Why tiger?'

'This is an anarchism,' said Leo, 'but amusing enough.'

After a while, two slogans appeared: 'We are all slaves of the tiger', and

'The tiger is the refinement of human nature.' The tiger itself seemed to stir: two counter-slogans could be seen in the crowd, 'We are slaves of the slaves of the tiger' and 'Refinement is not in the nature of the tiger.'

Polarisation set in. The wrigglings of the tiger became wilder – it was clear it was impelled by humans. Troops appeared, bearing the emblem of the tiger. Revolutionary flags were broken out – and the two sides began to stalk round each other. The tiger soldiers moved behind the cruisers, so the police were in the middle of the armies. Huge amplified snatches of the *marche militaire* played and distorted on infernal horns, roared out. The police moved towards the armies to keep them apart.

'This is where it starts,' said Leo. 'I don't really think the play was worth intervention – but it was splendidly noisy.'

The construction workers, miners, meat packers who stood around watching did not seem amused or irritated – the scene was familiar enough from television, even if the play had been wildly curious. But the police were certainly annoyed. They started to chase the actors. One fell, and a policeman started hauling her to her feet, but in such a way that she could not in fact stand. She was crying and frantic.

'Time to be brave,' thought Leo, as he seized the policeman by the waist. He felt someone else grab him, and giggled as he thought of them as an illustration of the team that tries to pull up the biggest turnip, or Rabbit's friends and relations trying to uncork Pooh from the burrow. Someone was kicking him, and twisting something.

'Stop! Just let's everybody stop – it's too uncomfortable like this,' shouted Leo. His hold broke, and like a string of fish on the bank, everyone fell over and thrashed about. 'So, this is political activity?' he thought wryly. Not many were arrested, and at each stage in the police procedure there seemed fewer accused and more police. 'We'll get security on him,' said the desk sergeant. 'Illegal entrant, I'll bet. Terrorism, bombing, his specialities.'

'No, inflammatory plays is my worst. And I've seen too much terrorism to want more.'

'Why can't you live like decent people?' asked a young policeman, 'Why can't you be satisfied?'

'I feel we've had these arguments millions of times here and there. I'm for what you call decency so long as decency isn't for barbarism, and if passivity solved problems I'd choose passivity, I promise you. But the "day of the tiger" was unexceptionable, a joke! Kids in high school read more intense and uncompromising stuff than that. It seems to me quite impossible to have less than an armed struggle with you people – even in the premature stages! You're so jumpy, you make me jumpy.'

'Is that a threat?'

'Yes,' said Leo. 'Of course I'm threatening you to hurt me, or jail me, or fine me. Aren't you intimidated?'

The magistrate fined them without comment.

'Shirley – I think I've come to the end of this attempt,' said Leo. 'I've been complaining that Peggy has no contact with the awfulness and sadness she's supposed to be embattled with. But now I don't feel I can contribute as a man of action. I think that our little group will have to work itself out without me – it's too various to submit to a rigorous discipline, physical or intellectual. It's hard for someone like me who's tried so hard for unity and understanding on the left to accept that kind of unsophisticated diversity – various kinds of brutality, despair, withdrawal, even irrationalism. I think the best thing for me is to withdraw before I do more damage ...'

'You may withdraw, but you can't escape – you're a man of the century, after all. But I know what you mean: I can't help you, and I wouldn't disgrace you by sympathising with your failure. You've tried to be unselfish – and that's nothing. You were lucky to be in a position where you had something to give.'

'Yes. We're like two old narodniks come home to daddy's estate – patching up the fences till the whirlwind comes. But at least it brings us closer together, Shirley. If we have no language of action, we do have an encyclopaedia of lyricism. You are so self-effacing, so understanding – I don't know if your husband accustomed you to the second best, or whether maturation brought you to embrace disillusion.'

'Leo, you're absurd. You laugh at your despair with such bad grace. Can't you relax? Can't you try for an existence less dense, and more lucid? Have you nothing to offer yourself? If not, there's certainly nothing for me.'

'Shirley, I'm convinced that from complexity will indeed come simplicity. But I'm afraid my simplicity is one I'm reluctant to admit. Mine is the restlessness of the man on parole – I couldn't live placidly with you, for instance …'

'I wouldn't ask you that. Why don't you use the past, instead of letting it torment you, and try to create something which would satisfy you?

'You mean – destroy the "something difficult" room? What should we do for conversation then?'

'Leo, you're so bitter. You don't turn the point of your irony like a hook – it's like a spear. You thrust it in, and pull it out without waiting for the laugh. You despise your contempt. You're totally frustrated – and too proud to say "Listen to me somebody." What we'll do is this. We'll go to my parents' cottage. You'll write there, or drink. Listen to the fish plopping up to look at you. Amass the material for a new idyll, to enjoy when we're back in the city. We'll spend our money, and that will avoid any feelings of indulgence. I'll employ you – as visiting playwright.'

'Shirley, I don't mean to be harsh – not especially, anyway. I feel I'm almost at the end of something – either something in me, or in the total society. I know this is very Slavic. And rather arrogant – society always has somewhere to go, even if individuals feel there's nowhere. But I'm not used to this feeling of uselessness.'

'Can't you start with something simple – try to be useful to me?'

'I'll try. But I'm not sure if I can.'

And Leo thought – so it's off to the 'something difficult' cottage!

The smoke from smelters, forest fires and garbage dumps rose all round them, like the smoke from burning dachas, reddening the sun, making the sky purple and coppery. Shirley smiled at Leo with all the tranquillity he had ever seen.

aleya

Waking boldly after too little sleep, Aleya thought, 'I wonder who it is that sets my life to music?' Someone was completing a long weeping song about a batyr, a warrior-hero:

'Condemned to impotence his legs
Grew into the ground like ivy roots,
His black horse grey, bones sliding
Under the skin. 'Aiieee, I am destroyed –
My horse, my armour, blood-flecked, rust-stained.
Never again my horse's neck, bow-arched,
Taut against the plain ...' His strength
Gone out into the thorn tree, our batyr
Locked in the tree – he cannot free us
Until we free him from the thorns,
Bitter thorns.'

Katya said, 'I remember it used to be a point of honour with us never to sleep before dawn. Ah well, our honour was cheap then. We were always more fortunate than the rest of the poor. Though we cheated from necessity like them, we had a panache which let us work with more style. After all, many of us were the things they pretended to be – princes, generals, for what that's worth. We had no compunction about stealing from the rich – we were fully aware of their mortality. But the men who'd been poor all their lives – they stole from each other, and so stayed poor.'

'I often forget, Katya, how hard your life has been. Odd that you should take a further risk?'

'Aleya, my husband laughed one day, and told me a story. There was a farmer in a village in Anatolia. And he had terrible luck. His crops were blighted, the animals savaged each other, he was plagued by beetles in the fields – he used to say it was fortunate he wasn't a sailor or the sea would dry up. Eventually he had to leave for the town – one of those blasted little Turkish towns – when you step in from the blighted countryside, it's like stepping down a hole: it's like a sore on the festering land. But it turned out that the man had some skill as a coppersmith. Not much, but enough to keep his idiot children and his sick and helpless wife in misery on the edge of existence. He lived the kind of life which Turks call modestly affluent, but the rest of the world thinks worse than torture.

'But one day the rest of the smiths got together and drove him out of town – not enough work for them all. He tried begging, but he'd been unlucky enough to keep his limbs and his sight. All went badly until one day he joined the army. He, of course, was so inured to bad fortune by this time that he was able to spread it about. He found he had a talent for making other people unhappy. He became a sergeant, and lived happily unhappy ever after.'

Aleya smiled and went to work. Two days seemed to make a routine. The shepherds were away, building little shelters among the blue flowers, where the yellow and black crickets clicked like bones or sticks, snapping themselves together for the highest leap. The trees were alive with chidder and chirr, falling silent only when the leaves tossed silver in the breeze and the insects concentrated on holding on. One of the young technologists came in, and said, 'Aleya – you remember saying we were to have all the possible deformations in a very rapid and compressed form? I don't think I agree – but I can raise one problem for you ...'

'Leonid – you know we're a collective – why do I always have the problems? Problems shared are problems doubled, you know – but problems given over to the collective are simply routine!'

He laughed. 'Laugh at me, then. After, you'll be able to help. The drivers and some of the other groups want to be represented on the leadership by occupation. They say they want their interests represented as fruit-growers, dairymen – not individuals, or communists. They say occupational differentials are the form the class struggle has taken on the *sovkhoz* in general, and they want your recognition of this.'

'But we're so small! Anyone who wants can do anything, make any suggestion.'

'They say they know all the arguments about differentials and division of labour. But they want an organisation which does not reflect differential and division. They say they want a society of producers, with each branch of production having equality – in planning, especially. They say that you have a planning job which you base on skill: they say you've made management an occupation – governing them is your function, being governed theirs.'

'Do you agree, Leonid?'

'I'm from Leningrad. From what I can see, it is impossible to have that system in Leningrad – but yes, we do also have it. Everyone plans, everyone is governed. I think in theory they're mistaken, but that theirs is not such a big mistake. They believe in a seamless technique – cobbled together from all kinds of arbitrary needs.'

'Leonid – how long have you been in Kazakhstan?'

'A few months. I left everything, everyone. I'll confess, I'm pretty much on my own. Did you find it hard to adjust – or perhaps you've always lived here?'

Aleya remembered leaving Moscow – Sergei hurt and embittered, forever silent. Dimitri, puzzled and wistful, pressing his face like a cat's against the railings of the Institute as she left him.

'I think everyone adjusted to me,' she said. 'I'm just about ready now to start my new life. But that was my fault. I was getting control of myself, so that I could go where I want. I used to be a single-paced horse – only the gallop. I got tired easily. Now I can go all day.'

'After sheep?' asked Leonid. 'Or just trotting about, sniffing and snuffing? No, Aleya, you have the chance to speak out here. Tell us where you stand.'

'You're so much like me, Leonid – and that's something I don't care to approve of! Your world of asking questions is not much admired – especially in everyone else's world. When I was younger, I thought marriage was like this – the death of questioning – jogging along, with no interruption but the occasional comma, until there were only full-stops ... And I still feel this about marriage – but less about questions. I'm more cautious, because I know how much people hate being asked questions – me? I love it.'

'Aleya, this is enormously encouraging. Everyone seems to work so hard here, to find you sitting like the Black Sea saying "just dive in" is splendid.'

'I've almost forgotten what a big city is like – have they changed? How I'd love to buy some big spike flowers in the evening, walk demurely by the river ...'

'And me – what could I do?'

'Well, Leonid, what can you do?'

'I could paint you, very badly, very formally. The kind of unfinished picture they sometimes have to put in local exhibitions to show that everyone has an ever-laden easel.'

'But to talk of deformations – we must have a meeting on this, with everyone.'

'Yes, I enjoyed the concert.'

'You find us very self-indulgent?'

'Amateur hedonists, let's say.'

'It's all very new, rather superficial. People are just beginning to see the possibilities here – and to resent the backwardness. It's not just smiling faces and folk-songs.'

'But you're glad you came here, Aleya?'

'Generally, yes. There's such potential. We don't have the kind of challenge and hostility here that I was conscious of in Moscow. There's a revolutionary excitement, but with a lot of the spadework done, and a lot of compromise. I certainly don't see myself as a meddler. People know what's expected of them, and they can make choices. I'm much cooler than in the old days.'

'It sounds dull – all passion spent.'

'Yes, I've thought that.'

'But not now, Aleya?'

'You make that sound very personal indeed, Leonid.' With a sudden flash, 'Dullness? You say that like a taunt! We're not drudges here. We try to meet the demands of others as willingly and vigorously as possible. If you're to stay here, better learn the lesson – the working day is a sacred truce!'

She remembered her own first days on the *sovkhoz* – desperate to seek relief from the sun, the songs, the wheeling specks of birds. She had missed her friends so keenly, until she could recover enough to start a correspondence, and adjust to its dwindling, she would rehearse conversations with them. And Leonid, smiling a little shyly, like a tiger meeting a tiger in the forest, just suppose he wasn't a tiger after all?

'Yes,' she said. 'We must have another meeting. And now – I'll show you the map of the future,' taking out the plan, 'and the part I've in mind for you!' She laughed, but he did not, looking hard at her, an eyebrow raised. 'I hope you remember to put everything in the plan,' he said. 'I wouldn't like to trespass on the sacred working day to force changes on you ...'

Yes, thought Aleya, he's a tiger, for sure.

aleya's diary

'Oh,' I said softly, 'the poor people.' Sergei had taken me to the theatre – stage machinery makes me cry, it's so physical. The villages were burning, silver sparks shot up like bullets. I seem to have seen the same device before – and how tearful I seem to be. In just a few days now, I'll be leaving, breaking through Sergei's resentment into the long slope to his indifference – I feel like a child coming out of the sunlight into the forest, running down to the green darkness. Everything seems bitter now – I'm so tired, though, it all seems comic. Dimitri wanted to come with us tonight, but I said two men and a girl put a constraint on the whole party. We have been trying to gather together all of Alexei's poetry, his jokes. There is not much and the range is small, even monotonous. Or perhaps that is because his is the only poetry I've read for weeks.

'Aleya, look at this,' Dimitri said today. 'A wolf joke dedicated to me! It seems that one day a wolf invented a violin. He immediately took it to show to the committee for cultural affairs. And the committee said, "Well done indeed! We demand that this instrument be used only for the playing of wolf music. Go ahead – you've brought honour to our culture." And the wolf said, "Don't be silly – wolves have no music." And the committee said, "But in that case – how come you invented that violin?" And the inventive wolf said "Damnation – you must be right!" I should show this to my teachers!'

'Dimitri – did Alexei ever get to England?'

'I don't know – I don't think so. He was always talking of travelling, though.'

'There's a poem called "London" here. Listen:

'Not the greatest workers' city, but still
we see where they worked and drank, breaking
all the gaslights in the street – now
Charlie and Fred, maned like lions,
chat about girls, rock, revolution, in the pub.

I'm so naive, and they're so gentle –
me their big prize, silver sturgeon
all the way from Russia!

"You should see the petrol-bombs," says Fred,
"The fascists use them on the blacks – but
"Your glass is empty." Here, my friends,

I sit, in my quaint suit, getting drunk.
So enthused – the splendid girls, the books,
the theatres – and just
one of me to say "'Comrades', I love you,
Your England is my Russia," and weep.

They laugh and say "Cheer up, Alex –
'We will win because
"we are the drunker."

I love
this half of England!'

'Alexei had such an impulse to enjoyment – it makes you ignore his irresponsibility,' I said. And later, sitting beside Sergei, I think it was pity for Alexei that made me put my hand on his arm. He looked so sombre, so awkward, so deeply set in despair. I don't think he was considering me, our own relationship, at the time – probably just counting over his anxieties.

'Sergei,' I said, 'because I'm leaving, that doesn't mean you can't have any human contact with me at all. I'm not trying to hurt you – on the contrary, I'm hurting myself. It's like amputating my whole body!' How foolish to think that a pat on the arm can cure that bleakness, though.

He looked at me as though I were an empty seat. 'Oh yes,' he said, 'I'm fully aware of that. You seem to think that all will be well if I understand your motives. I do understand them – and nothing is changed. You speak of leaving as though you are conferring immortality on us both – but that's very far from the truth. I'm not like you – I've no time for poignancy.'

Then, oddly, he said almost desperately, 'This migration – it makes us seem like animals, forever jostling away from each other to get to the warmth – sacrificing every contact to lie stretched out in the sun, alone. Life is full of savagery, and the only way to meet one's fate is by rigorous intellectual methods.'

'Sergei,' I said as gently as I could, 'I can't feel guilty for causing a little pain and disturbance. You're wrong to project onto me your sadness and resentment. Try to see the whole thing clearly. Loneliness is only a symptom of our independence. If we were together, I'd *need* to be your Larissa – I'd have to give you huge sections of my life because they would be intolerable to you if I lived them out. I don't want that any more than I could live on the edges of Dimitri's silence, his privacy – always feeling an intruder on his central concerns.'

Sergei looked away. I could see he did understand, that he'd planned the next days as a kind of ritual, as though I were a tribal chief whom it takes ten days to bury. I was moved, but not with tenderness, only apprehension. Why was he so certain these must be funeral rites?

The last act was short. The characters came out of the smoke like butterflies or snakes slipping out of their worn skins. So – all wars have to end, and the moment of hope. There comes a time when in our struggle to understand, we see like Sergei that further activity is impossible, is not required. Someone on the stage said, 'We who have beaten fascism – we leave the work in your hands – it is unfinished business,' and I thought of Alexei's reflected Marx and Engels soaking away at their minds in London, but still able to make the Russian visitor goggle.

Where was there for Alexei to retreat to but his own pleasures? There was a sweetness in his impatience with what he sees as our foolishness, our saintliness, our savagery. It's as if he's saying – look at the ideas you're supposed to be feeling, look at their complexity, their variety – and then look at the botched version you've created. Alexei sees us as children – you can't blame a child for drawing without perspective. To him we're wolves – occasionally witty, but with the wit of people crippled by nature. And I know I'm not like that. No one I know is like that. Alexei was our spoiled priest – everyone was a priest or a spoiled priest to him.

After the play, we walked down to the river. A few drops of warm rain fell, and I turned up my face to them. Sergei pulled me along, 'You'll get wet.'

'When I was little I used to think we were like trees, and the rain made us grow – that was why Englishmen were tall! I used to think the rain was coloured too – green rain on the grass, and so on – and wondered how the rain was so consistent in its falling. Or perhaps I used to pretend I thought that.'

'So you've gone from aesthete to ascetic in a dozen years – not bad.'

'Please no, Sergei. It's been such a difficult summer.'

I watched the familiar scene with such keen pleasure – I shut out Sergei's indifference. The little families on their late walks – it's too hot to sleep. Cats busy with a game with a wizened potato. Is this really what Alexei called 'the universalisation of the bourgeoisie'? I can't recognise myself in anything he wrote – I recognise the landmarks, but he leaves the faces of the people blank. Only Dzerzhinski is credible, because inhuman. He hovers over Alexei's life like a pair of black wings, and try as I can I can't frighten him away ...

And I'm so volatile myself these days. Sergei won't give me reassurance. He seems to hate me for causing his fondness for me. But I need his encouragement, and he's insulted by my need. Well, I'll have to do without him. But I remember one of our teachers saying something very moving. He had been discussing some problem in ethics, and he broke from his text – 'The realisation that one is not needed for one's own sake comes to some people as a profound shock. But wasn't it Plekhanov who said – we ourselves determine our value as individuals. That is what being an individual means. Of course, we are open for the judgement of others, but that judgement does not affect us independent of our valuation. This is the challenge, and the only reward, of independent existence.' And I said, 'Yes – but is this a consolation or an additional challenge?' And he said, 'If I am right, you've merely restated the conclusion ...'

But how little comfort this gives me now. And Sergei – staring at the orange and blue of the river, the twinkling red lights and stars on the skyline – how completely he can withdraw from judgements ... Why does he make me feel I'm torturing him ...'

feodor

'Poor Feodor,' says Grigor. 'Still looking for the key to all our hearts?'

'Not today – I'm down in the archives where all madness starts. Still searching for primal coherence.'

Grigor looks complacent – neither concern for himself nor ferocity towards me in his indifference. They make me feel like a policeman, trying to penetrate disguises – increasingly isolated myself from all the undisguised. I always seem to be struggling up river, to spawn or to die ...

Aleksandra will soon want to take care of my isolation. At present she finds my seclusion delightful. It gives me over completely to her investigation. But as my affection starts to decrease her vulnerability, to firm up the flabbiness which, after all, attracted me to her – she'll start to become impatient. Out in the provinces – our fewer problems are presented steadily, like the wind which is still swirling in with snow this morning. And this isolation – where does it spring from? Not from my America – beer bottles stuck upright in snow banks, the cities desolate with rebuilding and firebombing, jackrabbits printing their peace signs over the parking lots. From the reveries about the sun? – no, for I feel I'll never see those warm blue seas again, the cicadas like limpets on the sea-green trees, the big ants carrying away raspberries from the tangled fields ... Not even from Yuri and Ilich, who tell me so little – perhaps because they too are searching for primal articulateness.

Ilich said to me yesterday, 'Feodor – I don't envy you. You work alone, and yet you depend on other people to make use of what you produce in isolation. It's a solitary life all right ...' Always this word – solitary, isolated. And yet – for everyone who is isolated, there is a community of those who isolate.

It is clear that what I'm looking for is something total and dismissive. Something which will say – everything is an illusion, everyone is deceived. But I don't believe this. As they say, 'when you chop wood, the chips fly': we've chopped a lot of wood, and used some blunt axes. Through the wall I can hear a film show – I think it's on Asian politics. How keenly people are trying to feel close to the people on the film – to grasp some image of comradeship. How odd – in my America there has been no one to speak for the casually dead until so recently: their 'twentieth congress' is held underground, though. What do capitalists say about their 'deformations', their mistakes? I have the picture of men denying with easy minds their path to subhumanity – the substitution of technique for sensitivity. What would be possible for me in America but the wildest fantasies? What a rewriting of history they've had! What a negation of men's lives, a blunting of needs – the continent an open camp. And yet – come on, Feodor: the answer is not sensitivity alone! I've not even begun to enquire into the lives of the people here – how can that be possible? Instead, taking refuge in pedantry – I am at fault!

'Well, Feodor,' says Andrei. 'Did you find what you were looking for, and why?'

'Andrei, I don't understand you. You seem irresolutely to be pushing me into unresolvable questions, unsubstantiated contentions. What do you want me to say – that the factory's beginning was unauthorised, even criminal – and that this is, or is not, reflected in our current practice? Are you concerned at all about yourself? Do you want additional proof of the illegality of your own case?'

'I'm only asking – what do you think of all this? Are you satisfied? Are you afraid? Who do you trust? Can you live with us as an intellectual? What do you have to offer?'

'You mean – how can I make whichever truth I choose to tell useful to you? And what in any case would be useful to you?'

'I remember, Feodor, my grandfather said to me once, "There are two sorts of people, those who die with their eyes open, and those who die with them closed. But the first sort have them closed anyway."

'And I said, "That's very fatalist," but he said no, it was breaking through to realism, the making of realistic choices. But I could never see that this was a realistic choice, My grandfather was one of those old specialists – the kind who could impress you with effort which was really no effort – growing a beard, or moustaches, say. Or whittling a stick. I'm still waiting for someone – someone, perhaps, like you, not to expose efforts like this – but to suggest a more brilliant future.'

'No, I don't understand.'

'Ah well, someone else will.'

I am very puzzled. Responsibilities of an entirely new kind are being forced on me – why can't I bear them? Or discharge them? We need for this a new type of intellectual – more refined and sensitive than me, yet closer to the people and their concerns. It is what I tried to be – but I've failed. Not dishonourably. I have abused no one, despised no one. True, I've been negative – but that's been my worst fault.

Timofei looks in. 'Perhaps I was too forceful yesterday, Feodor. I think, after all, we'll still have to cooperate, help each other along. I don't know yet what I'm ready for.'

My précis of the question reads, 'In the setting up of the factory, gross inadequacies and infractions have been hinted at. In view of the relative early success of the plant, however, these mistakes were either concealed or overlooked. This success was probably bought by directors both forceful and unscrupulous. The cost of this in material and human terms is lost –

only prolonged hearings could establish it. The Party organisation must have connived at this, or been slack – or more probably ignored all wider implications. Are there continuing effects on morale? Does this story belong in a history of the factory? What are we to do – and to do in the future?'

'It seems to me,' says Aleksandra, 'that the answer is clear. Everyone will promise to be more watchful – and assert that they are anyway. Your charges are not part of the history – which can be written in less brutal but still suggestive terms. You will write a colourless brochure – thinking, after all, what does it matter. You'll have a lot to drink, and feel maudlin. I know you, you see!'

She smiles. I don't want to be known in that way. 'Aleksandra – if the solution is to be collective, I don't carry this weight of responsibility.'

'But you choose to do so. Alas, it's only a burden. But it is early yet. What can you expect – you are so alone here. Grigor is busy and satisfied. Andrei can't help you in the technical matters. Nor can I. We just keep pushing your discontent along, hoping that one day the lightning will come! You have not yet begun to recognise the vicious people. But Timofei will help you. This business is just a test. But you've been tested a little at last. The Sophie nonsense is over ...'

'But why should you think I have potential? I have two highly organised daydreams, that's all ...'

'You have discontent:, and isolation. That's why I am so deeply divided about you. All my life I've needed these things, to be in touch with a toughness, with independence. But there's not much future for me with someone like that. I need also a sinuosity ...'

What a strange girl she is, looking for a man as though she were a chemist analysing a compound. But at least different from Sophie, who treated men as though they were rocks, banging them with hammers to see if they'd break! And I'm still up to my shoulders, like a deer in the thicket, in dilemma. What a harsh and tedious day this is – and so cold: soup and pasty for lunch – time Aleksandra got round to the cooking. At least Sophie stood up well to my exploitation – said shopping made her head ache.

Aleksandra – she's so far from Pushkin and the yellowing of leaves on the birches – what kind of life could we make together? The days I most lack inventiveness, she's happy, and I'm most discontented. Tomorrow – the meeting, Stumbling in tomorrow through the drifts, a sky the colour of liver from snow and pollution. Well, no one can complain if we have a meeting to determine the level of their consciousness. As long as they've no concern with mine. I bought some stewed cherries today – I remember eating sweet cherries, looking out of my window only a few weeks back.

Aleksandra holds my arm as we lurch out through the snow, down to the road where the buses and trucks run into town, like animals herded into the barns from snowy pastures. This is an evening for musky wine, brandy, declaiming Maiakovsky with a gut loaded with goose and cream. Soothing away old tragedies, taking startling new decisions for tomorrow, with Aleksandra so close her breath has not frozen when it reaches me.

leo

On their second night by the lake a storm passed over – smacking in the windows like an open palm stinging against thin ice. Leo had been dreaming – 'never to start anything – no reassurance – no forbidden fruit' – when he heard the glass on the porch hitting the walls, like bats blown in.

'Fortinbras is here,' said Shirley, as they felt the cottage shake, a ship turning into heavy head seas.

In thirty minutes, they were safe – the moon, sailing safe too into harbour. They felt totally cut off. There were shattered trees all round, like spears tossed unavailingly against a magically protected fortress.

'Another twist to the idyll,' thought Leo, sourly.

By morning, nature and the chipmunks had forgotten the convulsion. Bitter and frustrated at times, dismayed and denatured by the monotony and scale of his surroundings, Leo wondered why this countryside should seem so disturbing, so difficult to enjoy. Strange animals came to sit on the chairs by the dock, and only boats disturbed the eternity of writing-time.

Their first evening, Leo said, 'Yes, Shirley, I think you could live in Moscow without being crippled by disillusion or idealism. I'm writing a novel about those days – the last days of the Mongol occupation and my wife's existence ... it's hard to avoid being blunt and threatening.'

'So, you've brought your wife here too?' Shirley said. 'Well, I don't mind. I'm happy you can write. I see the delight in your face as you establish control over your notes – that's all the pleasure I want.'

But for Leo, Shirley's husband lurked about, a giant and brutal face leering in hairily, in a hat like a canvas bucket.

'Leo,' said Shirley, 'I think it's about time you showed me some understanding. Already you're turning me into material for reflection. Here, surely, you're free from everything but me – you can do and say exactly what you like. Yet always I feel you're too polite for a lover: it's as though you're waiting to be repaired and sent on your way again. You can't pay a debt to your wife by withholding chances of happiness – or even pleasure – from yourself and everyone else.'

And Leo thought – how hard to think back to Moscow in the early fifties – we lived on the far side of any conceivable surprises. The crowds hustling past each other – ambiguous citizens of the earthly city: our civility seemed so hard won. We lived in a world of such primitive and precarious concerns – it seemed possible to revert to anything at all in such a demonic world. There were so few verities – the most pessimistic could not believe the scale of the catastrophes they predicted. How old-fashioned we now seem – we, the intellect of Moscow, with our bemusement, our pride in interpreting the incredible. How little we knew of the struggle, if there was a struggle, in the

Party itself. We were always in shock – like the people who protest publicly now, we felt our demands so modest, our remarks so reasonable and necessary, our impact so tiny, so misinterpreted. But in these spasms of archaic indignation we were disoriented. Who knows what we wanted or feared? I don't remember, and I don't believe I knew then. And to be married at that time to a trusting wife – disastrous. Waiting for betrayal – or reproach. Impossible to add that to the other perils. You can't get more self-effacing than to die, thought Leo, but self-effacement is no basis for a life.

The outline of the novel took him back twenty years – the story of his wife's love for him – during the most difficult years, and the period of relaxation. He was surprised at how simple his wife's emotions seemed – really, how reasonable. She asked of him no talent, nor even passion. How difficult to present the erosion of popular courage through the eyes of someone who had confidence only in her feeling for her husband. For Leo began to recognise that his wife's loyalty and strength were the very political virtues he'd sought and failed to find in himself at the time.

'My mode is the weakest,' he thought, 'but hers is unbreakable. She knew how to wait, to concern herself only with the limited aim of keeping us together so long as the terror lasted. And I wanted a response she couldn't give, and which was in any case inappropriate. I wanted merely to understand what is still incredible – I wanted understanding because I lacked guts. Now – I lack appropriateness. To write plays – that requires no courage or even understanding. I've stood on the periphery of my wife's memory and studied my reflection so long, but it was the depth that mattered ...'

He rambled through a maze of political errors become emotional commitments. At times it seemed as though his wife's tenderness had been a mark of her resistance to Stalin, at times Leo's refusal to tolerate her limitations seemed a paradigm of Bolshevism – she became the peasant cart which the bony donkey of the intelligentsia dragged forward. At times he resented Shirley's patience – angrily he said, 'When I talk of my wife's courage, I mean her political fortitude, not her forbearance of me! We didn't in general lack courage – it was unavailing, because the question of cowardice does not enter into our analysis. My wife is – in the novel – the one who sees straight. And in the end – yes, perhaps really the only emperor is the emperor of ice-cream. The ice-cream neither I nor Stalin could produce to satisfy such a tiny desire.'

Leo stared out over the lake. Here, where one was really alone, one most missed the cheerful dismissiveness of one's friends – this monastic withdrawal soon exhausted the most carefully hoarded resources. The lake was low and livid: frogs with ninetyish hips hopped and belched in the shallows. Shirley busied herself with holiday tasks – tanning, Proust, reminiscence.

'Leo, isn't this perfect? You writing at last – both of us with so few cares!'

He had been looking gloomily across the fish pools, each with a halo of flies, trying to visualise the restaurant they'd visited after their marriage, the irritable but pitying waiters, the discouraging food.

They'd walked down by the river, past the great closed fort with the mausoleum outside – Joshua had been silenced before the walls could even tremble. Leo saying, as he always seemed to these days, 'I don't know what to think, but...' The horror of opening the paper and finding one could no longer read between the lines ... Of sensing the need for a much purer analysis to stop oneself becoming terrified, or even worse, becoming briefly successful within the system ...

And now, with a start, he realised Shirley loved him – the cure from her old, distorted marriage had been as easy as making love. What could he offer her? An interlude of severe introspection that he'd avoided so long. He remembered saying to his wife, 'We should push old Lenin inside the walls: a Trojan horse and a resurrection – bigger miracles than that are unmasked daily.'

'We've only to hold on,' she'd said. 'It can't be like this for ever.'

'On the contrary,' he'd replied cleverly, 'we have the experience of living with eternity, we just face minor problems of adjustment ...'

They were both relieved when Peggy came to see them – Leo because he could avoid discussion with Shirley in which from politeness he'd be forced to present himself as the least worthy of men, Shirley because her happiness could be protracted only by interruptions.

Peggy said, 'Oh – I see something's come out of the theatre's collapse!'

'Yes,' said Leo, 'the stage cat and the stage mouse – gone down the trapdoor together.'

'I don't like your teasing,' said Peggy. 'It has something mean and European about it. To me, Europe is the place where all battles were lost in the first place. The trouble with you, Leo, is that your sophistication hides a complete absence of simplicity. You've cultivated an Olympian melancholy – you're an old god come home to enjoy your twilight. And you, Shirley – you encourage him.'

'Exactly right, my little chicken,' said Leo.

They drank their large drinks and watched the other lake-dwellers come to check the bolt holes. Leo felt a long way from home, and for once not enjoying it.

Shirley said, 'Leo's writing a novel, Peggy. He has to be alone. With me, that is.'

And again Leo said angrily, 'Let's not be foolish – no one wants to read a novel about the Soviet Union in which people are neither good, bad, nor judicious. Novel readers hate to be embittered by their hobby. They want to see more clearly than the characters – but the characters have actually to live in these confines. So of course their sensibilities are needle sharp ...'

'Well,' said Peggy. 'I see you're lost to us completely. No point in my staying.'

When she'd gone, Leo said, 'An emissary?'

'I think so. We've only our own resources now, my dear,' said Shirley.

They both felt a constraint. Night was falling, and the lights of their neighbours splashed across them like naphtha. Leo wrote, 'They stood pressed together outside the post office. A soldier, his purple greatcoat dark with melted snow at the hem, stared at them, as if he sensed they were using their intimacy to exclude enquiry ...' – and wondered, 'Isn't this the way we all end? A stab in the back with a blunt pen ... Except that I'm doing it later than the others. And I'm falsifying the whole thing too – I was prepared to accept as much as possible at the time. I was irritated that my wife would make so little effort ... and now – am I not still in the same battle, with people I can rely on less, but trust more?'

'Shirley,' he said, 'I'm not writing any more.'

'OK – it's near enough bedtime.'

'No, not that. I can't be a traitor – not because I'm not capable of treachery, but because the syndrome bores and displeases me. As they say,

'My friends I can betray,
Sure of their weakness.
But those I do not know
Leave them in darkness.'

'Better not to risk it.'

'But Leo – this is all you can do – write! Don't you see – without this, you're ruining yourself.. You have to compromise in writing, as in action.'

'The compromises are of different orders. There's something shameful in pouring out this weakness for the stereotypers – for people like Peggy, who'll read into the book any message she wants to send it.'

They went to bed separately, angrily. Leo listened to the cicadas until he could fall asleep and dream of cypresses and his wife dancing alone among the cornflowers.

aleya

'A goat's a goat, whoever his father' – Aleya heard two men shouting. A goat, its horns curled like French pastry, scrabbled and glared outside. It seemed to her it was trying to look in through the window, flashing its yellow eye like a quince ...

'How many hours I've spent already with Leonid,' she thought. 'But how many more do I want to spend?' Katya told her the story of the brave horse. A horse who had lost his hero, but been asked to carry on the trade of heroism. The horse had galloped into battle, striking out with its hooves, always wearing its fine silver saddle, in memory of its batyr. At times the horse had misgivings about its dangerous profession. But success and custom impelled it onwards. And one day the emir sent an ambassador to ask the horse a favour – to be allowed to ride it into battle. And the horse was angry, and said, 'No – I'm a professional, not a servant.'

'Foolish horse,' said the emir. And the emir set a trap for the horse – spiking one of its hooves with a long silver spike. As the horse lay helpless, a soldier put his arrow into its neck joint, and as it died, the horse said, 'I had no choice. I carry no one but myself into battle – but who cares about a horse?' And the horse was stripped of its saddle and left under the thorn trees.'

'You mean I'm the horse, Katya? I don't see the silver saddle!'

'You know my stories aren't like that, Aleya. I don't believe this mystical stuff about Kazakh literature. I can become a part of any literature I choose – and keep to its rules. But I remember a friend of mine took a lover. A very exhausting Turk. And one day she thought to herself – why should I burden myself with all this pride and puffing? It is just too exhausting to do what I want to do.

'Ah, Istanbul, to be drinking raki down by the sea – and have everything – fish, dust, palaces – turning into every memory of the colours of the sea. When I was young, it was so easy to be wicked that it became very easy indeed to be good!'

And now, Aleya could look over and see the future scratched into the earth like the lines of a map – the surveyors like mariners with telescopes, while their crews squatted purple, green, silver in their caftans.

'Do you ever understand what Katya is saying?' Leonid asked. 'You Muscovites are all the same – look wise and burrow away is your motto. Never say what you think – just tramp up and down like a horse threshing grain – you wear everything away in time, but you never shake off the harness.'

'Leonid, you must understand me. When I was leaving Moscow, a friend told me, "Stay here. Whatever is going to happen is going to happen first in

Moscow." But by then I'd realised that I wasn't the kind to wait for history to play its hand. The people I knew well – they all had ways of acting, of acquiring self-knowledge, control – through the discipline of their professions. I didn't. I was wild. I couldn't provide answers. If someone had a lively sensibility, instinctively I felt drawn to him. His questions and answers I accepted uncritically. And I'm still the same. I'm for commitment relieved by sensitivity – intellectually, I have almost no range. I can't generalise ...'

'How odd that you should sound proud of that. It's my position too, but I've always apologised for it.' Leonid smiled at himself.

'I always had reservations about my friends, of course. But I entered their lives as imaginatively, as deeply as I could. This is very demanding. It leaves you with nothing of your own. Passion becomes total immersion. But now I believe I can accomplish things for myself. Life is perhaps more monotonous, a little drier. The fire remains – but less like a pour of slag, more like a volcano.'

'Well, the volcano's been exploding lately – I don't think the young Aleya would have removed a director!'

'The young Aleya was very defenceless.'

'Not now, I hope. There's more to be discussed tomorrow at the meeting. Complaints that the unit is too mechanical, too industrial – that the voices of the farmers themselves are outweighed by the technicians, the drivers, the mechanics. The farmers say – we'll use machines – but they and the operators are worthless without us. We're not the slaves of our implements. Why should these people come from far away and tell us how to work? And, you know, they have a point. It's so easy to build tiny cheap cities in areas like this – imaginary cities with mechanical demands...'

'We'll discuss it tomorrow, Leonid. If seems to me we can't make many adjustments to our work here – these complaints are coming to us from history. One feels like asking history to solve them. I think our bigger question is the Party. It was the Party that saved me from priggishness and despair or perhaps you find that priggish too? There was a song Sultan used to sing, to the point of madness:

'I despair of you, my love –
You mock my laughter and my bitterness.
My head is heavy on my neck, I sing
only sad songs, my fingers
blurring the notes. I am become
less then a man – and you
my love, even less than me.'

'You see, Leonid, I have passion, but no anger. When I wake in the mornings, I wait for my routine to start. A routine of typewriters, of walking to the hilltop, seeing the plains rich with geese and poets, the trees brushing the ground with their fruit – like pregnant sows. I have helped to produce this. It's really very simple. It ignores most of what I can't change. My horizon stops with the director, with the neighbouring *kolkhoz*. You see, I'm still defenceless. I don't even have your talent for bad painting – I have to live my life in the open. Any hawk can see me from his morning hover. I have to develop my own means of evasion.'

'One technique being obliqueness?' asked Leonid. 'But Aleya – spring's long gone – we're in the heavy centre of summer. How can you harvest if you've planted nothing?'

'My harvest will be widespread this year.' She thought of Dimitri and Sergei – no one would know now they had all been friends. 'But the fruit may be a little hard, I'm afraid. Tell me about yourself, Leonid.'

'I have your passionate concern for action too, Aleya. As soon as my time here is up, I'll leave, willingly or not. I have to push myself to reach my limit – so that I can go beyond it. I look a quiet and conservative type, Aleya. But in fact I've done this before. I broke with my girl in Leningrad before I came here. And she clung to me, saying, "How can you leave me? Do you have no sense of justice, or compassion? You use me up, then reject me. You'll go out there, among the apricot trees, the vines, the flowers like trumpets – leaving me here like a stone in a hole. How can you wound me and torment me?"

'And I said, "I really don't know why I'm doing this. It hurts me too – and I know I'm not callous. It's like the proverb – 'Show me a couple with the same problem, and I'll show you a couple who hate each other.' We present ourselves with tasks – we can't make all these tasks collective. You can't share my autobiography."

'And she said, "Well, the rest of the world manages very well."

'And I said, "Look, I'm not throwing myself on the mercy of the rest of the world. I'm hopeful, but not philanthropic. Please don't feel badly," I said. "Suppose I'd been killed! Pretend this is a troop train ..." And I chattered on – because I really had no answer. I was dissatisfied with what I had, I felt it had no potential. Unless permanence too is a process, I don't want it. Mine's a hard creed, Aleya. And it carries little enough certainty with it. We should have been artists, so that the struggle would have produced its own record. As it is – we're just seen as hard and unrelenting.'

'But this is what we are. We've chosen a life away from the city, away from the option of gentleness. I believe you're hard. You're the flaw in my argument – you exclude yourself from the commerce of tenderness. When we meet, we meet as two savage animals. And this is wrong. It's true that here we are, so to speak, standing on our heads. It is hard to come from a city and live here – it's a leap backwards. No philosophical simplification can take us back to a world alien from us and in any case dying daily. But to those who've always lived here – the world of change is in the present and future. To us, perhaps, it's wholly in the past. And we're constantly scrutinising our own passports to see if they're genuine. I find you deeply disturbing, Leonid. If I have neglected emotion, it was not because it was lacking – there was simply no occasion for it.'

'Well,' said Leonid, 'so long as I'm here, we must see each other a great deal.'

And Aleya thought, do I want that? I've always sought knowledge, within my limitations. It is not for knowledge that one would search in Leonid. Indeed, he seems rather immature, even colourless. Compared with Sergei or Dimitri, he's rather philistine. Why did he recognise himself in me so instinctively? How absurd to live as though dead loves were always best! Alexei's life, for instance – how precarious an existence, so suspicious, so unyielding. And Sergei – he'd be lost in these hills and mountains, impatient with the herdsmen, obsessed with his own transfer – so ruthless in the rooting out of custom.

Dimitri would say, 'Aleya, my dear, so you've really made the change! Roasting sheep, the bright jangle of the dutar and the syrynx clear across the steppe – I hardly recognise you. You were always our little northern deer – those great eyes of yours pinched against the sun now, your thin little body, forever bursting out of lectures and slipping like a leaf against the crowds – so much shivering with excitement, now it's grown quite sturdy.'

And yet, will I ever forget those last months in Moscow? Every evening the gardeners sprinkling the flowers so solemnly, bringing up the scents of the evening like children crayoning. How good it was to run from the world of lectures to walk with Dimitri – in his eyes, some young cat taking home the day's goodies became a kind of wild horse, carrying legends through the squares like banners or icons. I was so young, so inchoate, so anxious that nothing should be easy. And I know I was right, even though I tell Leonid I've no answers. He'll see what's become of me at the meeting tomorrow. Alexei could still be right about politics – and I'd still have something to be proud of...

Katya said, 'That Leonid's arrogant, don't you think?'

And Aleya replied, 'Yes, I think that's the difference. We genuinely struggled – we expected things to be difficult. Leonid invents difficulties, and exults in overcoming them. He's like your horse in the story – one can only ask him, why do you go on fighting when the batyr is dead? Why go on killing; when your own fate is death? I'm sure you were never like that? A struggle for existence isn't a struggle for the extinction of others.'

'I think you exaggerate, Aleya. He's not so savage and frightening as you say. But he recognises no curbs on himself. In the early days he would be fine – but he can be vicious – with himself, as well as others ...'

And me, thought Aleya, when will there be peace for me? When will I go the way I wish? When will we be happy together again, the four of us, disputatious in Moscow? When will I come to accept the rejection of my old life? How sweet it was, and how long ago ...

aleya's diary

Dimitri was drunk when he came to see me. I was very disturbed and upset. I suppose we allow ourselves few enough indulgences, but Dimitri does not enjoy drinking, and his deliberate decision to drink seemed as self-destructive as Alexci's to kill himself.

'There's a lyricism of coherence, and a lyricism of drunkenness. I seem to attract the latter,' he said, looking drowsy and startled, like an owl fallen down the chimney, staggering away from the fire. 'Two people have said I was beautiful,' he went on. 'And neither of them was you ...'

'That self–congratulation's rather out of character,' I said, half teasing.

'It's a line from my opera – the only place I'm allowed to say meaningful things. Or at least. If only we could say more,' he flapped his hands inexpressively round his head, and repeated, holding out one hand likc a woman holding out a peach to a customer, 'If only we could say more ...'

'Say exactly what you like, Dimitri.'

'That's the trouble, I can hardly speak. I remember. I remember two of Alexei's wolves – one white and one black. And the black one frolics around the white one, trying to be noticed. And the white one pretends not to see.

'Finally, the black wolf says – just like me – "Look. Look how pretty I am."

'And the other says, "Not against the snow, though – you're not pretty then."

'"But in summer – so cool."

'"What summer? Who cares about summer? Sleeping and panting under the trees. It's hunting for food in winter turns us wolves white." Well, Aleya, I've turned a little whiter today ...'

He's almost asleep. But he is beautiful, and I wished I'd been one of these who'd told him so. Even though I'm writing this hours later, the memory is so clear, so dismaying. I sat waiting for him to wake up, reading a half-finished poem by Alexei.

'The house I live in
bursts with people like a pomegranate –
sergeants, store-clerks, engineers,
– silent when we meet outside, here
they're boozing, laughing, sneezing,
dreaming of Sochi ...

From the house that I live in,

you can see Children's World,
beer bottles, samoyeds, theatres –
drama, heroism, doggy devotion,
children scattered like seeds
(growing into fruit I'll never gather –
some of it rotting, bitter, on the bushes).

What keeps this children's world turning?
Half light, half dark, the world
hangs like a nectarine, the halves
clasped round that hard central stone.

And you, Astronomer – glued
forever to the telescope, watching
us children on the world!
From the house I live in
I see your eye, prismatic
through moonspace –
glinting like a speck
of mica.

Poor Alexei – his sly and tender wolf jokes – he allowed himself to comment on us all only with such oblique irony – one laughs at them delicately. Are they at all funny? This obsession with Dzerzhinski* – 'Astronomer' was one of his underground names – and the toy store in Dzerzhinski Square, Children's World – are these even obsessions? We must try to find the main poem of the sequence. He was so frightened, and frankly, I don't know if his fears were justified. Was he frightened of his own emotions, or of Dzerzhinski? His concerns were old-fashioned – but there's nothing wrong in that ... I'm not political, and I don't think Alexei was: no one could have been less threatening than him ...

Dimitri woke up. He seemed sober, but very depressed: 'What did I say? Was I unkind to you?'

'Nothing. And not directly unkind. You're unhappy because I'm leaving, and that makes me put a higher value on myself which makes me feel conceited. The world turns in a vicious circle, as Alexei would say. Should we go for a walk?'

'Aleya, no one asks us to reflect. We seem to be required only to

---

* See note, p. viii.

assimilate and give out information. And yet – you remember Yevtushenko – "in every real Russian there is somewhere hidden a Decembrist". Alexei was like that – a man with a secret too big to keep, killing himself to avoid the possibility of betrayal, or treachery.'

'You think he was right, then? That the revolution was dualist, not dialectical?'

'Alexei had no patience, no capacity for acceptance. As for his secret – things that are secret aren't necessarily true. I don't think Alexei ever had time to do much thinking. He certainly made himself mentally ill – not that that's proof of anything.' Dimitri asleep – his face glowed like marble, the drink faintly colouring him like an oxide. He refuses to communicate when he's asleep. Soon the train will be parting us, and he'll be talking of me as though I were some lost object. We've exhausted ourselves this summer. I feel we're incapable of further suffering. I'm so tired – when we went for our walk, Dimitri and I, we both staggered along like invalids. And I can't even hear the music which runs through his head like a taunt, a torment. Soon I'll be away – able to think, to reflect. For the rest of my life ... Dimitri says – 'Why leave – whatever happens will happen first in Moscow ...' what better reason could I have for leaving?

feodor

'All over the world, comrades are asking these unanswerable questions – are we to treat Feodor's dilemma as one of personal judgement or as something to be taken for collective resolution?' We are in the meeting, and the meeting has resolved the question already. We can't have meetings to discuss privacy.

Timofei continues: 'I have no doubts about the correct answer. I have always felt that Feodor was looking for some personal formulation perhaps literary, perhaps ethical – which would lighten his melancholy, his anxiety. But I feel he himself realises that his research is not a private question. For instance, how is it, Feodor, that you have been sidetracked from questions of socialist relations in the factory to those of the earliest years of the plant's operation? Are you not saying, "I don't know how to evaluate human relations – instead I'll consider a problem of historical interpretation," and isn't this a totally new dimension of the problem?'

There are masses of snow piled up in the lilac clouds, and the last fly in the world is sitting on my arm. Grigor, Andrei, Aleksandra – all are here, solemnly watching a lost cause evaporate. In the birch-woods the wolves will soon be coming for a late evening howl – first one, then, timidly, three or four: if they're spared, they should make a fine quartet, well-rehearsed, by next spring. The river now is stiff enough to take a horseman – and we too slip from building to building, afraid of being locked in the winter like fish in the ice – the circulation just a creeping tide.

I say, 'I am grateful that: there should be an open meeting, that the proceedings should be so careful and gentle. It is true that I have personal concerns – how to make my life, how to speak, when to be silent. I think my comrades are right in saying I don't have the attitudes of a Soviet intellectual. I'm not even sure I'm an intellectual – my concerns are not collective, nor am I individualist. I find my problems of no importance. I think Timofei's right – I've no idea how to write on human relations. People come to me – and how various they are. Socialist relations in this context – is simply to be able to talk, it's the absence of constraints. But people don't talk about: the same things. My explanations sound weak, I know. I feel I've been useless this summer – but I'm not sure how to change, to develop. I'm looking for some stimulus.

'I'm stronger than you suspect. Questions still have to be answered: have the errors of the early years been overcome? How much are we affected by institutional changes – can we use the institutions as they were intended? We can, for instance, cooperate with Grigor but can he cooperate in criticism of himself? It's my problem, not his, being discussed here. Frankly, I don't know what more we could do – but this factory is not the world ...'

When this is over, Aleksandra and I can continue our idyll. Andrei says, 'My own position is clear. I don't have to prove anything about myself. There's enough public life that I don't have to produce a private one. My efforts do not go in the writing of history, so much as its production ... But we still have questions to ask about ourselves. To pretend these are personal would be absurd. It is a mark of Feodor's flexibility, his desire to please and understand – some would say, his distance – that he's ready to have these things reduced to the personal level. Myself, I feel he has too much perspective! It is his job to struggle, to follow his convictions as far as possible, and as wrong as they may be. We learn from the exposure of mistakes more than from misplaced loyalty. But that is his decision. He will not take it alone – so put a committee on it. Give him an editorial advisory board. Perhaps he'll say more if the responsibility is less.'

'That is unfair,' says Grigor. 'Unfair to us all, We have nothing to hide. We don't want: to conceal the harshness of those days, nor suffer vicarious guilt either. We have had a long battle against the distortions – but from the base laid down by the distortions. And we are still in the middle of this effort – in every sphere, from the imaginative to the technological. As Timofei says – all over the world, men like us are discussing what can be done with their institutions – which we inherit – and their human resources – which are created collectively. My advice to Feodor would be – gain experience of the society which surrounds him.'

'It seems to me,' says Aleksandra, 'that there are two questions here – how to interpret Feodor's findings, and what to do with Feodor himself. He's desperate to be used, to be useful. But as soon as he starts to work, he finds big, vague dilemmas to speculate on. In many ways, he's straight from Turgenev. He's a sharp nose for difficulty, but the weight of even the smallest social insistence is too much. He's imprisoned in reservations, revulsions, evasions. Having rejected dogmatism, he comes to see that the only possibility of action lies in dogmatism, or collective decisions – no decisions. He needs centralism, that is, more than democracy. To him, democracy means submission to the wishes of the majority – and the majority he sees in narodnik fashion, it's a symbolic litter of small warm animals. He needs coercion, because he shrinks from using violence against his own doubts.'

Aha – so the drink has started to worry her! At least Sophie said 'Soak away – but I have my own forms of intoxication. Say and do what you like when you're drunk – and so will I.' But I can't see Aleksandra saving my soul for the Party – surely she wants a dressmaker's dummy at home, trying out her counselling on it, till the stuffing falls out? How many more winters will we spend cosily twisting each other's tails, replacing courage with devotion, strength with loyalty? We're becoming a nation of committees, producing nothing but decisions, guidelines. But who are we who sit on these committees?

There's a complacency, a narrowness about Aleksandra – she's too easily satisfied. Andrei carries on a private campaign – he's the only man who knows where he's going. For the rest of us – even Timofei – booze, volleyball, shopping for pickled fish, reading the chess section in the paper ... That's a fairly immature notion – but that's all I'm asked to have. They've given me an editorial board. We'll make a compromise, but everyone will know it's a compromise. Between them and me – not between realities.

They avoid my eye as they leave. Too bad, I'll soldier on. What a sad year this has been – even Aleksandra's humility has the power to irritate. 'I'm sorry, Feodor. It's so hard to know what you want, what challenge can unlock....'

'Let me remind you, Aleksandra. When I lived in Moscow, there were so many thousands of people like me – frankly, we were always rather boring. We had only two songs, and we sang them over and over. But what we meant to say was this – "Where has the vanguard gone?" We desperately wanted to be part of the vanguard – like students everywhere. But the vanguard was huge. All our desire was to be part of an active minority. We had no understanding of Marxism, we were a memory of a moment in the history of intellectuals, we had passed away before we were born. We were born for dissatisfaction and waste, for hedonism we despised, a speciousness in which there was no chance of isolation, or enjoyment.'

'And now you can't enjoy my company? You feel discontent, ennui?'

'Not at all. I feel tremendous energy, boundless inventiveness. could gobble you up in an instant. It's like the lines:

'Between our fingers – pours hydroelectricity:
our feet – planted like pylons: our arteries
carry a million volts. We are the giants
lighting feeble lamps in noisy tenements ...?

'You can all criticise me, help me as you can. But the only criticism which matters is Andrei's. He's the only one who still belongs to the vanguard. He's not afraid, because he's been fortunate enough to use his strength as a victim. You're afraid of using your power because you're convinced you'll abuse it. You're not gentle, you're passive. So long as someone else uses coercion – you're happy, because it's not you. But I'm not like that. I'm going to get to the bottom of you all, sooner or later.'

And Aleksandra is disturbed. I'm not ready to formulate what I mean.

But I'll not be put down in such a craven way ...

Dying in the sun, like that shattered dog: that's the lesson. Not to think one's legs are long enough to outrun the truck. Remember how quickly corruption sets in, among the melon rinds, the rabbit-eared donkeys. For the present, relax, drink in the sun – wait for the evening, the silver leaves, the silver fountains, the pewter stream from the teapot, wait for the hot evening calm. In my America – that's the hour when the new shift of cops comes on: thousands of faces watching from fire-escapes. The cropped college kids swapping drugs in the two-car garage, and talking of dollars. Hippies looking for the frontier, and finding it in each other ...

'I'm not beaten, Aleksandra, you know. Do what you can – even incoherence has its own defence, you know.'

'I know you're not, Feodor. And. I'll try to live with it.'

But now the wind is cracking down: smelling of snow. I feel we're all going under the ice, Sophie, Yuri, Ilich – all of us. Where is the scent of apricots, of cherry-blossom, of the grass one has lain on till drunkenness sets in? It's so hard to be alone. To be alone and still a good communist. Or even a bad one ... To survive, like lichen under the snow, shrinking from the touch of paw or hoof – waiting for the sun: what kind of life is this, after all? In America they persecute you if you're a bad communist, winter or summer.

leo

'I'm really too fat for poetry,' quoted someone in Leo's dream, 'And so are you – in your head, that is. Why do you know so little of all the modes of contra-bourgeois art? You must write only what can be attacked. That, my friend, is guerilla theatre ...'

Leo heard himself say, 'The dialectic is – what will you do, what shall I do, and, the negation of negation – what shall we do. At present, I'm still awaiting my synthesis – you write first, then look for the dialectic ...'

'But you don't trust what you write,' said the first.

Leo awoke, irritably. The dialogue would have to be completed without its main character. He looked through the membranous plastic over the window frame. He could see the island and the promontory – on the first evening he had made love to Shirley, and the boat leaving the island at the beginning had reached those rocks by the time it was over. Poor Shirley – when he said, 'I can't think dialectically,' she'd been impressed by the confession ...

'It's not up to me to distinguish between love and illusion, or affection and suspension of disbelief,' he thought. 'Why is it so hard to trust her affection? Perhaps, as the dream says, because I don't trust her art of life. It does not assert itself by hostile acts. Or perhaps after all, I don't trust what I write. So, what then? A demotic novel about Canada? Well, in a sense you must not only "love the people" – which means you must be lovable by them, which I'm not – but you must write for the bourgeois who read you. I'm not wanted by my social base, my proletariat: this is my fault. It is my deliberate choice to be estranged – at least subjectively. But if it's my choice – it's also my problem.

'There's no shortage of things to do: revolution is a multiplicity of actions and processes – inventiveness is at a premium. The movement does not end with revolution, nor is revolution the sole aim of the movement. And yet – I seem to stand on one side. Why? Isn't it because "first one thinks – and then one sees the purpose", or rather, first one exists, and then one reflects upon oneself – I feel like I did when I undressed one night, so as not to wake my wife, on the stairs. Completely drunk, but thoughtful, leaving my clothes in the kitchen … And our neighbour came in next day, "You meet have left these in my bedroom last night." Truly, the man without underwear.

How odd, to come to terms with one's wife so many years after her death ... 'The incredible times in Moscow – if this was betrayal, who betray-ed who, who betrayed what? Perhaps my wife had the only coherent response – politics sublimated is emotion, after all. My wife believed implicitly in the reality of what was happening – and I did not. I was ready with my analysis before the first leaves had reached the ground.

'What, after all, did Lenin say, something to the effect that unless the workers of the more developed capitalist countries come rapidly to our aid, our work will be incredibly difficult, and no doubt we will commit a series of mistakes … But what can I now make of myself, who cannot account for my own experience ? It is easy to talk of the deadness of being sad, critical – and dispassionate. But surely, I must now be dispassionate? I have to accept the coherence of my wife's response – and its uselessness to myself – and then to look for some people whose discussion I can share.

'Here, I'm so peripheral. As I said to Shirley last night, "I can't talk to you. You're not mistaken, and you can touch me, but I've blood in my nostrils." How peacefully she sleeps. How removable her discontents, her sadness – there's no trace of them now. So much eagerness to redress the balance of the past. To choose someone so unlike her husband.'

The day before, they'd walked to a nearby village of fundamentalists – 'all dressed up in bonnets and bows,' said. Leo. 'But if there are no zips in the bible, there were no battered derbies either.'

Later – 'Look, they're cheating – all of them! They're fantastically eclectic. Religion has been so subsumed that they can use the history of inventions like a grab-bag.'

'Leo, you'd find a completely literal interpretation quite reasonable, wouldn't you?'

'Of course, yes. One's life, if nothing more, should he literal. But yes, one set of rules and exceptions in this kind of community is as good as another. As claustrophobic anyway – they're a means of sublimation like any other set – only here, there's not much to rise above. Independent farmers, you know ...'

'Except that they cheat: other people too – they bargain and do down the outsiders.'

'There are no outsiders. But yes, I could live under commandments like these – the more the better. Men are most free where there are the most rules – it's such an encouragement to theology ...'

They sat in a pub like a chalet and ate roasted pigtails. Shirley looked at Leo tenderly. He said awkwardly, 'How far from everywhere, even Moscow, we seem here. How I long to join in a metropolitan discussion – power comes from the cities, not this universalised provincialism.'

And Shirley smiled distantly. 'You want so much to be hard and powerful. Perhaps you can be – though you dissipate yourself. Stalinism, guerilla theatre – it all seems to come down to moralistic generalisations and condemnations. You are in danger of missing the real, positive significance of the changes you've lived through. You hurried back into history – yet remain indifferent to the changed world, the potential, of your contemporaries.'

'That's because I have no contemporaries. But yes, Shirley, you're right. And there's an. urgency about this, too. Whatever I'm to do, I'm starting late.'

'Can't you write about the lives of people here?'

'Horse buggies and the forswearing of electricity – soviets, minus electrification, in fact? Novels for whom – for me? Better than a dispassionate sellout, for sure. And we can't all be lucky enough to be forced to compromise. But it seems to me we can either fight our enemies or help our friends. I tried to do both, and the task was too much. Or rather, I understood my enemies better than my friends. Like all those who live by the word and die by the word – I'm better at fighting than helping.'

'You flourish on abrasiveness – and that's why you can't have friends?'

'I can have them – I need them. But though I admire the people who can exhort the weak, those experimenting with their strength for the first time – my place is with those who attack the entrenched. I'm a swamp mosquito, and I bring the fear and the trembling.'

Shirley said, 'It's so strange. With my husband – you penetrated the crust of urbanity – and there was a sad beast, cowering on its straw, unable to smell its own stench. But with you – layer on layer of gentleness and gentility – and distance. The nearer I get to your centre, the further away I am from myself. It gets darker and darker – and you tell me there's something granitic down there? But long before I can approach that, you're lost to me. I can say nothing to you! I can't touch you deeply – my arms and fingers aren't long enough. You're a constant reproach – not just to my superficiality, which I grant you – but to my simple perceptions and pleasures. You're like a shell – so spiralling that no pin will ever winkle you out.'

'You mean my shell's too large for the little vulnerable creature within?'

'No, I have faith in you. You will produce something – it won't satisfy you. It won't strike people, perhaps, but it will carry a conviction and a directness that will surprise you.'

'And could you live under the shadow of this volcano?'

'You mock me, because you want me to say no. But I could live like that, yes. You would be my code, my commandments. I would live with your moods and modes – just like these people live with their literalness. But I would be no good for you. I've helped you understand your wife and her strength. You don't understand my strength. You see only a sacrifice – from which you want to save me where there is affection freely given. You can't understand this – you assume that in a hostile world, affection is given grudgingly. My husband thought it had to be seized by force or cunning. You both miss the point, but I prefer your error – since you wish 'me to be spared the contact with you which you think breeds melancholy. Disillusion and rupture are the way of the world, you say – so be it. But I'm not like that. I don't care about the way of that world – even if I'm the ant scurrying about under the universal descending foot, I'll scurry till the last.'

'And I – I have to write. To write in search of a theory. To avoid the market – no dead art for me – no excrement. Mediocre perhaps – but never successful.'

'Leo, your wife was happy with you. Your unhappiness wasn't hers. Her pleasure didn't extend beyond being with you. I seem to see so clearly those frozen streets, people huddled against the frost and the fear, the restaurants with the thin soup, little puddles of grease on its surface like worn kopek pieces. How to be big enough to see what you've built, when you've built so large ... But how will you deal with the people here? They've not even a literature through which you can approach them.

'You are not one of their needs. When you die, they'll abandon you. The lumber workers round here drive their cars for the last time till the gas runs out. They roll them in the ditch, take what they can from them, like a rider saving his saddle from a dead horse. Then leave them to the vultures – and hitch a ride to the next used car lot.

'This society is not gentle and reflective, Leo. It has never been organised to commit cruelties – but have no doubt that it would without hesitation or regret commit any atrocity. It's a society of peasants and workers, not jurists and litterateurs. You don't begin to sympathise with their forbearance, their generosity, the best they make of their bad jobs, their militancy, the halting steps taken against their condition.

'You're an animal who's seen a forest fire. You don't "love the people", because you've seen what happens to the people "the people" hate – or to whom these "people" are indifferent. You are resigned to the necessary directness of the masses, and its justice: but you fear it. You're right – it's to be feared. It takes no time to reflect – it doesn't measure and evaluate. All the things for which you live – it ignores. And Leo – you fear my directness too. And again, you're right. I could submerge you – we could fester in domesticity. You have to struggle against me too. Poor Leo – all these battles against appetites as a good hedonist you'd love to satisfy.'

'Brecht talks somewhere of man's supreme desire for happiness. Perhaps I'll celebrate that in my writing. But where does that leave us?'

'Just enjoy the present, Leo. That's all I have for you.'

And Leo sat uncomfortably – remembering the times his wife had cooked him some delicacy – waiting in line for hours. And he would say, 'Why waste your time on me? Other people would appreciate that more than I.'

And his wife said, 'I want you to enjoy it so that you can be one of those other people.'

And now – was a piece of goose liver to be the fruits of socialism in one country? For his wife – yes, and for Shirley too ...

Lying in bed now, he thought of Walter Benjamin's notion that the proletarianisation of the intellectual had not proceeded because its means of production, Culture, had become a constraint.

'How can I doubt the existence of things which don't exist?' Leo thought. 'In order to question my literary and political worth, I must start writing. I must finish my novel, so that its autocritic can begin.'

The sun harshly flashed on the lake: the cicadas, poised like plectrums in the pines, prepared for a day of whining and jangling. Leo sat again at the typewriter, a surgeon ready for the kill.

aleya

The stars were as precise as an astrologer's chart, silver bees on a dark honeycomb. Aleya thought, 'How full of pastiche our lives are,' as she heard the beginning of a new day of competitive song. A man sang,

> *'Blue bowls drying among the cornflowers*
> *your blue eyes and hair like corn.*
> *You came as a tyrant, stayed as a slave of my heart*
> *– not for you conscripted, dying in Galicia,*
> *learning to trust, and whom not to trust ...*
> *Poetry saw us through – redressing old wrongs,*
> *not speaking of new,*
> *learning to glorify menial work, mourning*
> *the death of the horse –*
> *as he once mourned our deaths.*
> *Learning to smile at whatever is new,*
> *and whoever brings it ...*
> *The land is full of strange things –*
> *some I don't care to see.*
> *I'm not a dog, I want more*
> *than a rounded gut ...'*

Katya walked with Aleya to the meeting. 'Building a city – a socialist city – is as precise as the fretting on a favourite instrument,' she said. 'Ah, Paris, my dear! The capital of the world, as they used to say. They said that Moscow was burning, while there was always bread and wine in Paris. Well, perhaps there was, but the looking for it wore out even our sharp noses. I remember, a friend of ours had a performing dog – and the dog had seen everything.

'As a puppy it had survived civil war and famine, exile and anathema. Mere domestic tragedies left it quite unmoved – the cancers, miscarriages, drunken stabbings, the sexual rivalry – all the things that most affect someone who lived under the bed. And it kept performing – a little barrel-balancing, general fetching and carrying, grinning and rolling. Nothing complicated.

'One day, this man, its owner, said to the dog, "Damn you – why should I have to watch your performance all day – boring old rat that you are. Get out on the streets and do it yourself. And call in at the corner shop for the bread on your way in."

'The dog looked at him and said, "Go to hell. Even an artist has his pride. I'm giving up the drama and going in for straight scavenging. I'll do better that way." The odd thing is – and you'll realise, my dear, the whole thing was a little odd, but that's the way with friends – that the dog prospered mightily. Took up with a gang, and stuffed himself with food all day. And his master nearly died with mortification and hunger ...'

Aleya laughed. 'You really think we're a lot of children, don't you, with our meetings, our objections, our pride in quite ordinary achievements? You'd say, "Of course, if you plant cotton or grain – you get a crop of cotton or grain. Eat it or pick it – don't sing a song to it!"

'I think you're one of the last people to sing songs, Aleya. You've no idea how bursting with green shoots you are! You've a delight in conforming and opposing which is wholly naive, and wholly spontaneous. I trust you. And my trusting you cancels out the dangers which arise from your trusting everyone – I think you've a very powerful armour. I stand behind you in my soft old body, and watch the missiles bounce off you!'

At the meeting, Leonid began: 'As it is still before dawn, let me make some preliminary remarks. Aleya says this meeting is called to remake, remould the base. But we're not concerned here with global matters – or analytical ones. We come here to work, and to enjoy ourselves. What is the point of pretending we can change things which are decided far above our heads? What base can we change – we had nothing to say about the director. When the conversions from *kolkhoz* to *sovkhoz* took place – you did nothing, said nothing. This is an agricultural experiment, not a social one. If the *partkom* secretary wasn't so lazy, all this talking would have been. stopped! We're just weeds in the cracks – grow too tall, and we'll be nipped off ...'

Aleya said, 'Leonid – I must reject that. Of course we're insignificant – we're working at a level so low that the Party is not interested, the local committees don't interest themselves in us except to evaluate our success or failure. But this is why we have our potential – we can re-enact the growth of a community of socialists—'

'You remind me,' interrupted Leonid, 'of someone in a book I'm reading, who said, "Like a foundering ship, the sinking theatre concerned itself with the possibly very difficult but basically unimportant question, whether it was better to sink to the left or to the right" – that's exactly the same with this theatre we're living in. It's staged – we've not stepped out of history into criticism! The same pressures exist here as elsewhere – and they're not primordial questions, but those of this year, these people, this organisation. We have our own busybodies, our own lechers and drunks – quite contemporary, I assure you.

'Grow up, Aleya. I came here for adventure and to pass the time. Do you really think it's possible to reinvent Marx, Aleya? You're like the Moscow students, with their neo-Dzerzhinskism, their class analyses of the level of proletarian development, their Hegelian nonsense about the realisation and subsuming of philosophy. They can see everything except what exists – not the negation but the unreality of their ideas.'

'So much for effort and striving, then,' said Aleya. But Leonid had hurt her. 'The conditions under which we struggle and strive – and the form of the struggle are of course only of historical interest. But so are we. We study our own actions historically as soon as we can. But what you suggest is an end to life!'

Gelderan said, 'Let us not forget that this kind of meeting is commonplace. All over the world, people are meeting to discuss the bases of their existence, their labour, the investment of social capital. We are at the awkward beginnings of an experiment – and frankly, I am bewildered. No one knows what will happen, except that these meetings are in some way at the heart of the experiment. Now, it could be true, as Leonid says, that we accomplish nothing here. But first I must know – what is it that we *cannot* accomplish here, and why? Why have we failed before we start?'

Kulkul said, 'Why do they call us social-democrats? We've not even been proletarians. How have I ever been a revolutionary, or even seen one? The question is inappropriate. Other people's revolutions are long since over – I shall not experience one, I don't have the possibility of being a counter-revolutionary, or a bystander. I am seeking questions appropriate to my historical experience, my social condition – and Leonid and Aleya cannot speak to me of this ...'

And Aleya thought of her rejection of Alexei, his opinions, his intellectualising. These had brought him the isolation which he hated, and the only solution was silence or suicide. These things too she found in herself – hard on herself, she was so tolerant and undemanding of others that they scarcely affected her, did not become objects for a serious judgement. Yet she fought against Alexei's solution: 'it must be wrong – to think oneself to annihilation – to punish oneself, or anticipate the punishment by others ...

She said, 'We are real types. Socialism is concerned with us – we who are typical – not with abstractions, not with the "innumerable millions". Are we conscious of what we are doing, of what we can do? We are one of the few communities which starts a hundred per cent active and interested: We have all of us lived in societies where the only struggle was to keep alive, to keep independent, to preserve one's identity and integrity to avoid complete extinction, to avoid being used for shabby purposes. But we no longer need to feel that. We can honestly work for the collective here. It's an academic question as to whether wages should have disappeared – we know that for the first time we here can build by ourselves, together avoiding isolation, avoiding self-destruction. Perhaps we are the only artists – we can look over these valleys and know that physical labour, the created labour … – we can know that we have directness, purity ...'

She felt confused – she was talking once more to Alexei, the first time for years. 'We can work together in comradeship, produce and be rewarded in comradeship: we have lessened our exploitation of ourselves and each other. We're not social-democrats – we don't have the comradeship of individualism … I'm sorry, I've expressed this very badly. I always think of the passive ones – perhaps I enjoy them ...'

Leonid asked, 'You mean, goods will be free, but labour will never be?'

'I don't understand your bitterness, Leonid. You see constraint everywhere because you give yourself no social, no typical, options. You choose a life for yourself alone – then complain that it does not please you, and that no one cooperates to make you happy. You have to reconcile yourself then to being used by others, and using them, in ways which express no one's real purpose, so long as you ignore the real possibilities for fulfilment, for achievement.'

'You amaze me,' said Leonid. 'You've really built a life from other people's expectations? Miraculous!'

Sultan said, 'Aleya is our voice and spirit – even though we do not know her well. She is serious but anxious. We don't look to her for orthodoxy, only for an admirable passion.'

'Enough congratulation – everyone shakes hands before the fight – will we do so again at the end, that's the question,' said the man from the Ukraine. 'We never face our problems – we play with them. Emotion and concern – but never action. Action is last on the list, and when we reach that, we're exhausted, and botch our tasks. We plan and scheme and debate – and then in the hour before dark, we say "Well, no time to think – what will get us the most money to last till next year" – and we plant sunflowers on the building lots because the price is high.

'You talk of the dangers of bureaucracy, of industrial drudgery – but what is that but order and discipline? Talking about discipline merely delays the time when you have to submit to it. And now you'll say, "So you think nothing can be changed by us, we have to be pushed to do everything?" No! I don't believe that. But we're like the donkey who said, "Sure, I have to be beaten before I'll walk: and I have to be beaten before I'll eat and sleep too. If ever my master got the idea I like carrots – he'd make me walk everywhere following a carrot, and never need to beat me at all!"'

'Enough time spent today,' said Sultan. 'We know three deformations – the bureaucratic, the apolitical, and the industrial. We must watch what we delegate to our specialists: we must keep our eyes on the political aspect, avoiding the preponderance of any one group, or interest. And we must be progressive. We've seen in Leonid what we have to avoid, from the personal point of view. And that's enough for any one day.'

As Aleya went back to work, she thought, 'Poor Leonid – having failed to impress me, he can't even mock successfully ... But he's right – I mustn't become sentimental about our experiment. I have a lot of work to do on my own life. How far I am from the company of anyone but Katya! How impossible to think of spending my life with anyone I know – and this is a lack, a fault. This is a part of Alexei, still, this impatience, this restlessness: vital but destructive.'

Trees sagged under the heat. 'Not to take the second best …' thought Aleya, as she heard the man singing again,

'I have sung my songs in contests everywhere –
and never won another song ...'

aleya's diary

I heard Larissa and my mother talking about me. My mother said, 'Dimitri drinks too much – but that Sergei would tame her down.' Taming! The last thing I need is extinction.

I broke in on them – 'I want neither of them, I want no one.'

What a blasphemer I seem to Larissa – she dwindles before your eyes, creeping into marriage like a vole into a burrow. Quite accustomed to a life of martyrdom, she can't understand why I don't adjust myself to any man. She plays on my mother's anguish until I seem to be some kind of public scandal – but I'm not responsible for my mother's discontents. She's bored and lonely, but why should I let myself be tormented to give her some diversion?

'I'm afraid Aleya is still too selfish,' my mother said. 'She won't even satisfy her needs!'

'What man wants me?' I told her. 'I don't know what I shall be tomorrow. There's no reason for me to be a married woman. I've nothing to give, and I want nothing for myself.'

'Is it still Alexei?' Larissa said. 'Are you still loyal to him?'

'What do you know of my loyalties?' I said. 'I'm not a writer, I can't sit for hours working out: my beliefs and perceptions. Why do you seem to attack me when you try to help? If Alexei was so wrong and foolish, why could no one accept or tolerate him? Why, if he was so harmless, did everyone treat him like a virus – and why must my affection for him be seen as a crisis for me?'

'But you are in a crisis, Aleya,' said Larissa. 'You're leaving for complete isolation, your body and mind seem to be constantly alight with passion – but passion for what, for whom?'

'For understanding, and for a means of expressing myself. That's why for you to leave the theatre is an act of destruction more ignoble than Alexei's. You're mistakenly trying to win the approval of a boor – the philistine audience to end all audiences. Alexei couldn't decide if suicide was the last gift of protest and wonder – or a private surrender. All the signs pointed to suicide – but he didn't follow one of them consistently. He was cowardly with himself. But – the poor boy! He was so exhausted, so desperate. But don't get the idea that's why I'm going to Kazakhstan – to re-create Alexei's loneliness – I've no wish to play in other people's dramas.'

I remembered the poem, the triumph, Alexei had left. It was a version of Lenin's last letter, written to his friends in the Georgian party, encouraging them against Stalin.

'Dear comrades, I follow your problem

With all my heart. I am disgusted
By the brutality of Orzhonokidze,
The connivance of Stalin, and
Dzerzhinski.' So, in the last line –
Caught you, old Felix! Where's the piety
Now, as you pass
Into dust?'

And when I showed this to Sergei, he said, 'Of course we know what Lenin thought, and couldn't stop. And also what he connived at too! You have to get used to it, Aleya – in revolutions violence can't always be resisted. And it becomes a means, sometimes, of continuing the revolution. When people are too tired to keep on making difficult choices, when they start saying, "Just let me count what money – if any – I have in my pockets before I decide what comes next" – then a little prick from the spur helps them along. You deplore – as I do – the glorification of violence: but it's a useful lesson, and one too easy to forget. It's better to keep moving than to have to be pushed forward.'

'Don't make too much of it,' I said, 'this "Violence" you talk so glibly about. Alexei was capable of using violence – and I shrink from his use of it, against himself, and all of us. But I'm sure he felt vindicated by Lenin himself, in that last letter. And it changes the whole weight of Alexei's attack: this shows Dzerzhinski as weak and shabby. Alexei used to argue from the position that the Bolshevik dualism was between coldness, conspiracy – and self-sacrifice, nobility, purity. Now – he finds the respite from that duality is shabby compromise ...'

'But,' said Sergei, 'his charges are global, and archaic. They're a literary convention, no more. The question is, Aleya, what are you to do? How will you make your shabby compromises, how will you live with this dualism?'

And I told him Alexei's story of the wolves – boastful and wealthy, much concerned with private possessions. And the husband and wife both decided they would work hard to save money for a car – 'no more slinking about in snowdrifts – we'll be able to ride about on the highway, swift and warm'.

But the husband said, 'Of course, it's a pity, but in order to save, you must be exploited. Freedom only comes with a material sufficiency – and to get that, you must suffer, or make others suffer.'

'In that case,' the wife said, 'I don't care for a car. I'll go naked. That's why we wolves have fur.'

But Alexei hadn't any fur to protect him. He was chilled to the bone from going naked. He chose cowardice sooner than compromise – that's the worst you can say of him.

There is so much I don't know about those dear to me: even about my mother. I'd like to ask her, 'Why did you want me, as your child? Were you frightened of what I'd be, while you were pregnant with me? How do you face your old age, alone here in Moscow, knowing pretension will die with you on your deathbed – dying without issue...? Did you have expectations for me? Why do you think I'm foolish to belong to the Party – is it to spare me difficulty and strain, or jealousy of my activity?'

But I can ask none of this. She doesn't think me capable of making a judgement about her. Sergei is the same – they resist my criticism because they'll not change themselves.

I went to a concert – quartets. Alexei's poems in typescript have a scent of the eraser, the faded ribbon, worn through in places. But the quartets had no contact with print and revision. Smetana, Janáček, Shostakovich. Listening with the conviction of conviction – at the interval we stood smiling, proud that we'd merely clapped, and not interrupted 'Stop! Enough! I understand everything.'

The music was like an invisible acrobat balancing on wires – you could see his weight sagging the wire, the imprint of his hands and feet tautening every slackness ... How I shall miss this concert hall, the oak crowns over the organ recalling the primal acorns, the gilded trumpets on the light fittings so familiar – the busts seeming to listen, relaxed and approving. I'm sentimental and foolish about it – but I've made my life's friends here. You find nowhere else in Moscow – my Moscow, that is – this relaxation, this concentration which lets you read the lines on the faces. You feel – my, what a hard war she must have gone through – how many people trembled before his desk. How soft the women's faces become, away from the noise of their apartments. Tonight there were technicians back from Vietnam – the music filled them out like a transfusion. I shall become so provincial in Kazakhstan – my concerns still more concentrated ...

Coming home, I blushed at my clumsiness. To tell Larissa she is marrying a boor – am I really so cruel? But he is a boor – I have spoken and saved my soul! He can feel passion only for flesh – he wants children so that he can be surrounded by parodies of his own flesh, he wants to keep Larissa off the stage – so that her body will be only the one body, it won't deceive anyone by playing a part.

In the underpass I smiled to the flowerseller by the metro entrance – it's a point of principle. A million people pass her every day, but I believe I'm the only one who smiles – every day. I hope I'm wrong. Or perhaps she doesn't care. But we shouldn't look so intent – only visitors smile in Moscow. Then I saw Lev – he left the institute last year, and I thought he was in Chelyabinsk.

'Aleya, living and breathing still!'

'Only just – a few more days only. I'm leaving for Asia.'

'A big place to leave for – you should find at least a part of it! But partial discoveries never satisfied you, I remember. "Give me Asia, or nothing" – You're Napoleonic, Aleya. But never prettier.'

'Lev, you look so much older – your hair's almost grey,' I told him.

'Yes, Aleya – and my face completely? We have to grow old, you realise – it's a way of establishing relativism.'

'Don't talk like that, Lev – you make me sound so clumsy. I meant – I was sorry to see things were so hard with you, that's all. I was very sorry when you left.'

'Yes, we all burst out of Moscow – like a seed-pod bursting at the end of summer. But things were hard this year.'

'Things or people?'

'People, mostly. I was married and now I'm not.' He smiled wistfully. 'My fault. Too bad. What is it that drives us to these things? To live with someone – that's a big responsibility – and so's driving them away ... I'm not a healthy person to be with, Aleya.'

'Are you serious, Lev? You were so quiet, so gentle – now, you seem beaten. How could you let this happen to you? Was it self-disgust? Why?'

'Aleya, the world's very different from what you fancy. People like you aren't appreciated. You tell people what they think about themselves, but we don't want that, you know. Employ yourself with technical questions, Aleya. That's where we need honesty. Clip your wings a little – and keep your beak closed. It's a better weapon that way.'

'Lev, I'm amazed! This bitterness! In just one year. If I'm fanciful, I could never have imagined this. You were so good at theoretical questions. I envied you!'

'Well, Aleya, now you see me changed. Don't rely on my judgement of theory. Keep quiet, that's my advice. Travel alone, and travel fast.'

Then he left, and I stared after him. Will my life be hard in Kazakhstan, a life like his? I'm ready for physical hardship, but mental? I thought I could be spared that. My life will be technical, precise. My loyalties will be concrete: I shall enjoy the fruits of my labour, and if I'm unhappy, it will be my fault and mine alone. But am I not to talk, to be loved, to be angry? ... How beautiful those flowers were, the scarlet on the spikes like butterflies unbudding – such colours, against the bread-brown brick. These details – I fix them in my mind as though I'll never again have anything to remember. I'm scared of leaving, of seeing Dimitri and Sergei for the last time, of finding them, touching and wounding two saddened men who can't understand why I should leave them. And yet – how my head is burning with longing to be away ...

feodor

Children are rolling a snowball round the yard, big as an antiworld. I am impressed today with my responsibility to remain silent. Under the snow lie all my memories of oil-stains and the sparrows' wallows. And what do they produce for me – memories of wine drunk but not paid for, the purple dog with two streams of purple – blood, wine, urine, there's no end to this speculation! – running across the square. Nothing but melancholy, Aleksandra would say.

'You don't speak my language,' I tell her. 'Language is what everyone speaks – otherwise, what's the point?'

Are we so evenly matched, reconstructing Yuri and Ilich's asymmetrical game of volleyball, asymmetrical because they are good players? No, I'm not a crippled sensibility. How to turn a question of truth into a question of conscience. Why ask the question 'ought I to tell the truth?' – when I could have told it and taken the consequences, if there were any? I suspect my motives – you don't establish contact with a social base by inviting the world to take your decisions of conscience for you! Still less when it is their lives you're examining. Have I learnt nothing from the Party?

I need a situation which is simple, in which I can learn from experience. But is this experience of myself – in which case I should have learnt a lot recently – or of others? In that case – who is concerned to talk to me? In any event – how spineless that experience would be! The forests, the wolves, the melancholy cages of my culture and Sophie's squirrel – 'it was so tame, I had to kill it, how would it survive away from my affection?' – these don't help me to ask appropriate questions. But what is the responsibility of the Soviet intellectual? To be silent sometimes? To drink with Yuri and Ilich – hardly a responsibility? To write the history of the factory, these sheds, in committee? To listen to Timofei? Now I know why everyone takes to writing poetry and mapping the apocalypse! I'm not so easily satisfied. After Sophie, superficiality will never seem the same again ...

Yesterday, Aleksandra and I went to the ruined mansion. The sky is so heavy with snow these days, one is almost bowed under the threat. She frisked round me like a cat. I said, 'The Germans were here.' The place is almost beyond restoration – the blue of the walls has oxidised, and the interior is spotted with rust like a book left through the winter in the forest. The Germans hanged a lot of people here – some of them old enough to be my elder brothers. And the building is dead now – the mould trying to carry it beyond the point: of restoration. There were other couples poking about – speculating about the ordinary experiences – death in action, servitude, decay – as though they'd been forever transcended.

Aleksandra said, 'Will you always stay out here, in the provinces? It's hard for you to be happy here, you know.'

'I'd go back to Moscow – somewhere I can live on other people's talent, like ivy.'

'Feodor, you didn't go wrong with your history. People aren't ready for it – why, an article in *Pravda* yesterday criticised these lavish factory histories, published in huge editions, and full of errors, and praise for all kinds of slackness, and nonentities.'

'And mine would have been different?'

'Different – and unpublishable. Your trouble is you're secretly gratified and reassured that it's not published. It seems to prove something, and you don't know or care what. The passivity of editors can't excuse your self-effacement.'

'You're quite right, Aleksandra – the only way to resolve these classic dilemmas is to ignore them as though they've never existed.'

I remember a friend of mine who went to the virgin lands, suffering who knows what. His enthusiasm became an obsession. He turned into an explorer of pedantry: he'd use nothing imported – food or literature. Life became very complicated for him – his obscurantism contributed, in its insignificant way, to the very slackness he'd gone out to remedy. He was a bore who felt everyone else had an obligation to pardon his boring them. Beside him, the man who collects his wages in kind from the warehouse, the guerrilla bureaucrat fixing favours under the noses of the official paper-hounds – becomes quite congenial. The first type subdues his audience by boredom, the second robs them while they're asleep – they work over society like a gang of pickpockets.

And Aleksandra said, 'Feodor, what's to become of us?'

'We'll go on like this, I imagine, until something happens.'

'Rejection hurts you so much, doesn't it? It's more than bitterness, it's despair. You're broken because you're ignored.'

'Not broken, Aleksandra, just latent.'

Now, today, Grigor asked to see me. 'Feodor, what do you think of Moscow – a little change, perhaps?'

'Why?'

'I'd like you to shelve the project here for a while. There's a friend of mine who can use you. Journalism. Research. More in your line generally.'

'But why? Are you transferring me? Is this a punishment or a reward?' He grimaced ambiguously.

'Several people told me this is what you wanted. So, I did what I could.'

There's not much more I can say. Grigor won't admit to self-interest and none seems to be involved here. Why should I stay? Aleksandra must have suggested this to Grigor. I feel the dignified thing is to walk out like a soldier under orders. At the worst, I'm being given another chance, and at best, someone is trying to help. Andrei already knows.

'So,' he says, 'You're leaving us. Too valuable here, eh?'

'I feel I've failed you, Andrei, but I don't know how.'

'To be honest, Feodor, I don't know either. I've learnt to rely on myself, to concern myself only with my limitations, and be tolerant of those of others. I think you did what you could. You lack a tactical sense, that's all. You dream and call it speculation, you suffer wounds, indignities, and pretend you're too insensitive to feel them. It's a mark of strength, but also one of cruelty to yourself. You'll never accomplish anything while you're so far from efficacy. It's too late to suffer vicariously with me – you must invent a new, bolder language. The people here have spoken to you – now it's your turn. Are you going to tell them nothing is worthwhile? The best won't believe you – and there's no point talking to the worst ... Your privilege is that instead of calmness and docility, your life can be volatile – it leaps forward, it stumbles. What will you do in Moscow?'

'Much the some as here, I think. But I'm under no compulsion to go – I can stay here if I want.'

'No, you must go. Moscow will suit you. We will wait with interest for anything you have to say.'

Aleksandra knows. She looks cheerful, too. 'Aren't you delighted? Just think – you're missing the winter here – it's so dreary.'

'Aleksandra – can't any of you stand me here? Am I so disturbing? You could have sent me to the Caucasus, or to America – that would keep me out of your way. I'm beginning to think there's a Sophie in all of you.'

'We're pleased because this is so right for you. We'll have a party to send you off. And when you're successful – you send for me.'

'No, the truth is – you can't stand to live with me, afraid of what I'll pry into next. Is there nowhere I can rest, nowhere to share some of the tranquillity you drank in with the honey and the golden dust of your interminable childhood?'

'Feodor, there's something in what you say. You're very exhausting, very demanding. A little of you goes a long way. You're like a bolt of lightning – you split clouds and frighten horses, but you end up burying your nose like a kite into some quite insignificant bush or piece of rock. You are disturbing – but only because you have the air of one who knows important secrets which he can't decipher.'

'But, pretentiousness apart, there's nothing incongruous in my chasing an illusory talent all over the world?'

'Feodor, you must know how much I'll miss you? I'm not sending you away from me – can you imagine how impoverished my life here will be? Please, Feodor, don't be cynical, don't be hurt.'

One can't be exiled to Moscow, I suppose ... Better to dissipate one's energies in Moscow than attempt an amateurish dissipation in the provinces. And so – new life!, perforce.

'Aleksandra, I never really told you what I thought about you. I think we go well together, and I'm relieved at how unpoignant it all seems. I should have gone long ago. When there's not much to do but drink, some of the savour is lost, one is forced into oblivion ...'

She's crying now – we'll not be apart for long. And she's wrung a little honesty out of me, which is better than conscience any day. Back to all those strangers, with a heavier burden, but more confidence.

It's really quite exciting! In an obscure way, I feel things are moving again. I've made some contacts. What I've lost on compromise, I've gained through Aleksandra. I'm not entirely unprotected now – all that turmoil was necessary after all. In my America, vast numbers are preparing themselves to die, as casually as they put out the garbage – content to become historical marginalia. They've not undergone even the little I have, the vicarious suffering, as Andrei would call it.

There's something terrifying about men prepared for death without literary conventions, without the approval of history, dying of despair, fully armed. Will it stop the other Americans dying of hope – helicopters over the mines and banana plantations, spraying Coca-Cola on the foliage till it flames and withers ...? Over there – so much misery, so much which wakens the agitator in me – and here, so much which stirs and attracts my attention. At last, I feel fully awake, recovered. Isolation is at an end, and my letters will keep Aleksandra close to me – closer even than when we talk ...

leo

Leo wrote, 'We don't always say things as precisely as we can – and this marks our backwardness. But at the same time, we have to take care of ourselves if we're not willing to die – and this too is a source of irritation to people. They don't like us to ally with people in arms. Perhaps this was once a mark that civil society was civilian – but not now. Who is ready for devastation? Not I, says everyone, hoping to be the last on the list. Writing? That's not a revolutionary trade any more. For one thing, the root of radicalism is teaching people to read ... And yet – if that is one's interest there is no shortage of real revolutions – and real apathy.

'At present we have the revolution of the armed against the unarmed. How long will that one last, I wonder? How easy it is for us to become the gentry of the bureaucracy – everyone of gentility uses a typewriter nowadays. The lesson is, perhaps, that one is always inappropriate. "The History of a Hole" – where we all fell and went on falling, falling through Moscow until we reached the bottom of the shaft and could start mining again ... Leaving Moscow – a retreat to the far side of the world, to a country where people remember only the primal insults, the deportation of the Acadians, the battle of the Boyne, where

'among the wrecked Chevs
and blackened house-frames
I rub away
the patina on the blueberries
the poor Indians sell.'

'Remember, the Mexican working is the States, telling me "The lightning fired the garbage dump – our best goats and favoured children came back to us as greasy soot – the cops billied us back. It was their right, but myself – I don't feel grateful."'

He remembered his wife's attitude to informers: 'We're a survival unit – I can keep you alive in the forest for years ...' and how easy it was not to cheer, nor to run, but to become accustomed.

'The problem is,' he said to Shirley, 'that until you have accomplished something of value in your own eyes, you can't recognise the permanent and positive value of anyone else's accomplishments.'

'How could you accomplish anything – except survival? You merely tried to do the wrong things in inappropriate places.'

They looked at the lake. Leo watched the proud little frogs, half-immersed. Every one looked like a prince – too few princesses to do the necessary loving.

'Shirley, I think this affair has not taken fire. I feel for you a tenderness, and in you, a great wistfulness for me. To leave you – well, for mc, it has been a qualified success, for you, another episode of failure. What can I say? You know these episodes never end – but that just makes it worse. I've discovered three things with you. That I misjudged my wife. That I've made not attempt to come to terms with this country. And that I'm not a demagogue. Easy enough, you'll say – but there's learning and learning – better to learn than to know.'

'Leo, I knew this would happen. How could I hold you? I could give you no memories of hilltop Georgian churches – as for seeing Stalin, I'd be as impressed if you'd said it was Genghiz Khan – I don't even know the ghost stories of the Atlantic coast, the routes of the trappers, the Indians' languages ... I'm a child of the shopping plaza and the drive-in. I can't help you to adjust – all my originality comes without reflection, without comparison. My heritage is disinheritance – dynasties have been founded on worse, but it's useless for you. "Sure, let's get married, sure, let's have a revolution." It doesn't satisfy you, this unconcern with the experience of others. You've an eye for detail like a schizoid – I haven't, and I know no one who has. We don't observe each other as reflectively as you do – we don't have that love for ourselves that you do. We don't get lost in the dark like you. Now, I think we're right. We'll do more than you ever will, without fuss or remorse – haven't you noticed how simple are the things the most coherent are saying? They're childishly simple – but they can instantly be put into practice.'

'Your husband? If I represent the ancien regime – surely he does too?'

'No. He was frightening because he was brutal. But he didn't think about what he was doing. He'd no more hostility than a cat that's gone back to the bush. He feared the world of analysis, sentiment, gentility. He was simple – you suffered from his anger, and delighted in his pleasures – that's all.

'I thought that under all your civilisation there was simplicity. But I was just another figure in the carpet – and I needed to be the whole carpet – as you would have been my whole life. I understand your wife now. She travelled light so that whatever you wanted, she could give you, or protect you from. You thought that was superficiality – really, it was comradeship.'

They drove back to the city, Shirley unemotional, almost placid. 'Why do you worry?' she asked Leo. 'I've nothing to say. I've earned no regrets. But what will you do, Leo?'

'The same – work at the theatre – that's my laboratory. One day, I'll create life there. It takes courage to realise that you don't have a complex vision, only an oblique one. But – I'll keep trying. I'll talk to people – see what they remember about their prehistories. Some weeks ago I met someone who'd walked from the Andes, through the States, to work in the mines here. Now – he longs to own a motel. He said, "They drink so quietly and when drunk, they fight so little. And the big cars, they all drive away when they're drunk, stealing so little. Ah, what a great and placid people." What would he make of our lawyers and executives, dressed in every shade of lime-green, only leaving their big houses in the evening to bend the knee before Beethoven or a visiting comprador? A motel with some bars – it's peonage in its most mobile form ...'

'Have I been good for you at all, Leo?' They sat in the parking lot, the car radio tuned down to a mumble. Some Ukrainians in ten-gallon hats in the next car were laughing as they opened a food parcel a grandmother had sent them from Kiev.

'We survived an experiment together – more than my wife did!'

'So – you're back to independence? Will you enjoy that?'

'What kind of life would it be for you? Sitting quietly while I go through the card index, remembering old friends who would never reply to my letters? The whole of your life become a "something difficult" room? Shirley – you'd hate being the silent servant of some formulation – not even a discovery – which served only .my purposes. You need a hedonist or an activist – you can't understand anything in between. Secretly, you think I'm useless. You'd like our problems to appeal to you as though we were in the States, or Haiti. You can't understand the many modes of conviction and resistance. You have the struggle before you – that's why you needed the theatre. But now – I don't believe the theatre can help you. You'll just have to face your cowardice or your crisis alone. But me – I've had my struggle, in Moscow, where it wasn't very courageous or dramatic. It did cost a life, I suppose, but then, we were all ready to be victims then – there had been forty years of being victims to look back on. And now, things have moved on. You've shown me what I've to face in this society, Shirley. I know it irritates you when I say, "There's nothing so inert as an open mind." But no one likes to be accounted useless – and my own mind is closed to betrayals.'

'You mean, you need my reassurance that you've not betrayed me? Well, Leo, how could you have done? As you say, this is only a rehearsal. You'll arise like the hero who breaks from the ice-mountain to lead the frost-soldiers to victory! I'm sorry, Leo. How could we satisfy each other? You have such impatience, you won't let us grow together. You've done no harm, so surely you won't regret the incident.'

'I don't feel that's wholly satisfactory. You make it seem that I've no private emotion. I think deep down I don't want happiness, so I'll not start looking. I've a conscience ...'

'Yes, Leo – damn your conscience. Nobody loves a spoiled priest. Your confessions are cheap.'

'I understand why you're angry, Shirley. But remember, there were millions of us spoiled priests. And look what cathedrals we built! If our theology was a disaster – look how many souls we saved. Can you imagine how tiny my personal weakness seems, even the sum of all our weaknesses, when you look at our achievements?'

Sadly, Shirley said, 'Not many achievements for me ... And you've missed the wildness, the urgency, the indiscipline here – even with me.'

Leo went home, alone: work to be found, thoughts to be disciplined – down on the floor of the cave again, the darkness at the back to be fought against once more.

And Shirley thought, 'He even didn't see it was me who released him! Should I have let him go back to isolation? Should I have withheld devotion, told him – I'll not release you from your first wife by becoming your second, and dying without asking even for ice-cream?'

She couldn't convince him of his imperfection – the fact that he couldn't find ice-cream: it's haunted him ever since. She couldn't tell him either – that there were things she needed which he'd not begun to understand: that she was dying voluntarily, as it were, to show him how small and how difficult the very last and smallest need was ...

And yet – devotion, certainly he arouses that. Without trying, however scornful, cynical, insensitive, we listen and reject him. And he's right – he does have a warning and a lesson – which I can't grasp. Unless it's the idea of these achievements, built despite weakness and insensitivity. But the achievements were needed! They were demanded! And perhaps that is Leo's concern – how can he be of use, how satisfy these human needs which he sees so clearly, and approaches so obliquely. And I've failed him – and he knows, and does not care. He expected too little of me, and wasn't disappointed – so my release of him seems petty. For him, 'one' is always too small an audience, and insufficiently critical. But he leaves me lonely, still as 'one'.

aleya

Aleya thought: 'Perhaps this year we shall produce enough to ensure another year's experiment.' The days had run together – the heat haze dissolving week into week. They had plans for a school, a stage for contests in epic. One of the competitors was singing,

> *'My head in history, my feet in criticism –*
> *modesty forbids talk of satisfaction,*
> *I'll mine for songs in Karaganda,*
> *bend my neck to the tractor like a horse*
> *to its harness – and afterwards,*
> *the difficult tasks completed,*
> *sleep under the almond trees –*
> *glazed skies stretching over the peaceful hills ...'*

Aleya said to Katya, 'This question of reconciling false oppositions has been difficult for us – how much worse it must be for young people elsewhere. I sympathise with the teacher who's to go into a *kolkhoz*, saying farewell to the decencies of urban life, suffering till he realises things are not bad after all. But even for me there were so many questions which were insuperable while I approached them as an isolated intellectual. Art and life, literature and practice, intellectual and proletariat – no resolution ever seemed possible, only some mechanical and brutal articulation, unsatisfying and crippling.

My friend, Alexei, could not achieve efficacy, couldn't build bridges between himself and others, was never content with less than global statements – and of course, missed the originality he craved for – there was no substance to him. Or – am I unfair? Am I really content here? I've no songs. These mountains, the herdsmen – I seem surrounded by indifference to my efforts.

But why should anyone care? It's exciting when you're in the early stages. Which Marx shall we choose – debates day and night, fantastic forms of organisation, modes of liberation so embracing one seems ready to burst through one's skin. Can we answer the questions of the French, the Italian students? I've not even read their books. But – I do feel for them. Because one day, they'll have to lose something of this exaltation, and this comradeship, to suspect each other – and above all, they'll have to go out, like our students, to the farms and factories. Katya, can you understand how hard it is, to adjust? How long it took me!'

And Katya said, 'I understand. You've renounced Alexei in order to become flesh and blood. But don't forget – he was flesh too – don't ignore unhappiness, Aleya, even an unhappiness which seems inert, passive. Misery is – I won't say the human condition – it's characteristic, let's say. You've managed to unite belief and action – but what of the millions awaiting their revolution – as you say, helplessly discussing the possibilities? Alexei is commoner than you'd like to think.

'It reminds me of a story – when we were in Istanbul, they told of a man, an exile like us, who had fantastic luck as an entertainer. Drums, bears, fire-eating, nonsense with daggers, parrots – he couldn't go wrong. And he always wore a big fur hat – bear, I should say it was.

'And I said to him once, "What's the secret?"

'"I get dreadful catarrh," he said, "it's this damned Byzantine sea, it even looks lumpy with germs. And I really believe it's this hat that gets me some relief. I couldn't perform with a cold – that's the secret."

'Well, that seemed to put him beyond imitation. But one time – he caught a terrible cold, nearly died. And he cursed his hat for failing him, and threw it into the sea. And then his luck stopped. I'm sure you've heard stories like this before, Aleya. But the point was quite simple: people came to see his act because of his funny hat – they didn't care about his catarrh! It was a case of obsession driving out talent – a lesson there for us all!'

'So, Katya – what's my talent? What's my magic hat?'

'Well, as they say, Aleya – seriousness. You're like the snail that climbed to the top of the sky by sheer perseverance, and got down again by strength of conviction. No one who looks at you could believe you demand less than the most of yourself or others – you push every value to its peak...'

They went to the meeting. 'How sad,' said Aleya. 'I feel we're saying farewell to the stage of meetings and entering that of material production. We'll become less interesting.'

Leonid said, 'Yesterday I was misrepresented. I don't believe in our autonomy here, that's all. You can't be an autonomous experiment – you're someone else's experiment. So – what do we hope to get from this solicitude – the heart of discipline is obedience, to start an old argument.'

'Not so,' said Sultan. 'Our development here has been political, it has passed rapidly through many stages. This work is work of essential preparation – not a story of direction meeting with compliance. We hear from his own mouth that there is Leonid and Leonid – so too there is discipline and discipline. We're running a group of farmers, not a government – our philosophy must be appropriate.'

'My life is of a piece,' Kulkul said. 'These discussions are tranquil – I mean, they bring me peace. I am reassured at understanding you all. It eases my relations with you – more people than I'd otherwise think of talking to.'

'I'd like to hear what Aleya thinks,' said Leonid. 'It was her idea to come here.'

'Leonid – I don't understand this spinelessness. You say, "Aleya is our leader – I don't follow her." I'm not coercing you – you have to coerce yourself! You can't live without coercion, Leonid – and when there is none, you resent your reluctance to move! Everything you judge too harshly, including yourself.

'Then you sit back complacently and say, "Well, that's clear. I'm a useless amateur. No point in analysis – I'm a broken reed." And you don't realise: all this harshness and vigour is a means of securing self-indulgence. You're a cosmic failure, so the little everyday deficiencies leave you unmoved.'

'More kindness, Aleya? You're happy here, so you feel everyone must accept you and your accomplishments – why should they?'

'I'm amazed you have this view of me. You're the first person to say I'm happy, or had accomplished anything! I feel as embattled as ever.'

'Nonsense!' said Leonid. 'You stand there, proud and beautiful – model for propagandists everywhere. I thought we could flourish together, because of your restlessness. But no – you're tamed. Perhaps your congeniality has misled you. You're liked, Aleya, and you're used.'

No, thought Aleya, you must be loved before you can be used – compliance gets no one what they want. But am I any of these things? – a tame tiger? Why did Leonid offer his companionship, and turn on me? Congenial – surely not! I have this power to wound – a useless power. I'm not a commissar with her troops – do I have the appearance of one? How incongruous! How banal – if it all turns out to be 'Aleya in search of affection, finds the world in Leonid's hard little head ...?'

'Look, Leonid, it is pleasant to work with one's friends and find them good workers,' said the Ukrainian. 'Even better to find the people you work with become your friends. Don't dramatise so much, Leonid. We should be discussing quite other questions – standardisation, specialisation – not your psychic epics.'

'I disagree,' said Sultan. 'If Leonid is out of sympathy with us – if we are wrong in thinking of ourselves as pioneers – he should tell us.'

'Yes. I am out of sympathy,' said Leonid. 'We can't take a flying leap into the future, just by accelerating the process of development. Aleya, your history is one without civil war, Stalinism, patriotic war – it's history without the prickles. Some day, you'll have to start something yourself, to invent, not copy and compress.'

And Aleya thought, yes, so far I've just managed to reconcile myself and the collective. What efforts to reconcile the other oppositions and only then to act!

'Speak clearly, Leonid,' said the Ukrainian. 'If we differ, how do you propose to expose the differences.'

'By exile,' he said. 'By simply withdrawing – leaving no record of opposition for you to debate over. Frankly – I think you're self-deluded. Aleya sees the whole scheme as an attempt to build Soviet Woman out of little girls running in frilly blouses to their violin lessons, the rest of you see wheat kernels till you must think like squirrels! No scheme is perfect – I'll be your first silent failure. You can send an order down for another Leonid to replace me.'

'Don't go, Leonid. There's no falseness in my asking you – I think you should stay, just because we're so far apart.'

'Aleya,' Leonid replied, 'you know things don't work like that. I'll go before there's trouble. I'm incorrigible – I'm the dead wasp in your honey. You're too sweet, Aleya – a fine furry fellow like me needs salt in the diet.'

'Let him go, Aleya,' said Katya. 'We can't all stay together quarrelling delightfully all our lives – dispute may keep you lively, but I've heard it all before.'

Leonid walked away.

'Well, this was hardly the way I expected this to end,' said Sultan, 'But after all, we're ready to go to work now.'

And the Ukrainian said.

'How demanding is this poetry?
We can reject our friends with it –
Between one rhyme and the next there pass
Battles, a blossom-season, and betrayal.'

The meeting broke up. Aleya thought: the discussion is over, the link is stronger. Always strength demands rejection, parting. Where will Leonid go? He has less hope than me ... How hurt was he? It's so sudden – things are accelerating, repeating themselves. The first time as tragedy, the second time as aphorism? How could I hold Leonid? And do I even want to? It would be disinterested indeed. He's too hard to have close to you ... And perhaps Sergei felt this about me, back in Moscow. He tried to argue with me, to make me stay, or at least avoid apocalypse. No one wanted Leonid to stay. The herdsmen are galloping off, pleased to be riding into the hills. And now – poor Leonid, who does not want my pity, and does not have much of it. He's not even begun to look for happiness – he's one of the millions I can't reach, even though my body aches with the strain. How hot it is today in the sun – there's no breeze to carry the scent of the apricots ...

aleya's diary

Sergei and Dimitri took me to dinner – my farewell treat. What a gruesome idea! – it must have been Sergei's. He's so bewildered by my leaving everyone, not him personally. And Dimitri is too kind to refuse him.

'I've dedicated my next quartet to you,' Dimitri said.

I laughed and said 'Why the next? It may be terrible! Aren't I orchestral? Can't I have a symphony?'

Always the wrong thing – I can't convince Dimitri I think he's brilliant. He needs more praise than mine – I shouldn't try to make him laugh at himself while so many others are doing so in earnest ...

He just looked at me. 'I may not write a symphony. Or anything more – it seems to be the fashionable thing, self-mutilation. It should be so easy to write for one's audience, fine majoritarian principles. But I haven't an audience – I've got three people who are interested in my work. What's wrong with these three – except that they're my friends? One's dead, and one's leaving, but otherwise they're sound enough. So, why should it make me gloomy?'

Sergei danced with me – and I let the champagne carry me, for he's very stiff and careful.. But everyone was watching us – I hate people who speculate silently when I'm trying to enjoy myself, it's like having my family before me. Dimitri was drinking. The whole affair was so awful – I wanted to shout out, 'No, why should I go? I'll stay here between tenderness and dependence, ensnared in these sentimental friendships till someone else breaks away.'

And yet – friendship has nothing to do with my leaving ... Dimitri invented a wolf joke – they're becoming a fashion, poor Alexei.

'There were, it seems, these two wolves. And one said to the other–' and Dimitri drank as though he were trying to drain the translucence out of his glass.

'"I hear you've been making all kinds of friends – bears, squirrels, dogs – a heterogeneous lot. I don't believe in criticising another wolf's friends – but since our intention is to eat these people, don't you think it's a little unfair to pretend you like them, enjoy their company?"

'And the first wolf said, "Oh, I don't mind them. They know where I stand, I don't hide anything. It makes the time pass more easily until I close my jaws on them that's all."

'And the other wolf said, "Fine wolf you are. You're disgracing us, and weakening the whole notion of predation. I'm going personally to warn your friends what kind of a fellow you are."'

He laughed, and he noticed people staring at him. He began loudly, 'It seems there was this roomful of busybodies, informers, parasites, cheap speculators – and the talented wolf drinking champagne...'

'Dimitri, this is my evening, please don't spoil it.'

He took my hand and squeezed it to keep his tears back.

'Really, Dimitri, this is too embarrassing, please decide what you're unhappy about, and let's talk, do something.'

'Exchange of gifts,' said Dimitri. He gave me a little book of children's songs – his own manuscript. 'You don't have to sing them to your own,' he said. 'Anyone's will do.'

Sergei read one of the verses:

'Gathering the one red mushroom,
Like the tree's first scarlet leaf –
Why pick the mushroom when
You know all leaves will fall?'

'It's just pretty, I'm afraid,' said Dimitri. 'But Aleya, when you put on the peasant smock and leave the mansion – you must expect your old servants to press slim volumes of advice on you ... A little rural lore comes in handy – though you'll probably only see coalmines.'

'I've nothing to give you,' I said. 'Only Alexei's last poem. And I know what Sergei will say: "As rough as the others … another 'honour among wolves' joke – another falsification, neither analysis nor direct emotion." Anyway, this is Dzerzhinski Square.

'The crowds flow into Children's World like pigeons.
Peace to the World. And innocent –
or ignorant – accordions sound
as workers dance,
high on the scaffolding, shadowed
by giant cranes' wings.

How does it look to you, Felix, old astronomer –
kids in the planetarium, stars like the red stars
you sighted on the Kremlin ...
Lovers in plastic macs,
Grannies taking home the dark sheep cheese.

Children file to see our Ilich –
did he really like you, your
pure and ardent blood? – always returning
from exile, each time

the leaders seeming younger, mere schoolkids.
You're exiled now from our Siberia –
new cities, the old school bullies dead.
Useless to doubt you, Felix – I forgive you,
whatever blows you gave you'd suffered –
tense, burning, balancing –
without accordions – so high,
just act of will, no girders.

tick lock, your Bolshevik heart
with one pulse in the grave –
soul damned, pure soul ... They say
you loved children, children's world.
Are we your children then, not knowing you,
But offspring of your frightening will?'

'The answer's easy for me,' said Serge. 'No, I'm not his child. Alexei had such a fear of any consciousness, and any judgement, but his own – he excluded all responses but his. You can't treat your audience like that. It reminds me of a letter of Marx to Engels – he's laughing at Hegel, because the words he uses to label the upper reaches of abstraction are in fact feudal property terms. Someone should do the same for Alexei – stand him on his head, because that's where his feet are.'

'Still trying, Sergei?' Dimitri asked viciously. 'Can't you see Alexei isn't your rival with Aleya, that no one is? You're both good Leninists – you know there aren't any more soft options. We do what we mean, we're sad or happy and say so. Dead men are dead – criticism is free.'

'Do you object to that?' said Sergei.

'No. But you make me tired with this endless talking around the realities of your lives. Aleya was fond of Alexei, but hasn't the slightest desire to accent his opinions. She hates cynicism, she wants. action. She doesn't want Alexei's type of *contra mundum*, the lonely visionary pretending to pierce the fog, but doing no more than repeating the stalest and most barren opinions of a liberal bourgeois whose experience is of survival, of success, good luck, sophistication, whose experience of politics comes from sipping wine with other bourgeois intellectuals and saying "dear me – the state of the world". And all the time Alexei wanted to perfect his technique – *his* technique.

'All these noble themes are just little squares of marble and glass – the mosaic itself is Alexei's alone. It's Alexei's will that's frightening – he holds Dzerzhlnski as long as the poem lasts. And Aleya rejects this. Just as she rejects me – she wants to overcome the self-absorption of the struggling creative artist – who in fact is the world's least creative animal, building fantastic lairs and nests, that no one else will live in. And she rejects you, Sergei, because of your damnable common-sense. She thinks you're waiting to justify yourself in some act of inaction or pettiness. You're not big enough for her.'

'Dimitri – please,' I said. 'You talk of me rejecting you – I reject no one. That's the trouble. I have to discipline myself – to live more socially, more humanly. One of my teachers said "The trouble with the coterie, the salon, is that it attempts to recreate the intensity of literal existence in real life. But characters in novels can have these intense and conscious lives because they disappear when they're not in the novel. Flesh and blood can't sustain itself in this literary fashion – so the coterie leads to exhaustion, to ennui, to a profound dissatisfaction with all types of activity which are not literary.

The most exalted form of action thus becomes the tea party, the *mot* not merely replaces, it seems to transcend, the manifesto. And then, in time, the manifesto itself becomes a form of action, it becomes the characteristic mode of action – that is, of literature – of intellectuals. And – it leads to ennui, exhaustion and so on. It's lost – through its very exaltation, its nobility – contact with the real world of human progress."

'And don't you see – that's the danger I see, Dimitri! And yet you persist in making things worse – of talking of my rejection of you. I don't want to transcend you, don't you see? But the only way I can avoid it – is to leave you, to solve the archaic problem of intellectuals in an archaic way – to leave the. city, to leave my friends. I'm not proud of this – it's anachronistic, and so is Alexei. But my energy is real, my conviction aren't brittle. Perhaps my act of creation will be to see fields of cotton, apricot trees, knowing that and my friends have produced all this ... You seem to need some childish idealism. Intensity should be expressed with wit and elegance – you force me into all kinds of sentimentalities.'

I don't know if that was what I wanted to say, but, for the moment, it kept us separate. Yet – Sergei and Dimitri are right – there is evasiveness in Alexei. He's not interested in political questions and so one can't follow him far. We sat in silence, I was heavy with my disloyalty. When we left, we could hear the band playing some small, sad tune, as though it were the last music in the world. It was raining, and it seemed as though everyone had forgotten summer. I wished I could stay in Moscow – doing anything, hiding like an old dog in its hole – just to be somewhere I knew. How could I say goodbye to them? Sergei's so clever after all – how can I leave them, leave everyone who cares for me?

I walked home between them, until Dimitri said, 'Well, Aleya – no more caring jobs for you. When you next hear of me, I'll be fifty and famous.

You'll see my dentures grinning at you all over Central Asia ...'

I know he said this only so that I'd share his unhappiness, so that our parting would be memorable because it hurt so much. But I broke away, and ran home. I just left them, ran through the rain like a fish plunging through the waves to find the dry beach to die on. And I cried ... Horrible.

feodor

It's my last morning. I feel like a painter, afraid that his hand will start to shake on the last strokes. People clearing snow always look so pitiful, like performing bears. What have I learnt, what has emerged from these months? Certainly, this time it is I who can leave Aleksandra – unfinished business is better than stale cake, as you might say. Rather – I'll be back for her. I think this has been a period of transition. I've made my contacts, tried out my strength in public. It wasn't a wonderful performance, but that was to be expected. I never found out much about Yuri and Ilich, and less about Sophie. But they enjoyed having me around to discuss, and discuss with.

Andrei says, 'A good man is always on the move. This talk about roots – I've never understood it myself. Everyone has to travel the breadth of the land. I knew a young peasant once – longed to settle down, but was always sidetracked – until he became a worshipper of the unexpected. In our country, you need the sense of movement – of trains crossing vast expanses, of cities pushing up like mushrooms in the tundra. You must get the bigness and strength into your system – only then can you understand the real processes, the real movement – only then can you begin to think dialectically.'

'That means you think I've not begun to think in that way?'

'You are moving towards it. But transitionary periods are the most dangerous – that's when the mistakes matter more.'

'You think I'm on a dangerous path?'

'Everyone who is dour and impatient is a threat to himself. You are, if you can be convinced of it, a dynamic force – but so is a stone falling on your head. You must learn to take responsibility for yourself – which involves being patient with others. But we may meet again.'

'Andrei –all this is inappropriate, and obscure. You make me feel like a student – in fact, one I asked what his ambition was. And he said, 'Gentleness and nineteenth-century literature.' I've no objectives – I've no answers. I don't envy Americans, I don't feel everyone since Herzen has been mistaken. All I envy are people in the sun. I have no ambitions. Raining simple questions, balanced between anxiety and conviction. And what have you to suggest, Andrei? Metaphysical stuff about patience and transition, debates in railway trains between old memory-bags? With our memories we live always with the second rate.'

'Now, Feodor, you've said it exactly. Good luck!' and he's plodding and hopping through the snow like a wounded raven.

Ah well, goodbye birch trees. No drink to be had this early. In Samarkand they'll have been using the sun for five hours already – that's why it's so damned cold and exhausted when it gets to us. One of those furry little creatures must be Aleksandra.

Last night Sophie said, 'I used to be quite frightened of you, you know. You were so taut – I felt I could string arrows on you and send them out of sight. You made me seem such a fraud – "go or stay – but at least feel," you'd say. I used to reply, you remember, "How can I feel if you give me that choice?"

'Be patient, Feodor. Let me make my mistakes if you like me, and have something more to offer than reproaches. But you never had. And, you know, I wasn't greedy. I never asked you for anything. You wanted kindness, but all you gave me was criticism, sets of rules, formality – you even despised me because you'd so little impact on me. All your rationality was selfish – you can't reason people into being gentle and receptive to you – especially when you only talk of sacrifice, risk.

'But Aleksandra's different – she'll examine you more closely than I could be bothered to – like a mouse with a nut, she'll look over your flaws, shake you to see if you're sound and worth the long effort of opening you up.'

'I must have seemed very strange to you, Sophie.'

'Totally absorbed in. something else, which you couldn't recognise. Nervous, isolated – very touching – but not useful.'

We embraced, each thinking about who knows what, like two animals keeping warm. In the days when I first met her, when she could remember her misspent virginity, Sophie fluttered like a bird that one closes over with one's fingers. But now – she's solid, domestic – looking for a hearth, perhaps. She invites vulgarity – because she's indifferent to it: vulgarity is the self-criticism of the genteel. Or perhaps I'm not really genteel, and not vulgar either, just envious. It was hard to say goodbye to Sophie – I could have done so much better with Sophie another time ...

Waiting in the museum for Aleksandra – she likes to come here with me. There's one photograph we enjoy – soldiers bathing in a river, under willows and poplars. Red cavalry – you can see men holding the horses. Aleksandra calls it 'the high-point of the nineteenth century', and it does indeed look like something by a Russian romantic painter, a stately exuberance. But I say 'they died in the twentieth century' – and the rest of the museum is an inventory of their equipment. The beautiful machines! Tiny steam engines from Petrograd, copper and brass, like stills. Rifles so cut down, they're just iron tubes ... decrees, illegitimate ruble notes, the hundreds of dead ... the early open-air meetings in the snow, with everyone standing about like currants in the snow, immobile under all that saturated wool.

And later, the factory meetings – enthusiasm, but less exuberance, the horses perhaps tired of waiting for all those dead riders. We are the survivors, we have come through by skill, or by cowardice. These exhibitions encourage one's inadequacy – what must I do before my jacket and shoes will be put on display?

I find myself staring at my clothes as if I am on show, though some quality in the leather and the cloth account for the mortality of its owner and the immortality of his clothes. One is left alone with one's tiniest thought in here – it looks as if all the good communists are dead ... But no – here are some survivors. Twenty years ago they looked like Grigor. When I thanked Grigor he said, 'You don't know how keen I was to help you, Feodor, to see you placed. With specialists, it's easy. But you – you're pure intellect, as you might say. We couldn't make proper use of you with the workers here. You need to go and be near other intellectuals – a bit more in the public eye.'

Well done, Grigor! Ambiguous to the end! I'd a big enough public here – just my intellect was too small. I think Grigor was afraid I found his achievements lacking. But I didn't. He was an excellent manager. He spent as much time worrying about my function as he did about his own. Was it jealousy that for a time he took my Sophie for his audience? She didn't seem affected by him – he satisfied her, but she gave nothing she didn't want to, and it was her he wanted, not to exploit her. He had something to give which I didn't. And in this way perhaps Aleksandra is, after all, more impressionable than Sophie? With her literary pretensions, her respect for a man of the intellect ... As one might say – the pen is mightier than the sword because writers find it harder to lift up ... Well, so Aleksandra is a mistress of a new type, suitable for the satisfaction of asymmetrical needs. Perhaps I resent having needs – especially needs so different from hers. We're like trucks using the same road but travelling in different directions – we think we need each other, but really, we only need the roadway. This would be freedom, then – to avoid head-on collisions?

Aleksandra at last, pressing her hands to the radiators, then to her cheeks. How different from my bitter daydreams of her she is! The little girl from the nineteenth century, her nose in Pushkin and her feet in the hot mousy dust – that's gone, though there's an exuberance left. 'How's the heart of the great Soviet people today, Feodor? Standing beside it so gravely, stethoscope plugged in as usual! Let's talk – I'm happy only because of the loneliness to come. We'll say goodbye as if we were to see each other tomorrow. And each day will be an absence of just twenty-four hours, and we'll never reach a total till we're together again. And look, here's a present!' And in all this rush, I didn't think to get her anything – well, that lapse will make her remember me more than any gift!

It's a notebook – a cheap paper – I'll have to write fast or the ink will run as thick as twigs! But what a thought!

'I have nothing for you, Aleksandra. Gallant to the last.' 'Nonsense! You'll send me this to read when its full, and then buy another to fill for me. The possibilities are endless.'

'And the potential?'

'As much as mine ... Feodor – don't forget me in Moscow. Big cities are so full of dead loves. I feel the night-crews drive around all night picking up the dead passions.'

'And the dead drunk too – I'll pickle my love, Aleksandra, and keep it deep inside me – in my liver. And any tears, I promise you, will be the best vodka, however high the price …'

'Well, Feodor, you are allowed a few tears now, you know.'

'If I were leaving for the front, perhaps. But to work in Moscow? I don't feel I've earned them – even though I admit there's a certain pressure ...'

'Feodor, you have to write – I've studied you so carefully. This bleakness, this withholding, this uncertainty – it can only be conquered on the page.'

'And on the factory floor? I'm so ambitious, Aleksandra. I want to stand up and say, 'Look, comrades, this is how it is. This is how I see you – and here you're wrong about me.' I want to be able to walk in the sun, pick up some tile from the Chinese mosque, hold it to the sky like a mirror, catch the kestrel on its broken surface, that kestrel crossing the jagged edges of the fallen cupola, forever trying to sort. out the mice from the men. And then, I think of Andrei, and of Timofei. They don't want this Weltschmerz and rant! They want my America, too – gunfire in the suburbs as the white housewives rehearse the apocalypse, brush-cut cops with doctorates in Panama. But mainly, they want something to be useful to them. Am I useful, Aleksandra? You've cured my loneliness – but at what cost to yourself?'

'Feodor, you're so harsh. I know all this – this museum, for instance – it demands harshness. And how to fit this with your appetite for happiness? Perhaps you have to urge us towards relaxation, so that you can shock us again with your bleakness. Perhaps it doesn't matter so long as you know what you're doing.'

'No, Andrei's right. Knowing takes a lot of experience and practice – and patience. These are big demands.'

'That's why I want to see you leave for Moscow. That makes a demand on me – and I want to share the demands made on you. I want to become a part of your anonymous and potential audience. I entrust you with my confidence, that you will try to serve me.'

'This notebook is feeling heavy already: blank pages are a big responsibility! I'll come back, Aleksandra, and I'll write.'

It's hard, struggling through the snow to the station. What does Aleksandra want of me? Nothing I can't give – or so she says. The militiaman at the barrier says something to his friend about students – flattery at last, as the train's about to leave. Leaving alone, as I arrived. Avoid the shrewd ones with the sacks of onions, try and find a threesome not too drunk. 'Moscow, eh, citizen? That's a couple of bottles away ...' The birch trees are flickering past us, like brooms stuck in the snow. Sophie's wolf had better be warm this winter ... Take the notebook: 'literature and the working-class: some methodological questions'. It's a start, Aleksandra. Just thirty minutes from saying goodbye – and how many years till I see you again?

Look at them all, our idealists, fresh from the last century, climbing aboard their trains, out to the distant lands, into transformation. What chance do we have, of reaching our goal, that other shore – what stands in our way? Is it History or history? Men and women, students and teachers both, waves in the sea breaking, achieving, dying, on that as yet invisible sand! What can pull us down, and steal the future that should be ours?

leo

Leo thought, 'Can I communicate with myself only through these lurid and inhuman dreams?' waking from one. Climbing up a sandy track to see the most skilful shepherd in the world – 'I'm an Italian, but not a member of the Party,' the man said, without being asked – he saw wolves guarding the sheep. One followed him, and the others stared with malign uninterest.

The sheep were heavily ruffled, thin ascetic faces framed by the thick neck-wool. They ate as though they were mumbling, sombre green and yellow eyes in clay brown faces – they looked like an assembly of Armenian scholars, surrounded by guard dogs. There were fires of burning straw on the path, and these forced Leo and his wolf to climb up through the pines. They dropped down then towards a mine worked by prisoners, and the wolf left Leo at the entrance to the shaft. In the control room policemen and guards chatted urgently. The chief wore shoulder tabs – 'Princess' – but it was not clear if this was a rank or a nickname. His face must have been mutilated, for he wore a blue facemask, like a Chinese theatrical warlord's. He was wrapped in a heavy blue and red police cloak, and Leo asked, 'Do you have sexual significance, or are you real?'

Not too difficult to read all these signs – even to the shepherd's row of children, wrapped like Aztecs in sheepskins, and stacked against the white daub wall of the peasant's hut. Firmly secured, they could only watch the thoughtful sheep being tipped in their hundreds from trucks, to be rounded up by the lazy wolves ... The previous evening, Leo had come home late – standing in the street, he looked up at the sky.. It looked grainy, two-dimensional, grey – like a print from a badly washed photographic plate. The industrial smoke rolled away on the horizon in the same charcoal and silver, in loops, like the sea in a Japanese woodcut.

'Home and something difficult this time,' he thought. 'So many signals of despair – but at least it's good to have spent my savings. Insecurity is the next best thing to travel ...'

Later, he tried to put himself on paper. 'Leo works alone, not successfully; but he is not a failure. He is not kept alive artificially, he is not subsidised by the people who should be hostile to him, and whom he attacks. But the price of the independence is terribly high. He's totally genuine, but not very nice. He can't experience a revolutionary movement – partly because of scruple, but also because it's pointless, and he knows it, to talk of undertaking militant activities in the same way as one talks of undertaking a revolution. Intellectually he rejects militancy, but accepts the revolutionary process which is independent of both his will and his intellect. Yet he cannot experience a capitalist society either.

'Can this process of rejection be made one of genuine intellectual refinement? It doesn't look hopeful. Where should he look – in the cities, the factories, the backwoods? Well, one can't live just anywhere – and what is so special about living in a place? But these dilemmas don't constitute a failure. He lives in a situation where both art and science are the special preserve of the bourgeoisie – everyone is at the mercy of the telephone and the hi-fi. Leo refuses to submit, or to become effete. He stands appalled by the casual and aimless philistinism of the proletariat, which does not surprise him. But the calculated brutality of the bourgeoisie effectively silences him ... It's like the silence of the sea – each wave a sinuous colloquy of tautologies ... And yet – what can be tragic about silence? Or useful? Or independent?

Shirley telephoned. 'So – I'm speaking to Genghiz Khan, really? Still paying the phone bills, Leo? Part of the cost of independence, would you say? How are you? I'm very anxious to know. We seem to have parted for such abstract reasons – plenty of people settle down and live in the concrete – up to their necks in it – all their lives.'

'Shirley, I'm having a period of vividness, and don't know that I like it. I was in a pub last night, and saw something very unusual. Four men were trying to unburden themselves of intimacies. One would say, "I never liked my father but he made me a boat while he was dying of cancer," and someone else said, "When I met my wife first, she was living with another man," and so on. They seemed desperate to establish a comradeship by putting themselves in each other's power. It's odd that miners should need this – you remember the Italian syndicalist miners who used to have the slogan – 'Safety measures mean all safe on the day of the great strike ...' Here men seem to ignore safety because the bosses enforce it for reasons of economics and public relations ...'

'Leo, I called to make sure you're happy with our decision. I met Peggy today, and she said something unusual for her. That "men who want their independence, for whatever reason, often take up with women who are weak and impressionable. They think they'll be able to dominate them in such a way as to retain their isolation. But they're wholly mistaken. That leads only to boredom and loneliness. Explorers need explorers, not natives: who know only the next: hill." Can you be happy in the life you've chosen for us, Leo? Or rather, should I accept the inevitable, when you offer it with such resignation?'

'Shirley – my school believes that you don't matter unless you're useful. I'm trained to withhold all kinds of conventional offerings, services.'

'But Leo – what's it all for? Who could you serve? You've already discovered your mistake about your wife. And you'll just reply to me bitterly, "So, I'm a comic figure, is that it?"'

'You put the problem excellently, Shirley. There's a limit to what I'll admit about myself. You can't play this cold and emotionless role with me – you can't live with me on some bargain terms. I can admit to disillusion when it's based on my mistakes – but frankly, you represent total capitulation. I'm struggling to keep just a part of me above the water – and you're the water. I was an interpreter once in a smelter in the Soviet Union – for a group of visitors. To me – the heat and the sound were fantastic. They had to stand me between the groups so I could hear, and shout my translations. And the whole smelter became for me a huge voice box, a gigantic bubbling tongue magnifying every human inflexion, every verbalisation from Sheffield to the Urals ...

'I was profoundly affected by this cauldron of human speech, this seethe of syllables – with myself in the middle, interpreting, sorting out the mechanical from the human. This was my adventure, this was the one Promethean moment we're all allowed. And I said to my wife, "That's my ambition – to be able to work and live and speak like the smelter workers. Imagine – to exist despite the terrible fragmentation of the simplest phrase, to have unions, drink vodka, play the accordion – and live in that crucible."

'And she said, "Another enthusiasm, Leo? They make steel there, Leo, not poems or new languages. Why do you want to be a steelworker, dear?" And I felt as though my adventure had been taken away – very childish. I'd rather be childish than resentful, or bitter. I can't see that I'm one of your needs, Shirley. Because I would be a drag on you, you'd become a drag on me – there's nothing so reciprocal as disappointment.

'I know I pay a high price for my isolation, and it's paid grudgingly. But what do you want me to say – that there is no more adventure, that I must strike a balance and write memoirs?'

'Leo – I'll say what you want me to. No, I don't understand you. But tt's you that's lacking, not me. Why can't you write a book about your wife and have me with you? Not everyone has that chance – a despairing mistress ministering to a desperate wife.'

'How can I tell you, Shirley? Yes, you're right. I'm a boor to refuse you. I'm objectively both ancient and immature! I don't want to discuss my emotional fortunes – there's no time for that. I could say truthfully, yes, part of me turned gangrenous that winter in Moscow, my wife dying to protect me against everything but her own death. That made a big debt, you know. Something withered in those long grey days – it seemed as though Stalin was making even the seasons bigger, longer. I used to shiver against the pipes, like a lung warming itself against the ribs of an emaciated man, dreaming of the sun and the south. Part of me will never get warm again, Shirley. You'd do well not to get too close.

'But another part of me says – well, so she's dead. You survived, you recovered. Just look at all the things available for you. Look at all these people ready to join in the adventure. In your Moscow now, there's ice-cream. If you want, you'll be able to go back and die there, you could spend your last days under a thorn tree, drinking that same sweet red wine, watching the ants on the bark going about their domestic tasks. You see, Shirley, I'm betrayed by my own high standards. I'm not a necessitarian. I can't recognise you as part of my necessity.

'All right. Flog yourself along the tightrope. I hope you make it on the other side. But if you fall, the water's really calm.'

'Shirley, you can't see the water through the fog and the distance any better than I can.'

'I'll call again, Leo. But without expectations.'

And Leo sat alone, and thought, 'Ah, but those were astringent, those years in Moscow – you could hear the world turning on its axle as those millions of shoulders heaved against it, pushing the great peasant cart of history bodily around. And you could hear the crack of the bones too. And I walked away without a bruise – you could see I'd not been pushing. And my wife – who wanted to spare me the effort, and took the weight on herself. The next time – I think a wheel will go over me. All those hungry, eager people – while I've been wringing my hands at the bedside of the old world. Perhaps the old world recovered – how should I know? And only my wife died. When it's my turn, I'll have the strength not to ask for ice-cream ... meanwhile, something difficult is happening, and one never tires of one's thoughts. Not every rat writes 'A History of the Cage – And of Its Architects'.

They began to pour the first of that night's molten slag from the smelter. The orange had dulled to red by the time yesterday's cliff was covered, and the heat had melted the snow.

aleya

Aleya thought of the loss of Leonid. 'The only way I can conceive of myself, winning or losing, is along with the others here, overcoming difficulties for ourselves, exemplary. And yet – there are so many like Alexei and even Leonid, marked and scared with the struggle to emerge from, or remain within, the womb! Alexei concerned himself with abstractions beyond the range of even theoretical enquiry. They could only be criticised and judged by action itself. I couldn't accept that melancholy of Leonid's, whatever other doubts and problems arose. We are still raising here only questions which can be resolved in our present capacity.

'But perhaps too we are presenting a history of ourselves as socialists written by ourselves as bourgeois. And just as no bourgeois sociologist has concerned himself with the bases of socialist society, so we find ourselves searching for a new language of happiness and disquiet. As Katya says – out in the mainstream of history, one learns to value the moments of tranquillity, and to fear that they may be moments of submersion. It's hard for me – how much harder for the listless millions who see in my activity only a frantic restlessness, a manic sentimentality?'

She climbed the hill above the farm – she smiled at herself as she thought, 'It hardly looks as though a struggle is going on down there.' Snatches of music reached her, like calligraphy – 'her eyes were black as two small beetles, her feet, small as a mouse'. Sultan came over to her. 'Aleya, do you think we're succeeding?' Two brown sheep, their eyes between yellow and green, stood pressed together in indecision, then wheeled and ran like bushes harnessed together, hobbled.

'I was just thinking, Sultan – how sentimental I am about the past, and the things that haven't survived the past. I'm all for pushing forward – but I regret the casualties. Perhaps indeed because the process seems too casual ... Certainly, we're succeeding. Here we are – just a few people – we've laid a foundation for the future – we've carved a nest for ourselves in the cliff-face of the accidental ... Yes, we'll succeed.'

'I ask, Aleya, because our concerns seem now so technical. I feel a nostalgia for my own inadequacy. There are so many ways in which a little effort can bring praise and success. I miss the government of accident, of effort for its own sake. I miss the feeling of irreducible privacy. Sometimes I stand up here and look at the patterns we've made, the moonlight striking the machinery like a sword striking armour, the ditches like graves, and I wonder how it is possible to be happy and transitory. I seem to have buried more than I possess – even the animals – I seem to have denaturalised them. I don't recognise these sheep! I've created them, but I can't locate my responsibility. You won't understand, Aleya. But I feel we're sometimes collectively selfish, that we're making things too easy for ourselves – we define the problem, and its solution – and there's no delight in the solving. I hate easy satisfaction – and distrust it.'

'I feel rather differently, Sultan. We all hover between naivety and surfeit – the choice of satisfaction is a difficult one to make. I feel we've not yet begun to approach the question of our needs and beliefs, to communicate them to others. We're like horses just unsaddled – we don't know if we want to run away unencumbered or to eat the hay which is our reward for submitting to constraint. Mentally we feel undecided – but we must make the choice a conscious one …'

Later, Katya said, 'A phase is ended. What will you do now, Aleya? How will you collect your rewards? When I came back to the Soviet Union, I thought, "You believe you're making a choice. But you're too old to be making a choice about economics – at your age, that's ridiculous." So why was I coming back, why did you come here? And the answer – we're forever inquisitive. My husband had a dream. He was standing by the sea in Istanbul – that glaucous sea, like peeled grapes, or the eyes of dead rabbits – the colour of that grey-green stone there, it always reminded me of soap cliffs, around a huge soapy sea of bathwater...

'And my husband said an old man came up to him, and asked him, "Would you like to look through that circle that gives onto the sea, or to the land" – holding up the fingers of both hands, so twisted that they formed complete loops. "The left hand – is the land: you can see in that your own future. The right – that is the sea: that lets you observe the future of anyone you wish."

'And my husband, cautious even in imagination, said, "What do you advise? Which gives most people the more satisfaction?"

'The old man replied, "Most people want their own future. Some are afraid, and ask for their husband's or children's future – but that is often worse."

'My husband thought – and he said, "I'd like to know what happens to Colonel Kowalski, a Polish gentleman, an acquaintance of mine who makes evil-eye charms in a hut by the railway station."

'The old man was furious. "Go to hell," he said. "Anyone will tell you what will happen to that old fool! If you've no more respect for the future than that – you deserve nothing from it!"

'He could well have been right, for much as I sympathised with my husband's curiosity, the Colonel was dying of ulcers and mysticism, and my husband died that same year. So you see, Aleya – one has to take one's chances, when it comes to a science of the future.'

But Aleya thought, 'However precarious, I have my independence, my happiness ... I have completed myself, and I'm ready to become useful. I can now attend to the technical problems.'

A breeze brought the scent of warm blue flowers, and someone singing

'I wakened to accept my new life –
from war to the first thin shoots
– a new harvest coming, of plants strange to me ...'

aleya's diary

No more poetry. 'Forward to the victory of communism', say the signs on the factories as we trundle out through the suburbs. Lines of pine and birch. How cosy to be those people – stopping their bicycles to watch the train pass, buying sausages and sour milk ... They all came to see me leave – Sergei, Dimitri, Larissa, my mother.

Mother said quietly, 'Look at her! Unmoved even to the end! My poor Aleya,' as I sat stiff and silent, like a new widow, wept out. Why do they overdramatise? Can't they think of me as one of the oppressed, going out to rule? To govern myself, fighting bureaucracy from the bottom ... In any case, I really have no choice. I wouldn't make the choice to stay in Moscow if it were offered – so after all, I do have the choice to go to the South.

I can feel the first change of the season today. The summer is ending here – but in the South, the horsemen will stand like rooted giants on the long blue-green ridges above the farms. How long will it take me to recover from my summer in Moscow? How precious these memories are, how deep the feelings we have shared, how exhausted our resources ...

No more poetry – I have exhausted Alexei. I have hunted for his life's activity – and in finding it, I'm grateful. He gave so freely – he gave a lifetime of comment, of disillusion, in those few months. We shouldn't minimise the benevolence, or the torment. But I'll not follow Alexei's path – and perhaps my intensity is cowardice. I can't imagine such isolation, such a useless, profligate vision. But what an example! To live one's life at that pitch – to meet the demands of one's life with such determination, it's a frightening notion.

I am standing on the rim of these mountains, looking down into my Kazakhstan – my choice is to spend a lifetime close to people who may not be my friends – overcoming friendship perhaps, refined, austere, controlled. Dimitri and Sergei – they want this for themselves, but they can't sympathise with me, I who have no special talent of creation.

Dimitri said as I was leaving, 'Aleya, the hardest, but the first, thing you must control is fantasy. It doesn't matter what motives you think impel you – so long as they're not fantastic. Lives based on error are commonplace – those based on fantasy are a universal disaster. You can't live the life of everyone. I've said this before, Aleya – but make sure you are going to live your own life.'

And I said, 'That's it, Dimitri. Friendship seems to exclude dependence and independence. It stops me either living a private life – because you're such public people – and it stops me paying attention to my social duties. You, Dimitri, when you join the creative intelligentsia, you will live, through and for your music – but what do I have? Alexei was dragged by his poetry like a charioteer by his two horses, and they split him in half – but I don't have even one horse. I'm running along, trying to keep up with you on foot. But I won't let you help me ...'

Sergei said only, 'You underestimate yourself, Aleya. You're testing yourself beyond the limits of your strength – but the test will be a long one. You're going out to die – in some confused desire to atone for Alexei...'

And I said, 'No – I may have spoken like that in the past. But I'm now very hopeful. I won't forget Alexei, but I'm free of him, I'm free of despair. And of dualism. It's not my idea of socialism that's wrong, Sergei, but Alexei's dualism, and you're falling into his trap. My efforts will not destroy me, but strengthen myself and others ... Dimitri can pursue two themes at once in his music – so shall I.'

Dimitri said, 'You're going on to the steppe to make music, then, Aleya? The music of tars and rebecs, or whatever? You see – fantasy! What part will song and dance play in your life, do you think? We no longer set the sounds of our factories to music, you know. Will your desk calculator manage a concerto? I'd love to put music back into your working day, Aleya: but I've only the chance to put it in the concert hall. We have to fragment, reintegrate, before we can meet your archaic demands!'

'You sound like one of the teachers who said, "Economies should deal only with qualitative ends, like music. When one is given an assignment, one should compose a riposte. But it's never quite like that. Are we aspiring to the condition of music – or music to that of economics?"

'And I told him I thought that confused all the issues.

'"Maybe so," he said, "but there was a sociologist who once said that every banality, every platitude, every tautology, held some fresh and illuminating perception. Go away, Aleya, think that over for a dozen years – and see if your profession is sounding more musical ..." And I will.'

Larissa was the only one who congratulated me – and I've treated her worse than anyone. 'You'll be lonely, Aleya. But yours is curable – and you tell me mine is not. Marriage to a boor excludes politics as well as drama. So I envy you – because you think I should.'

'The station was so charged with emotions, mine were almost purged. The immanence of movement seemed to overcome our shabby and grudging farewells. Soon we'd all, for good or ill, be moving in the same direction – the waving hands back at rest before the train is out of sight. Sergei and Dimitri will have lunch together – and in a few months, they'll drift apart. I'm breaking the threads that hold all these people together. In winter, they'll hardly recognise each other, have forgotten that the snowbanks ever held scarlet flowers in long hot evenings when we talked of Herzen and counterpoint.

We are already a long way from Moscow. In Kazakhstan they'll be resting from the heat under the apricot trees ...

Dimitri said, 'Remember, you can always come back ...'

But no – no, I shall never come back. Today, I alone have become responsible for my future!

Written in 1970–1971

about the author

John Fraser has lived in Rome since 1980. Previously, he worked in England and Canada.

www.ingramcontent.com/pod-product-compliance
Lightning Source LLC
Chambersburg PA
CBHW020551310726
48979CB00008B/1167/J

9780956140975